A DANCE AND A DEAL WITH A VAMPIRE

H. S. LUNA

Contents

Author's Note

This paranormal romance is meant for a new adult audience and is not recommended for readers under the age of 18. As a vampire novel, it will feature scenes involving blood, violence, murder, and descriptions of consensual sex throughout.

There are two brief mentions of miscarriages in chapters 1 and 20 for readers sensitive to that content.

Your mental health matters.

"There are only two tragedies in life: one is not getting what one wants, and the other is getting it."

ix

OSCAR WILDE, LADY WINDERMERE'S FAN

One

Isabelle

1897

A piercing scream rang in my ears. I let out a long sigh before muttering, "This night will be the death of me." I braced myself before rising from my seat in front of the vanity. The auburn curls that had just finished setting fell around my shoulders, still needing to be pinned in place. But Irene, my older sister-her needs came first.

"Isabelle? Where are you? I need your help picking a dress!" Irene shouted from down the hall. Her cries for attention could always be heard through the thick wall that separated our rooms.

Quickly, I threw on a silk robe, tying a knot around my waist before shuffling down the hall. I had been talking my sister in and out of dresses since we were both little girls. She always needed someone else to validate her so I was well-versed in what she wanted to hear. The sooner she settled on a dress, the sooner I could retreat back to my room. As I entered, she was throwing another dress into a pile on her bed.

"Irene, what seems to be the matter?"

She whipped around, her brown eyes focused on me like a judgemental bird. "What dress will you be wearing tonight?"

"The new one that father brought back from his New York trip."

"What color is that one?"

My eyes grew with excitement. "Black!"

"Black?" She scoffed, "to the Autumnal Ball?"

"Yes, I felt it embodied the death of summer."

Her light brown curls shook as she turned back around. "You are entirely too morbid. I doubt Ashley will approve of you wearing that tonight."

It was hard to resist rolling my eyes, "Ashley does not get a say in what I wear."

She giggled as she turned back to face me. "Yes, he does, considering he is practically your husband."

The same retort I always used when someone brought this up started to roll off my tongue, "A proposal when we were children hardly-"

"Hardly counts blah, blah, blah." With her hands on her hips, she looked hard at the pile of dresses on the bed. "You are his. Everyone in this town knows it to be true. And I cannot understand why you fight it so much. I would kill to be attached to a man as fine physically and financially as Ashley Johnson."

"I suppose you are right." There was no use arguing it. Irene saw Ashley the way everyone did. He was every father's dream man for his daughter to marry and every woman's secret desire. He was the best option if I had to be stuck with a man forever. But something about how he claimed me when we were just eight years old never settled right with me, which is why I fought out union in any way I could.

"I suppose I am." With a triumphant smile, she plopped herself on the empty part of her bed. "Now, help me decide what to wear!"

I went to my sister's already opened wooden wardrobe and thumbed through the dresses that were still hung up. Satins and silks slipped under my fingers until I settled on a dress that I hoped would satisfy her. "What about this one?" With a flourish, I pulled out a deep rusty orange dress with beaded floral accents trimming the corset and a skirt lined with frills. "This color will be ravishing and bring out those beautiful brown eyes."

"I have worn that already." Irene's face scrunched with uncertainty.

Whether that was true or not, I did not care. I wanted to get her dressed so I could finish getting ready myself. "No, you have not. I would have remembered if you had worn this already." I paused before adding, "You will look stunning!"

Irene stood staring at me, pursing her lips. She moved them left, right, then left again before announcing, "Very well." As she snatched the dress out of my hands, she smiled. "Thank you, sister. Where is Mary?"

Sighing, I went to the door and poked my head out into the hall. "Mary!" I called, hoping my shout would reach her in whatever part of the house she was.

Within a minute, Mary's pale, hunched frame came to the end of the hallway. She smiled quickly, but the creases around her eyes and lips let me know she had been fussing over something before she heard me calling. "Yes, Miss Isabelle?"

"Irene is desperate for your help."

Mary tried to hide a smile as she entered the room and the pair got situated in front of the mirror.

My feet started to move towards the door, "I'll be in my room if you-"

"Oh, I still need you." Irene's impish smile disappeared as Mary heaped the gown over her head. When she was free from the fabric, she asked, "Ashley is coming tonight?"

"The last letter I received from him indicated as much." Ashley and I had spent the last few years mostly corresponding through letters. He had gone down to Williamsburg to study finance and just recently graduated in the spring. Instead of returning to Alexandria for the summer, he had spent the time in Washington establishing himself at his new job. When I asked him what he did, I was told it was 'too complicated to understand.'

Irene continued, "Do you know if he is bringing anyone with him?" That was the real reason Irene cared for Ashley was because of the eligible bachelors that he was constantly parading in front of her.

One of the excuses I gave Ashley as to why we couldn't wed was that I wanted Irene to be married first. After what she had endured over a decade ago, I was almost certain she would never find a suitable man to marry her. It was how I hoped to ensure I never married Ashley.

When Irene was eighteen, she fell in love with one of the men who worked in my father's tobacco fields. I understood the appeal. He was tall, broad, and gorgeously tan with a smile that made Irene forget to finish her sentences while speaking with him. He'd barely been working here a month before my sister was sneaking out in the middle of the night to meet up with him.

It wasn't too long after they began their secret rendezvous that Irene confessed to me that she was pregnant. Neither of us were surprised, she had given me the explicit details and revealed that they weren't being careful. What was surprising was when she informed her lover of the pregnancy, he left that very night and we never heard from him again.

Irene tried to hide the pregnancy. Mary helped her fix her dresses to avoid showing off the growing bump, but my parents eventually figured out what had happened. They stashed her away in the house hoping to avoid the whole town knowing what their daughter had done.

The baby ended up coming a few months too soon. Irene survived the birth but the baby didn't. After grieving the loss, she decided to start fresh and see if she could find herself a suitable husband. But so far, even with Ashley's help, she hadn't found another suitor.

"Well," Irene asked again. "Is Ashley bringing a friend with him this time?"

"I believe he is bringing one of his colleagues from work. They are coming down from Washington tonight."

"Has he bought the house he sent you a drawing of?"

With a dismissive wave of my hand, I replied, "I believe so."

Her brown eyes went wide. "I am so envious of you."

"As I have said countless times, you can have him."

"I would have him if that is what he wished, but he wants you."

Feigning happiness was an effort as I said, "Yes, he wants me. I should be so lucky."

"Yes!" She smoothed out the front of her dress. "Now, go get ready so you can help me find a husband!"

Irene pushed me out of the room with Mary following. The door was abruptly shut behind us.

Alone with Mary, my body relaxed into her comforting presence. She had been taking care of my sister and me our whole lives. The years had taken their toll on her body, giving her a hunch and wrinkles throughout her pale face, but I could always count on a bright smile when I looked at Mary.

What Irene had said about my dress choice made me rethink my plan for the evening. Black was not the color many would choose for a party, but I loved this dress. It had a lattice corset with lace draped along the neckline and throughout the dress. The bustle in the front revealed more intricate rows of lace, swooping down in layers that created a train.

When my father brought it back, I tried it on right away and fell in love with the woman I saw in my reflection. I didn't look like a little girl or even a young lady. No, with that dress I looked like a woman.

My mind was made up. Irene's and Ashley's opinions be damned, I would wear that gorgeous dress and feel gorgeous all night long.

With a quickness that came from years of practice, Mary helped me out of my robe then lifted the dress over my head, tightening up the strings in the back of the bodice.

Mary's voice had a hint of awe in it as she commented, "You truly look like a woman now, my dear."

Slowly, so slowly, I turned to face myself in the mirror.

I fit into the dress like a wick in a candle. The corset gave my body a voluptuous curved waist I didn't know I had. After a few adjustments to the top, I could breathe better, but my breasts also heaved over the top making me look older than my twenty-three years.

Mary adjusted bits of lace along my neckline. "It is perfect, Miss Isabelle."

I felt my cheeks heat as I whispered a thank you to her.

"Do you need help with anything else? It is almost eight o'clock and guests will be arriving soon."

"No, no, I'll finish everything else myself. Thank you."

Mary said no more as she left the room.

Carefully, I made my way back to the vanity to finish setting my curls so half were pinned up and the others were loose around my neck. With a practiced precision, I lined my eyes with the same black mascara that I used on my lashes. The dark makeup made my blue eyes stand out. I put just enough blush to match the red that painted my lips. It was a bold look, but it was what I wanted.

With a quick step into my matching black satin heels, I was out of my room heading towards Irene's door. Stopping in front, I gently knocked then called out for my sister.

She didn't even open the door, instead shouting, "You go first! I want to make a dramatic entrance!"

"Understood!" I rolled my eyes before I headed down the stairs to the front of the house. As I went down the hallway, the smell of tobacco grew stronger. The murmurs of a few guests could be heard coming from the ballroom and the smooth, sultry notes of Beethoven's Ninth Symphony were filling the halls.

My parents, who were greeting guests at the door, stopped and watched with admiration as I walked down the stairs towards them.

"My beautiful baby girl!" My mother cooed before giving me a kiss on the cheek. I could already smell the wine on her breath. Her face was just beginning to earn a rosy tint, meaning she had only drank a glass or two. I did a quick spin as she continued, "You look exquisite!"

My father gave my cheek a pinch. "If I had known this dress would make you look like this, I would have never bought it. "

Mother gave a coy giggle, "I'm sure Mr. Ashley will enjoy how you look in this dress."

"It doesn't matter to me if he enjoys it." I took a glass of white wine from a passing server.

Father cleared his throat, "It should matter greatly to you."

"Why is that?"

"Isabelle," Mother's eyes rolled along with her glass. "You know that he has spoken to us about-"

"Hush," Father cut her off. "It isn't our place to speak about that yet." Ashley had spoken to them about our engagement. As I started to shrink, my father started again, "Go enjoy yourself tonight."

"I shall, father." After a long drink of wine, I continued towards the ballroom.

The front doors opened and revealed a new line of familiar guests coming to the party. Everyone always looked forward to this party every year. My parents had thrown their annual Autumnal Ball for as long as I could remember, but I was only allowed to begin attending when I turned sixteen.

Irene was allowed to join the party when she was sixteen and I waited in her room eagerly anticipating the news my sister would bring back. That night, she had constructed a decadent dream of all the gentlemen and ladies for miles coming together to share drinks and dances under candlelight. She was allowed to have six glasses of wine that night and she could not recall what was said but remembered everyone laughing and smiling as they twirled around the room.

Four years later, when I was allowed to come to the party, Irene's description was completely spot on. I remember a swirl of lace dresses in every color, people folded over in laughter, and my parents dancing in a way I had never seen before. It was a magical evening, like one I had read about in my book of fairytales.

I took a few more quick sips of wine for courage before gliding into the ballroom. The massive carved wood doors that contained the ballroom were closed most of the year, but tonight they were flung open revealing the candlelit decadence. A dark wooden floor stretched between the burgundy walls that were decorated with filigree columns. In the center of the room, a classic crystal chandelier caught the light from the flames that danced amongst the guests. Each corner of the room housed a bar filled with imported wines and liquors. As the evening was just beginning, everyone was crowded around the different bars greeting one another as they grabbed their preferred drinks.

The ballroom was beginning to fill as I scanned the room, but didn't see Ashley. He towered over most guests with his big frame, and his bright blonde hair was easy to spot. My whole body relaxed as I realized he wasn't here yet and I still had a few more moments of freedom.

Irene had paused in the entrance of the doorway to the ballroom. Her painted red lips curled into a bright smile as she locked eyes with me. That was my cue.

I disguised my voice and shouted, "Oh, my goodness! Who is that?"

All the eyes around me turned to look at Irene. Those looks attracted others around them to stop and stare, and soon the entire ballroom was gazing at my sister.

Her smile was coy, but I knew she was relishing all the attention as she floated over to me.

"Thank you, sister." She flipped a loose curl off her shoulder.

"Anything for you."

I heard Irene say from behind me. "Now is the time to relax, have a few glasses of wine, and when Ashley arrives you will be ready to dance!"

I straightened up and gave my sister a convincing smile. "But whom shall you dance with?"

"I have found my next target." Her hand waved loosely towards the south corner of the room. "I have never seen that man at any of these parties. Someone from out of town will be perfect."

In the corner, three men were standing together locked in conversation. Two of them I recognized: one was Mr. Smith, who was in his forties, and despite claiming to be happily married, always danced with every girl at every party. Next to him was Mr. Middleton, who in every respect was a true gentleman, but also had more money than any one else in Alexandria, even my own parents. No one quite knew how he had amassed such a fortune but everyone loved to make outlandish guesses. Bootlegging? Illegal weapons from the war? He never confirmed or denied any of these, which only led to more speculation.

The man I did not recognize couldn't have been more than twenty-five and was dressed in an excellently tailored tuxedo. He was taller than the other two men and had the lean body of a man who doesn't over indulge. His features were dark with naturally tanned skinned that didn't look like anyone from this town. Perhaps he was from Europe? I had not seen many people from places other than Virginia, so I could not even guess where someone with his strong jaw, aquiline nose, and thick brow was from. The dark brown hair shined in the candlelight as it curled in soft waves at the top of his head.

I found him strikingly handsome and hard to look away from. The longer I stared the more guilty I felt, but I was mesmerized by this stranger. It had to have been because he looked so different from Ashley.

"He is quite...handsome." Was all I could muster before finishing my glass of wine. He was more than handsome. He was unique. In this endless parade of pale faces, his gloriously tan one stood out in a remarkable way.

"Oh!" Irene quickly turned away because the stranger had caught the two of us staring at him. "That is quite embarrassing. Do you think he caught us?"

Moving just my head, my eyes caught the stranger's gaze again. I swore the faintest smile danced across his lips.

Irene softly shrieked as she smacked my arm, "Isabelle?"

I was forced to look away from the stranger to reassure her, "What? Oh...no, no he did not see us."

"Perfect," She smoothed the front of her dress. "Where are those servers with more wine?"

"Here comes one!" I waved a server down then grabbed two more glasses of wine.

We gently knocked our glasses together before indulging in hearty sips. As I drank, I dared a look back at the corner.

The intriguing stranger had disappeared.

"Where did he go?" Irene began eagerly searching the room.

I couldn't find him in the growing crowd either. "Let's not fixate on that right now. Shall we go say hello to everyone?"

"Oh, yes! Perhaps we shall run into him!"

Two

Isabelle

Irene and I made our way around the room exchanging pleasantries with the guests. We said 'thank you' to everyone who called us beautiful and tried to genuinely laugh at the awkward jokes. As we circumnavigated the room, Irene, who was obviously trying to be discreet and thus not being discreet, was searching for the stranger. I was looking too, but mainly out of curiosity. How had someone like him earned an invitation to this party? Normally, it was only people we knew from town or father's business acquaintances.

After we finished waltzing through the room greeting everyone, we realized the stranger was nowhere to be found. He had completely disappeared and was no longer in the ballroom. Considering how starkly he stood out, I couldn't imagine where he was hiding now.

We were talking to our friend, Jane, when Irene aggressively grabbed my arm. "There he is!"

"Ouch!" I pulled my arm out of Irene's crab-like pinch.

"He's back!"

"Who's back?" Jane was always one for gossip and eagerly leaned in.

Irene cooed, "The stranger!"

I chimed in, "We've never seen him before and Irene wants him to ask her to dance."

"He is quite attractive!" Jane agreed, joining in the ogling. "Do you not agree, Isabelle?"

"You know she has eyes only for Ashley." Irene spoke before I could.

For a moment I was annoyed, but I smoothed my face out so Jane wouldn't see it. It was better to go along with the charade in front of others. I let my disdain for Ashley slip out among my family because that was safe. They would never repeat what I said about him to his face. Anyone else in town would not show me the same loyalty. "Yes, if he does not show soon, I will never get the chance to dance."

"You could always dance with my brother!" Jane suggested with a laugh.

"Do you want Ashley to ruin your brother's face?"

She nodded and lowered her voice so as only we could hear, "He's been a real ass lately."

Irene loudly gasped. I almost dropped my empty glass.

She tried her best to whisper, "*He is coming this way!* How do I look?"

"A vision!" Jane elated.

"Painted by Da Vinci himself!" She truly did look like a woman from a painting with her perfectly curled hair and the jewels in her dress catching the light from the candles around the room.

After quickly downing her glass of wine, Irene spun to face him head on. Her painted lips were curled in a practiced, demure grin.

The stranger was gliding towards us with a curved, dark smile that brought out a dimple. When he stopped a few feet in front of us, I noticed that his brown eyes were the same shade as whiskey.

"Good evening, ladies," He bowed, then his eyes scanned us all before stopping on me. "Would you care to dance?"

"Me?" My shock matched Irene's contempt.

"If it pleases you." His voice had a hint of an accent, but I couldn't place it. His eyes bore into mine and I felt an unnatural pull towards this stranger.

I should have instantly rejected his invitation to dance. It greatly upset Irene that he asked me instead of her. She was the eligible one, not me. Ashley had made that clear to all the other men around town.

My eyes darted around the room to see if Ashley had arrived yet. If he found out that I had danced with this man while he was gone, he would be livid.

As I looked back into those deep brown eyes, I could not form the words to refuse him. My hand lifted and then lowered into his as I acquiesced.

That smile deepened, causing both dimples to appear.

Perhaps it was nerves affecting my body, but the stranger's hand felt cold in mine. I noticed the difference in our skin tones as his tan fingers wrapped around my pale hand.

I could feel the anger rippling off Irene, but I ignored it as the stranger led me onto the dance floor as a waltz began. His free hand found my lower back, stopping on the curve of my waist. He naturally took the lead and began spinning me around effortlessly. I had never danced with any man other than Ashley, but this felt right.

The stranger seemed content to let the music fill the space between us as he stared deeply into my eyes. The faintest smile still pulled at the edges of his lips.

There was a fogginess to my thoughts like I had already drank more wine than I should have. The fog was creeping from my mind down my throat, into my heart, and settled softly in my core. This stranger was affecting my entire body, and I still didn't even know his name.

The heavy fog was making me feel giddy. A giggle slipped past my lips. Those dark eyes continued their strong hold on mine.

I blinked once, twice, then three rapid blinks and the fog cleared from my mind and body. But the feeling in my core remained. My mind urgently ran through all the questions I wanted to ask him but I needed to know who I was dancing with first.

I dared to say, "I apologize if we have met before, but I cannot remember your name, sir."

"We have not met before. My name is Matias Ciervo." He answered, his eyes never leaving mine. "And you are?"

"Isabelle Haller."

"It is a pleasure to make your acquaintance, Miss Haller."

"It is a pleasure to formally meet you as well. I dare to ask another question, I hear a bit of an accent in your voice, where do you come from?"

"From Florida, my family came over here from Spain before I was born."

My curiosity was impossible to contain, "What brings you to Virginia then?"

"I have been traveling around looking for something I have lost."

"And have you found it?"

His dark, intense gaze finally left mine to trail down my neck and chest before flicking back up. Matias flashed a fully confident smile that showed off his perfect white teeth, "I might have."

I could feel the blood rushing to my cheeks turning them bright red. My breathing became shallow so I quickly lowered my head to look at the floor, unable to meet his gaze any longer.

He leaned so close to me that I felt the wisps of his dark curls against my cheek as he whispered, "You are the only woman I have ever met that can look more beautiful when she blushes." He sucked in a breath. His voice was rough as he added, "The way your blood heats your face, I wonder what other parts of you are heated."

"I beg your pardon, sir." I felt my stomach turn in a pleasant way, as I tried to feign outrage. No one had ever said anything like this to me, not even Ashley.

"Forgive me for being forward, Miss Haller." He continued to whisper and it made my stomach tighten, "But you are hauntingly beautiful. My mind keeps trying to picture what you look like out of this dress." Matias used his hand on my back to push our bodies together. Only the layers of my skirt provided any space between us.

There was no conviction in my tone when I whispered back, "You are too forward." I was pretending to be insulted for the sake of appearance, but wanted him to continue to talk to me this way. His words were warming a part of my body that was begging for more.

But I couldn't allow it to continue. Not here, where I knew hundreds of eyes were watching us. "Perhaps they have different customs down in Florida, but here that type of talk is unacceptable."

He leaned back and I wished he hadn't. "My manners escape me, apologies."

I took a breath to steady my heart and cool the warmth that was spreading all over me. When I felt brave enough to look back into his dark eyes, I saw they had softened. "You are forgiven, this time."

"Thank you kindly, Isabelle."

I felt the knot in my stomach tighten when he said my name. It rolled off his tongue, each silky syllable flowing smoothly into the next.

I wanted to hear him say it again.

Before the music could fill the void of our conversation, I started, "I would be remiss if I did not inform you that my sister desired a dance with you."

"Yes." He leaned in close to me again, "But *I* desired a dance with *you*." His breath tickled my neck as he lowered his lips closer as if he was preparing to kiss me. My body started to relax, my eyes shutting as his lips ghosted across my skin. When they opened, I saw how everyone in the room was cautiously staring at us and my body went rigid again.

I should have stopped our dance, slapped him, shouted at him, or done anything a decent young woman would do. But I didn't feel like a decent young woman anymore. The feelings Matias was pulling from my body were conflicting with the thoughts running through my mind. My body was winning.

Matias pulled away just enough for me to see his dimples were back. A deep chuckle floated between us before he playfully whispered, "I desire much more with you than a dance."

His arms wrapped tighter around me as he spun us around. When we stopped spinning, I locked eyes with him again. "Again, your boldness will get you in trouble."

"In trouble is my favorite place to be." He finished with a wink.

A gasp escaped my lips. Matias looked down at my left hand. "I see no reason why we cannot find ourselves in some trouble tonight."

I shook my head, "There are many reasons why I must avoid that kind of trouble." Ashley wasn't here yet, but he would be soon. If he walked in and saw how close I was dancing with another man, he would cause a scene that would rival when another boy from town brought me flowers.

"Please elaborate, Isabelle, because your words are conflicting with how tightly you are letting me hold you."

My body instinctively moved away from him, while his arm loosened to allow the room between us. "I would love to spend tonight getting into the *best* kind of trouble with you, but if that is not something you are interested in, then I shall be satisfied with our dance."

Matias was somehow the one doing the decent thing, because I wasn't exactly saying 'no' to whatever trouble he was going to suggest. The decent part of me was quiet, letting the curious part of me take over. What would Matias have suggested? He was right that I was technically not spoken for, but everyone in town knew that I was Ashley's, even without a ring to signal it.

No one had ever dared to try anything with me and Matias was a very tempting option to see what else was out there. But I couldn't do that. It would only end up with one of us being broken.

"I can only give you a dance."

Matias nodded, "Then I shall enjoy what I am given."

I let out a breath to calm my body as he continued to guide us along the dance floor. The first song had ended, but it bled into the next song so smoothly that we didn't bother to let go of each other.

I took the opportunity to compliment him, "You are an excellent dancer."

He laughed, "My mother would be thrilled to hear this. She always said I was a hopeless dancer."

I giggled, "Hopeless? No, you are doing a wonderful job."

He shook his head, "I am the worst dancer in my family. I have two left feet compared to them."

"I doubt that, you waltz perfectly."

"This is easy," He joked, "You just make a box. Where my family is from, they dance more..." He paused to search for a word. "Freely. It's beautiful to watch and hard to replicate."

"Could you show me?"

Matias nodded to the musicians, "I doubt they know any *bolero* songs."

"Bolero?" I butchered the pronunciation and he smiled.

"*Bolero.*" He said again, perfectly rolling the sounds off his tongue. "Spanish music."

"I cannot say I know much, if anything, about Spain, other than where it is."

"Not surprising."

"And why is that not surprising?"

He shrugged, "People only learn about what directly impacts their lives. You would have no reason to learn about Spain or even Florida. All you need to know is related to Virginia, to Alexandria. Beyond that, it doesn't matter."

"I know more about the world beyond Alexandria."

"You do?"

"Yes."

"Because you have experienced it? Or because you have read about it?"

How had he guessed that I had only read about what life was like in other parts of the world?

His finger gently lifted my chin so I was looking into his eyes again. "Go out and see the world. See for yourself what you have read about in those books. It is far more *pleasurable* to experience it all in real life."

I wasn't sure if he meant to be coy with what he said, but my body reacted to his words anyway, twisting my stomach and tightening my core.

While I was trying to think of something witty to say when the song ended. Matias let go of my waist, took a step back, and gently took my hand in his.

"I hope we can dance again." The confession left my lips before I could stop it.

"We shall." His words were a statement of certainty. He gave my hand a soft kiss before walking away into the crowd.

I stood there for a moment with my hand still extended out. I knew this dance was real, but it felt as if I had awoken from a dream.

A hoarse whisper brought me back to my senses, "Isabelle!"

Jane was quickly waving me over. I looked around to see if I could still see Matias, but he was lost in the crowd that was swirling to a new dance. "Yes, Jane?"

"Your sister is upset and would like a word with you. She is in the library."

"Very well." I huffed off while keeping an eye out for him.

As I left the ballroom, I recognized most of the faces that were passing by, and a few new ones were sprinkled in. Each received a polite 'hello' with a smile.

Outside the library door, I hesitated. What I really desired was to find Matias and ask for another dance, but instead I was doing exactly what my sister wanted.

It was my duty, though. It was easier for me to lie than for Irene to accept the truth. With a deep sigh, I slowly opened the door to the library. "Sister, are you in here?"

Irene slowly picked her head up off the couch she was lounging on. The tears that dripped from her brown eyes weren't genuine. "Oh, you are done dancing with my potential suitor now? *Dear sister*," She spat the endearment back at me. "If I may inquire, how was it?"

"Dreadful!" I began my routine. "He smelt of garlic, had no rhythm, and tried to discuss finances with me. When he was not stepping on my feet, he was boring me to death with numbers! For all those looks, one might think he would know how to speak to a woman but-" But he did. He knew exactly what to say to disarm me. I couldn't admit that to Irene. "He had no idea what he was doing!" I finished my performance hoping that she had been convinced.

She wiped the tears from her face. "It would have been nice to have been asked to dance. I spotted him first. Do I not look good enough to dance with?"

"You look divine! He is a fool, as I said."

"Perhaps it is better that you danced with him instead."

"I have spared you from an unfortunate ten minutes of your time."

"I am surprised he even asked you to dance." Irene leaned back. "No one ever asks you to dance."

"Well, he told me he is from out of town. He did not realize that I was spoken for."

"Ashley will be furious when he finds out."

"I'll figure out how to handle that."

Irene crossed her arms.

"Come back to the party. Ashley and his colleague should be here any minute and you'll never get a chance to dance with him if you are hiding in here. "

With a deep sigh, she conceded. "Alright. I need tonight to go well. I'll be twenty-eight in just a few weeks. This may be my last chance to find a husband."

"I'll make sure you find one." I held a hand out. Irene pouted before she took the peace offering.

"Sister, I need you always."

"I need you too, sister." We shared a quick hug and then headed back to the ballroom.

Three

Isabelle

On our way back, Irene stopped in the bathroom to fix her countenance. Alone, I walked back into the ballroom and saw our parents were dancing in the center of the room to a fast paced song as the drinks started to loosen up the rigidness in the air. Most of the guests had partnered off and were twirling around the room with smiles lighting their faces.

Instead of joining the dancers, I took a spot by the bar and grabbed a fresh glass of wine.

"You look like you could use a dancing partner!" Mr. Smith joked as he took an empty space to my right. His face was bright red as he asked for another glass of whiskey.

"Afraid I won't be able to oblige you tonight, Mr. Smith."

He leaned in close, "Ashley won't let you spare a dance for me?"

I smiled at my wine as I gathered my words. "He should be here any minute."

"I should have asked you before Matias did. If I had known you would only be giving out a single dance to someone else, I would have jumped on the opportunity."

The smile I was forcing on my face started to hurt. "Well, perhaps next time."

He tipped his drink towards me with a wink.

"Speaking of Mr. Ciervo," I dared to ask, "how are you two acquainted?"

"Ah," He said, taking a sip of his drink. "His family is in the rum trade down in Florida so Middleton knows them. He said he was traveling back down from New York, catching up with friends and acquaintances as he goes."

"So you only met him now?"

"Yes! Came into town yesterday evening and asked Middleton to dine with him but since we had this event to go to, Middleton just invited him along. Glad he did, Matias has delighted us all evening with his tales of traveling around the world."

As if summoned, Mr. Middleton appeared on my otherside. "George!" Mr. Smith smacked his arm. "I was just telling her how wonderful Matias is!"

"Yes," He paused speaking to us to order another whiskey for himself. Once he had the new glass in his hand, Mr. Middleton turned back to me. He did not look as intoxicated as his friend, but there was a looseness to his speech as he started talking. "Yes, Matias popped by last night saying he was in town on business and wanted to catch up. I recognized him right away when he showed up at the front door. Looks exactly like that last time I saw him when he came up the coast with his father."

"So you know him well?" I asked before taking a casual sip of my drink.

"Yes, quite well. His father and he stayed with me over a decade ago and helped me work out a wonderful deal with a Spanish wine supplier."

"I see."

"Why are you so interested in him?" Mr. Smith cocked his brow.

"I was just curious how someone from out of town managed an invitation."

Mr. Middleton perked up, "I did not mean to overstep when I invited him-"

"You know my parents believe the more guests, the more merriment." I said placing my hand on his to ease the tension. "We don't get many visitors like him in Alexandria."

"We don't." Mr. Middleton shook his head. "But he comes from good people." He nodded off to his left and my eyes followed his movement.

"Buzz off you two!" I heard Ashley's deep voice boom before a laugh followed. Turning to follow the sound, I was immediately surrounded up in his familiar arms.

"Hello, Izzy." Ashley whispered in my ear as he embraced me. I cringed at the sound of the awful nickname he had been using for me since we were young. I told him years ago that I didn't want him to call me Izzy, that I liked the way my whole name sounded instead. But he told me that he liked the nickname and it was just a special way for him to refer to me. No matter how many times I protested, he never conceded, so I just gave up the fight.

"Hello." I whispered over the footsteps of the other men retreating. Forcing some room between us, I noticed another man was right behind him. "And who is this?"

"Roger Rochester." The man smiled at me, his dark brown mustache curling. I offered him my hand which he gently kissed. "It is a pleasure to make your acquaintance finally."

"Yours as well," I looked at Ashley to explain.

"Roger and I work together in Washington. I brought him here to meet Irene."

"Did I hear my name?" Irene moved into the small circle we were standing in.

Roger's eyes lit up, "You must be Irene."

I watched a glimmer of hope sparkle across my sister's face. "I am."

The pair barely acknowledged us as they exchanged names and then Roger led them to the dancefloor.

Ashley's hand slid from my waist to grab mine before we made our way behind them. His straight blonde hair was styled but that one rogue strand that always managed to escape had fallen onto his fore-head. He had a new navy blue suit, his favorite color to wear. It clashed with my black dress as we walked in step out to the dance floor.

Despite our clashing outfits, we did make a fine looking pair. There were worse options of men to be tethered to. At least Ashley was a handsome brute.

His large frame eclipsed me as we took our spots on the dance floor. We moved until we were alongside Irene and Roger but not close enough that they could hear us. The music was flowing as we started to follow familiar steps.

"Does Roger know about Irene's past?" I asked in a cautious whisper.

"He does."

"And he is content with that?"

Ashley's grip on my hips tightened. "He has been given thousands of reasons why that shouldn't be an issue."

I stopped dancing. Before it completely threw Ashley off, his hands forced me to start moving again. "Izzy, what is the matter?"

"You are paying Roger to marry Irene?"

"If it comes to that, yes. He agreed to meet her first and decide how much it would take to make this arrangement tolerable."

My eyes went to my sister smiling and Roger twirled her around.

Ashley leaned in to whisper, "He's desperate to make a fortune for himself. And no one makes worse deals than desperate people."

"Ashley, my sister-"

"I don't want to talk about her now." He pulled me close so our bodies were flushed together, just like I had been against Matias. But that rush I had experienced earlier was gone. Instead, I felt a shiver of disgust creep up my spine. "I haven't seen you in weeks."

"We would go weeks without seeing each other while you were in school."

"But it's different now."

Despite how smoothly we danced, my posture went rigid. "So you'll stop entertaining other women-"

"Not tonight," The grip on my hip tightened, "Do not address that here."

I had asked him every now and then if he had been with another, but he always shut down that conversation, even when I told him I would understand. He denied it all, but I never stopped bothering him about it. Even if I could prove he stepped out of our arrangement, it wouldn't matter. What mattered to me was how uncomfortable he was at the accusation of being unfaithful. It went against the perfect image he had spent years perfecting for us.

"Apologies. It hurts my heart when you go away for so long." The hurt comes from knowing he will eventually return and continue his quest to take over my life.

The bit of freedom I had felt my dance with Matias was the only reprieve. The flirtatious words exchanged between us didn't change the fact that everything had been set in motion for Ashley and I to ride off into the sunset together as husband and wife. Nothing would change that.

Ashley would never allow it.

"It hurts my heart as well. We'll need to remedy that soon."

Before I could ask just how soon he meant, Ashley lifted his arms in preparation to spin me. After dancing together for over a decade, we moved perfectly in sync. Ashley twirled me out away from him and then spun me back towards him. It inspired a few of the couples around up to try the same move. Irene and Roger managed it well enough, but Ashley gave me a knowing look when other couples didn't pull it off.

"Another?" He asked.

I nodded before he twirled me out. My gaze spun and landed on a pair of whiskey brown eyes.

Matias was there, staring right at me.

His lips tilted in a smirk that made one dimple appear.

My breath hitched in my throat. When Ashley went to twirl me back into him, I tripped over my feet. Luckily his arm shot out to catch me.

I looked back up to see Matias was gone.

"Are you alright, Izzy?"

"Yes," I fanned myself with my hand. "I...I just got dizzy." The lie slid off my tongue easily.

"Let's get you another drink." Ashley led us over to the bar then ordered a glass of whiskey. I took the glass from him and let the warm liquid coat my throat. "Pull yourself together."

I nodded, forcing myself to look calm despite how I still felt inside. Matias had been so close to me. His fingers only had to reach out a few inches and his cool touch would have been on me. My skin heated at the thought of that happening.

"There you are!" My father boomed from behind me. Ashley's face lit up as he shook my father's hand.

"Mr. Haller." Ashley turned to my mother and kissed her out-stretched hand. "Mrs. Haller. You look radiant tonight."

"Thank you, dear." Mother's blush could've been from the compliment or the wine.

"How are things in Washington?" Father asked him. The two shared a quick conversation about business while I finished off the whiskey.

"Isabelle..." Mother chastised as I wiped my mouth with the back of my hand.

"Pardon." I looked down and set the empty glass back on the bar.

My father looked at us with a smile that matched Ashley's. Something other than business has been discussed between the two of them. "Ashley would like to come over for lunch after church tomorrow. He has something very important he needs to ask."

Mother's voice was loud as she cried out, "Certainly!"

My stomach sank as Ashley slid his arm around my waist.

"I'll come over right after church." He bowed to my parents before leading us back to the dance floor.

As Ashley began to spin me around again, my thoughts started to spiral. He was going to officially propose tomorrow. There was no more putting it off. No more excuses to avoid it.

I was going to become Mrs. Ashley Johnson.

The realization was causing my chest to constrict.

I had spent so much of my life trying to get out of this arrangement. I had put so many conditions before Ashley, the biggest being that Irene needed to be married first. That was supposed to be my way to avoid ever having to actually marry Ashley. But now, he found a way around that.

My body was barely moving on its own. Ashley's strong grip was leading me through the motions. As he led us through the next few steps of a dance, I tripped over my own feet.

Ashley managed to keep me upright. "Izzy," He leaned close and his breath tickled my ear. "What seems to be the matter?"

"Nothing, I am fine."

His lips brushed my cheek. "You need some air."

Loudly, so anyone overhearing would think it was my idea, I asked, "Perhaps we would go get some air?"

"Of course." With a tight grip, he led me out of the ballroom and onto the garden.

The full moon was high in the sky, illuminating all the trees and flowers as we entered the garden. It was a warm night, but the chill of fall was on the slight breeze that ruffled my skirts. The music from the ballroom was muffled by the walls of the house and replaced by the chirping of crickets. Ashley led me to one of the stone benches. I sat down first then he followed, his eyes focused on me.

"Are you feeling better?"

All I could manage was a nod. I wasn't feeling better at all, but the fresh air was helping to cool my skin.

"Why are you acting so odd tonight? Is it because I was late? I had to handle some business before-"

"Business is always your excuse." I waved a dismissive hand.

"Yes, but I hate when it keeps me away from you." His hand grabbed mine and squeezed. "I was too late to save you from dancing with another."

I tried to hide how my heart stuttered when he said that. "Well, he isn't from here. He didn't know that I was spoken for."

"You didn't think to tell him?" His tone was calm, sweet even, but I could feel the tension in his body.

"I did."

"So he kissed your hand knowing you had a fiancé?"

"It was a simple pleasantry. Aren't men supposed to kiss the hand of the woman they dance with?"

His hand squeezed mine harder. "Not in the way I heard he kissed your hand."

How dare he? Ashley had been able to do whatever he wished with whomever he wanted while away at school and the singular time I danced with another he chastised me for it. A flash of anger went through me, "I am not a dog that sits and waits for you, especially when you are running late."

Ashley straightened his spine. "I hope you enjoyed that one dance, Izzy. This time next year I imagine you'll be so swollen carrying our child that you won't be able to attend your parent's Autumnal Ball."

The laugh that bubbled out of me sounded manic. "You say that as if we will be married tomorrow."

"We will be engaged tomorrow. *Officially* engaged." My face fell as he continued, "I have met every one of your requirements. I finished school, secured a job, and purchased a house that is not my family home. The final step was getting Irene married, which will happen once I discuss the finer details with Roger. You have no choice but to say yes to me tomorrow."

His devilish smirk shone in the moonlight as his hand slid down my arm before grabbing onto mine. Ashley lifted my left hand. "Your father has already agreed to the marriage. Tomorrow I'll bring a ring to *officially* claim you as mine."

Breathing was becoming difficult.

His arms tightened around me, "I have been ready to marry you since I asked you under the willow, Izzy. I wanted you then and I always get what I want."

A suffocating dread was creeping into my chest. My already constricted throat was making it hard to breathe. This is what Ashley did to me. He made the decision and expected me to just agree to it. It had been this way our whole lives. No one understood why I didn't want to marry him but this was the reason. He stole my autonomy from me. He stole any chance I had to find real love. He stole my future from me.

And nothing I said would ever convince him otherwise. He believed winning my hand in marriage was the ultimate accomplishment because of how much I didn't want it. Forcing me into this was solidifying the control he had over me.

In the last few years, I had started playing along with the charade he was trying to show the world. After seeing what real love had done to my sister, I wanted nothing to do with it. I would never truly love Ashley, so anything he did would never really hurt me. I never wanted to experience the pain of a heartbreak, so I figured tethering myself to Ashley would accomplish that goal.

Becoming a docile and agreeable version of what he wanted me to be made interacting with him easier. So I slid that mask back on.

Turning into him, I leaned on his broad chest. I hung my head as I quietly confessed, "This is a lot for me to process in one night. I know marriage has been the goal this whole time, but I truly never thought Irene would find a suitor."

Ashley gripped my chin between his thumb and forefinger, forcing me to look back up at him. "That's why you have me. I can make anything happen."

"I suppose I am spoiled in that regard." My smile was fake but the one he returned seemed genuine. It really was this easy to bring his more agreeable side out.

He started to lean in closer, I braced myself for the kiss I knew was coming.

It was the same motions we always went through. Ashley's arms would wrap around my waist as my hands rested on his shoulders. His lips would move mine until there was enough room for his tongue to snake through. Once inside, his tongue explored my mouth like he was discovering it for the first time. After a few minutes of that, I pulled myself away because I didn't want this kiss to go any further than was needed. "You'll ruin my lipstick."

"You'll be my wife soon. Some ruined lipstick shouldn't matter."

"It does to me. Especially after what Irene went through. I won't have the whole town gossiping about what we've done."

"Very well." He loosened his grip on me. "Shall we go back inside now?"

Nodding, I let Ashley lead me back inside.

Four

Isabelle

I managed to make it a few more dances before I couldn't stand being around Ashley any longer. The whole time we danced I kept thinking about the impending proposal and trying to figure out a way around it.

Perhaps it would just be better to go along with it all? Ashley would provide me with a good life, but I wasn't even sure if that is what I wanted. I didn't want to be stuck with Ashley making the best of the life that had been chosen for me. I didn't want any of this.

But what else could I do?

With my evening spoiled, I made an excuse to end the night early. It was nearly midnight, and still early to be ending the night, but I was done with dancing and drinking.

After giving Ashley one more goodnight kiss just outside the ballroom, I shuffled back down the hall towards the safety of my room.

The sounds of music and laughter followed me as I walked towards the stairs. My toes were pinching in my heels so I carefully took the stairs one step at a time. I was tempted to just take them off, but the hallway that led to my room wasn't too long.

The sound of boots following me down the hall pulled my attention from my scrambling thoughts. "Izzy?" The familiar voice purred.

I whipped around to see Matias closing the space between us, his jacket billowing behind him as he walked. The butterflies in my stomach made my voice shake as I stated, "You do not have permission to call me that."

"Only he can?"

I nodded because that explanation was simpler than telling him that I hated that nickname. He took a few cautious steps towards me. My eyes scanned to see if anyone else was in the hall.

We were completely alone.

Matias's body was just inches away from mine and like a candle suddenly being lit, I felt myself heating at his closeness. This felt like when we had been dancing together, but because of where we were, it was even more salacious. To give myself some sort of reprieve from the heat, I took a few steps towards my door. Without taking my eyes off him, I fumbled behind me for the handle.

He asked, "Isabelle, are you going to invite me in?"

"Why would I do that?" My hand tightened around the handle to my bedroom door.

"Because I doubt you want anyone to see us together like this."

"How do you mean? There is nothing to see here."

"Yet." The side of his lip curled up.

That one word sent a shiver of anticipation down my spine. "What are you even doing here? The party is still going and I am certain there is no shortage of women for you to dance with."

"Allow me into your room and I will tell you why I sought you out."

Before I could second guess myself, my hand twisted the knob and the door cracked open. Matias motioned for me to go in first. Once I was in the threshold of the room, I looked back to see he hadn't walked in. With a harsh whisper, I commanded, "Come in."

That smirk turned into a smile as he crossed into my room. I shut and locked the door behind us.

As the lock clicked I realized that I had just shut myself in my room with a stranger who could do any number of things to me and no one would be the wiser. My hands reached for the gas lamp on my nightstand, but it was hard to get my fingers to catch the dial. Matias reached around me and without taking his eyes off me, he turned the dial so the flame ignited.

The dim glow of the lamp highlighted the edges of his dark features. With more courage than I felt, I demanded, "Now answer my question, what are you doing here?"

"To put it simply, I noticed you were upset."

"No, I am not-"

"You may have that buffoon fooled, but I can tell you are deeply upset."

I shook my head. "Why does it matter to you? You don't even know me."

"I have known many like you."

My eyebrows rose in a signal for him to elaborate.

"I have known many young women who have had their budding lives ended by the cage of marriage. I heard what was said to you out in the garden." How was that possible? I hadn't seen him out there. I wanted to ask but he kept speaking. "You wilted as he spoke to you. And based on what others told me after we danced, you've never even had a chance to truly be free. So I will make you a deal, *pajarita*, one night of liberation that no one will ever know about or even remember."

"Pardon?"

"Do I need to say it plainly for you, Isabelle?" Those whiskey colored eyes of his went to my lips, then made a slow trail down to my heaving chest, before snapping back up to meet my gaze.

My eyes went wide with realization that the liberation he offered was for my body. "You are far too bold!"

Matias lifted his shoulder, "I admitted I wanted to get into trouble with you."

My stomach flipped at his words. I had never been offered what he was offering me before. For fifteen I had been bound to one man. Even if I had wanted to experience others, Ashley ruined that for me. He had been able to do whatever he wanted with whomever he wanted all these years with no consequences. And now he was going to keep me trapped in a house in Washington as his consummate child bearer. So this deal for a free night that was completely about what I wanted, it sounded wonderful. I had all the power here. "Just one night?"

His eyes went wide but he quickly smoothed his features so he looked relaxed. "I must leave tomorrow. This party was just a way to keep myself entertained for an evening. One night is all I can give you."

I thought for a moment about the repercussions, but I could keep this secret until I died. "No one will know?"

"Your darling buffoon will still believe he is getting a pure bride on your wedding night. That I swear to you."

"Why are you offering me this?" I asked because it seemed too good to be true.

He lightly ran his fingers up my bare arm before playing with the lacey sleeve of my dress. This light touch made me shiver. Those fingers settled into a gentle grip around the nape of my neck. When his brown eyes found mine again, he stated, "Because I want you. You are imprisoned by the rules society has placed on you, but you cannot deny that you felt something when we danced."

"I..." My breath was caught in my throat. "I did."

He leaned in so close that his lips brushed my ear as he whispered, "So let me give you everything you want tonight."

"I haven't experienced *everything* with a man."

"Almost everything then." His deep chuckle went through my body and to my core. "Wouldn't want the buffoon to be robbed of what he thinks he is owed. I doubt that will end well for you."

I shook my head and felt the pads of his fingers brushing against the sensitive skin of my neck. Ashley would be furious if he knew I had given everything to another, so that couldn't be part of this deal. But there were other things that we could do tonight. I had read about the different ways to touch and be touched without giving up our maidenhood. And after what Irene went through, she warned me on how to avoid becoming pregnant.

This could work.

That silky voice floated into my ear as he asked, "Do you accept my deal?"

His body tensed in time with mine as we held each other's gaze. If just his fingers on my neck were making me feel like small fires were flickering under my skin, I couldn't imagine how they would feel along other parts of my body.

Finally, I breathed out, "I accept."

A smile split his face as he wrapped his arms around me. My hands landed on his chest as he pulled me closer to him. "And how does this-"

He cut off my words with a kiss. His lips, which felt much fuller than Ashley's, moved against mine. Instead of a manipulation of my mouth, Matias molded his lips to mine, gently kissing me deeper until his tongue gently twirled around mine. I copied what he did, matching the movements of his tongue. His lips pulled away to start a trail of kisses down my jaw and the right side of my neck. "You feel..." Matias moaned before he kissed up the other side. "So alive..." He breathed the words before placing a kiss on my pulse. I felt his teeth graze the sensitive spot on my neck before gently biting down.

The sensation of his sharp teeth on my neck shot down to my core and I squeezed my thighs together.

Nothing Ashley and I had done ever made me feel like this. Matias was awakening something in me with just his lips.

In one swift movement, he took a step back and then spun me around so he was facing the back of my dress. "So many layers..." He tsked as he released the first bow holding the bodice of my dress together. The tension in the fabric eased as his fingers slipped the silky ribbon loose. The tips of his thumbs tickled my back as he pulled apart the corset. At the base of my skirt, he undid the buttons. I sucked in a deep breath and inhaled the scent of him. He smelt like whiskey and spice.

Once there was enough room, I let the gown fall down until I was just in my slip. The silky fabric covered my breasts and the most sensitive parts of me, but my shoulders, arms, and legs were completely exposed to him. I had never let any man see this much of me.

My hands shot up to cover myself. The rashness of my decision caught up with me as cold air hit my heated parts. Matias's words had disarmed me and my body was aching for him to keep touching me, but my mind kept sending signals that this was wrong.

His tanned face crinkled with concern, "Do you not want me to see all of you?"

"No, it's just..." I looked around realizing that he wouldn't be able to see much with just the small lamp for light. If I wanted to take this deal, I needed to let myself enjoy this moment. This wasn't the time to feel insecure or afraid. This was my moment to seize. My hands fell to my sides as I stammered, "I've never...this is all just..."

His fingers laced into mine. Bringing my hands to his lips, he gently kissed my knuckles. "We can end the night here if you wish." With my hands still in his, he took a step back to put some space between us. "This is meant to be about your pleasure, so if you are not pleased, we can stop."

A mix of shame and weakness pulsed through me. Here was the deal of my lifetime, one I never believed I would be offered, and I was overthinking it. An extremely handsome man wanted to spend his night with me and there would be no consequences for this. If I didn't take this opportunity now, I would never be able to feel like I fully lived.

I pulled him back into me. "I want this. I want you."

"So let's take it slow." When I nodded, he shot me a smile that showed both his dimples. "Lie on the bed."

I did as he said, putting myself in the middle of the bed and resting my head on the pile of pillows.

Matias slipped off his black suit jacket then placed it on the chair in front of my vanity. He strolled around the bed, untucking and then stripping off his white dress shirt as he went. I watched his legs move to take off his black boots leaving him in just his dress pants.

He climbed into the bed and adjusted himself so he was sitting up against the pillows. I laid back down, nestled in the crook of his arm.

My body was stiff as I admitted, "You're the first man that I've had in bed with me."

His hand traced a line up and down my arm, "It is an honor."

I didn't know what to say next. It was my hope that he would take charge but I got the sense he was trying to make me feel comfortable again before we went further. My mind scrambled for something else to ask him but every thought was wiped away by the soothing stroke of his hand.

The arm not around me reached out to the nightstand. He grabbed the book at the top of my stack. "*Dracula*?"

"Yes," I blushed at his incredulous tone. "It is a favorite of mine."

"Really? Not *Jane Eyre* or *Emma*?"

"I like those as well." I motioned to the shelves of books lining the one wall of my room. It was where I kept all my personal favorites. Something about having them where I could pick them up whenever I wanted was comforting. "I enjoy reading pretty much anything."

"But your favorite is a book about a monster?"

I shook my head, "It's a book about love."

Matias lifted the corner of his mouth, just enough for one dimple to pop up. "You would think that."

"It is! Everyone in that story is motivated by love."

"Even Dracula?"

"Especially him."

Matias put the book back onto the nightstand. "I'll concede to you on this one."

"Good." My lips curved as I snuggled in closer to him. The heat of my body was being tempered by the chill of his.

A crisp breeze floated in through the open window. The night air felt warm compared to his cool skin that was making my whole body erupt with goosebumps.

Matias leaned in to whisper against my ear, "Would you like me to warm you up?"

I nodded as my fingers curled around his shoulders.

He leaned in for a kiss. My lips eagerly met his. It started out light and sweet, just enough to make me feel the heat between us starting to grow. His lips took their time, drawing out each kiss, moving our mouths wider until he could easily sneak his tongue back into mine. A small moan escaped my mouth as he pulled away.

"You're getting warmer."

He moved and settled his knees between my legs. The chiseled muscles of his chest were twitching as he steadied his breathing. Cold hands dropped onto my thighs. Another round of goosebumps erupted on my skin as he slid the edge of my slip up stopping before he revealed my undergarments.

I sucked in a shaky breath.

Matias's dark eyes focused on mine.

He leaned his body forward and used his arms to hold himself above me. "You." He kissed my lips. "Are." Another kiss. "Exquisite." He kissed me deeply.

While his lips had my mind distracted, I could feel the distant sensation of his hand moving. It landed on my breast, pausing there as he waited to see my reaction.

Even through the thin satin of my slip, every touch sparked something in my core. My nipple peaked under his cool touch as he started to squeeze and knead. My hips started moving against him, matching the pace his hand set while caressing me. He moved his head so his mouth hovered over my nipple for a moment before he took the stiff bud between his teeth. I moaned at the overwhelming sensation.

While his tongue worked me, his free hand went to my other breast. He twisted my other nipple between his fingers. The two sensations sent a shiver of pleasure through me and I let out another moan. I had never made a sound like that, but it felt so right at this moment.

He pulled his mouth away and swapped it with his other hand. The silk of my slip was moist where his mouth had just been. Another moan crept out of me as his tongue and fingers played with my nipples.

When he lifted up again, he was smirking and one dimple was showing. Those whiskey colored eyes looked dark as they scanned my body. "You are gorgeous when you're flushed."

"Am I?" I managed to breathe out.

He nodded, kissing each of my heated cheeks. "So full of life." His body slipped down mine, planting soft kisses along my covered stomach. I was beginning to regret leaving the slip on. What would his lips feel like against my bare skin?

I felt his breath tickle my core as he passed it. His hands stayed on my hips while his lips kissed up one thigh. It was such a light sensation but it sent a powerful ripple of pleasure to my core. Then he repeated the same light kiss on my other thigh and I felt my toes curl in response.

I wanted him to place one of those kisses on the part of me underneath my undergarments that was pulsing with desire.

Looking down at him, I tracked his movements as his lips teased kissing my still covered sex.

His dark gaze met mine and he stilled. "Last chance to call it a night."

I pleaded, "Don't stop now."

Matias bit his lip and groaned. His hands on my hips slid to slowly start pulling my undergarments down. The cool air felt warmer than Matias's touch as it met my skin. He pulled the fabric up the length of my legs before discarding it off the edge of the bed. Then he sunk back to his position, hooking his strong arms around my thighs.

"*Perfección.*" He whispered before his tongue met the already sensitive bundle of nerves. A gasp escaped me as his warm tongue met the wetness there. My hips instinctively bucked off the bed, but Matias held me in place. Another lick of his tongue sent my hips moving again. That glorious tongue of his was licking me like a metronome was setting the rhythm. My eyes closed so I could better focus on the feeling.

Slowly, he sped up the pace. His strong hands loosened up enough so I could move myself against his tongue. My hips went from bucking in surprise to grinding towards pleasure.

The moans and sounds leaving my mouth weren't coherent.

Matias lifted his mouth away from me. I opened my eyes and met his gaze. "*Cuidado, pajarita.*"

Through heavy breaths, I asked, "Pardon?"

"As much as I love the sounds you are making, you cannot be so loud."

"Oh, I hadn't even realized..." I started to prop myself up on my elbows, but Matias shook his head. I bit my lip, "I'll be quiet."

He made no movement to indicate he would return to what he was doing.

"I swear I'll be quiet. Now please..."

"Please?"

"Please continue."

His tongue darted out to lick me. My hand flew over my mouth to cover the gasp that I couldn't stop.

"*Bueno.*" He whispered against me before nibbling on my swollen bud.

My hand muffled all the sounds I made as his nibbles relaxed into his tongue drawing circles around me. As if he was mixing a potion, the swirls built up the pleasure in my core.

I could feel the wetness, a combination of the both of us, pooling between my thighs.

"Oh God!" I cried out as I crumbled around him. Pulses of pleasure spread out through my entire body. I hadn't realized that it would be like ripples in a pond after a stone comes crashing through the surface.

Matias continued working me until I finished. Then he pulled back and whispered against my skin, "God doesn't make you feel like this. This is the devil's handiwork."

I let out a breathy laugh, "He is very good at what he does then."

"Yes," He smirked. "Yes, he is."

My body was still tingling but the feeling was starting to fade. As long as Matias was in my bed, I could keep chasing this. "What else does the devil know?"

Five

Isabelle

He sat up on his knees. "Things that will lead to trouble."

I followed his lead and lifted myself off the bed, "I thought you liked being in trouble?"

"I won't face the consequences for this trouble, you will."

My face fell. The reminder of my impending marriage proposal had just curdled the satisfied feeling in my stomach.

Matias moved so he was lying next to me on the bed. Lightly, he grabbed my arm to pull me back down. Despite feeling his soft gaze on me, I kept my gaze focused on the ceiling.

I felt like a bird that had been plucked out of the air mid-flight. It wasn't Matias's fault. He was being the responsible one here. But I wanted to be free of the commitments on the other side of the door for just one night. I wanted what I had read about in stories where women were free to do what they want with who they wanted.

His hand reached out to grab mine and gave it a squeeze. Then I turned to look at him.

His dark brown eyes looked into mine. "There are a few more things we could do that won't compromise you."

I had to bite my lip to keep myself from smiling too big. His free hand grabbed onto my hip and pulled me so that our chests were flushed against each other. His cool chest was bare, chilling the skin that wasn't covered by my slip.

The pads of his fingers slid up my thigh, pushing my slip back up. My free hand grabbed on to his bicep.

He sucked in a breath as his fingers inched closer back to my core, slipping past that bundle of nerves, but pausing before going inside me. "You're already so wet. We just have to be careful."

I sucked in a breath, "Careful?"

He nuzzled my neck as he nodded. "We're so very close to breaking the one rule. I can't get carried away with you." One of his fingers slid into my center. "And it already feels like I am."

The fullness of just his finger was causing my whole body to pulse with pleasure. When he slowly moved his finger out and then sank it back into me, I moaned. His lips crashed into mine to stifle the sound. I could taste myself on his mouth as he swirled his tongue against mine.

He moved his finger so agonizingly slow. Before it was fully out, he would slide it back into me. Every noise I made was swallowed by his kisses.

Instinctively, I started to grind my hips like I had against his mouth. It made his finger touch more of me.

He tsked, pulling away from our kiss. "*Cuidado*, we need to be careful."

"It feels so good."

"I know," His voice was raspy. "But if you bleed now..."

He left the threat hanging out in the tiny space between our bodies. If I bled now, I wouldn't be able to bleed later. And it mattered greatly that I did when Ashley and I finally consummated our forced union.

Reluctantly, I stopped moving. He smiled before gently kissing my lips.

"Just hold still. I'll make it worth it." He emphasized his words with his thumb circling my very swollen apex. The feeling of his finger moving inside me while his thumb stroked me was an entirely new sensation. It was almost overwhelming.

My hand on his bicep was gripping it tighter and tighter as the pleasure built. Matias brought his mouth back to mine, but this time his kisses were slow and deliberate. It was like he was trying to memorize my lips with his.

I could feel the hardness of him through the few layers he had on. I had never seen or touched a man's sex before. Ashley had tried, but I always made an excuse because I never desired him that way.

But I wanted to touch Matias. I wanted to know what he felt like. I wanted our night together to help me understand what I had read and heard about. I wanted him to be my first experience with a man.

He was doing everything to make *me* feel pleasure. I wanted to give Matias that same satisfaction. I wanted to be the source of *his* pleasure.

I pulled away from our kiss to ask, "Can I touch you?"

He hummed, "I was just praying you would ask that."

"The devil answers prayers now?"

His laugh was breathy, "I suppose he does." He motioned to his pants with his chin, refusing to let his hand leave me even though he stopped moving his finger. "Go on."

Slowly, I slid my fingers down his arm, across the broad plain of his stomach. My hands met where his pants were fastened with a series of buttons. I felt my heart sped up with anticipation as I undid each one.

"That's it." His breath tickled my cheeks as he whispered.

There was a slight tremor in my hand as I pushed the black fabric down, exposing his undergarments. It was the only layer left.

"Keep going."

It wasn't a command, but I obeyed, moving the cloth until his arousal was free.

My whole body stilled at the sight. It looked bigger than the drawings I had seen of the male anatomy.

"Take me in your hand."

Gently, I wrapped my fingers around him. He was smooth and soft like velvet.

"Now stroke," He slid his finger in and out of me. "Just like how I am."

Slowly, I moved my hand up and then back down.

He moaned into my ear.

I moved up and down again.

"*Bueno*, just like that." His voice was like gravel.

When I moved my hand faster, he moaned again, deeper this time. He timed the pumping of his finger with the pulling of my hand. We were working each other in tandem. His pace picked up and I matched him.

Hearing him come undone by what my hand was doing sent a thrill of satisfaction through me.

"You...your touch..." He seemed to be struggling to speak. "It's like a drug."

Before I could say anything back, Matias's lips were back on mine. Just like when we danced earlier tonight, our bodies naturally flowed together. His finger moving inside me was building that pleasurable feeling up in my core.

He took my bottom lip between his teeth and sucked. With a barely audible moan, I felt myself succumbing to that overwhelming pleasure again. It rocked my body like a wave hitting the shore this time.

Matias's free hand covered mine still holding his arousal. "Don't stop."

As the waves of pleasure subsided, I kept pumping him in my hand.

I opened my eyes to find that his were closed. His full lips were tilted in a smirk. As I continued moving my hands, I noticed that the muscles in his arms and neck were tensing up.

With a groan, his eyes opened again. I didn't look down but I felt the pulsing of his release in my hand.

He placed a sweet kiss on my forehead before looking down. As he lifted his hand from mine, he whispered, "I'm afraid your slip is ruined."

"I'll throw it in the fire later." That would get rid of any evidence this night occurred. I was tempted to take it off now, but I wasn't sure how I felt about being completely naked in front of Matias. Something about the thin layer of my slip covering me made everything we did tonight feel less consequential, which was ridiculous because Matias had seen, touched, and sucked the most intimate parts of me. But with each of us still in an item of clothing, it wasn't as intimate.

He tucked himself back into his pants before lying flat on his back staring at the ceiling.

When I felt up to it, I stood, then I went around my bed to the nightstand and poured myself a glass of water. After eagerly drinking from it, I offered it to Matias. He took the glass but barely took a sip.

He motioned for me to come back into bed with him, so I did. We moved so that I was laying on his chest while he ran his fingers through my hair.

My body was humming with contentment. I expected some shame after what I just did, but it never came. I had gotten exactly what I wanted from this deal and it would be my secret forever. Only Matias and I would ever know and he would be gone in the morning. This worked almost too perfectly.

But as we settled into each other, I again found myself lost for words. What was one meant to say to a stranger that had just made them feel pleasure like that? It felt wrong to make comfortable small talk, but the silence was starting to weigh on me.

"Have you read all those books?" His voice brought me out of my thoughts.

"Yes," I smiled. "And then some. Those are just my favorites. You should see the library we have in the house. My father is adamant we have every book that is printed."

"Really? Is he an avid reader?"

"He is but he covets books because he watched them being burned during the war."

"The War Between the States?"

I nodded then lifted my head up so I could look at him while we talked. "He was a young boy, too young to fight, so he stayed here with the women while his father and brothers went off. He watched the soldiers come through and ransack all the houses. His mother, my grandmother, hid the valuables, but left behind the books. So when the soldiers got to this house, all they could burn were the books and that's what they did."

"He was upset about that?"

"I think it's more that the soldiers just did it and no one could stop them. He couldn't stop them from taking something from him. It wasn't even something he thought he wanted until he was told he couldn't have it anymore."

Matias nodded in understanding.

I asked, "Were you alive for the war?"

"How old do you think I am?" He laughed and it made my heart happy to hear that sound again.

"I don't know. You never asked how old I was either."

"I was born just before the war." Matias started playing with my hair again.

"You're thirty-seven years old?"

He nodded.

I sat up, examining his whole body now that I knew his age. "But you look like you're my age. I thought you were my age."

"Which would be?"

"I just turned twenty-three. How is it that you look so young?"

Matias shrugged, "I drank from the Fountain of Youth."

"So it exists?"

He simply winked.

I rested my head back on his chest. We laid together, Matias running his fingers through my hair, and I started idly tracing cursive letters across his skin. We stayed there, in each other's arms, for I'm not sure how long. We could hear the party dying down and then the music stopped completely. I held my breath as footsteps sounded down the hall but they never approached my room.

Matias's fingers found my chin and lifted my face so I could look at him when he stated, "I want to taste you one more time before the night is over."

Eagerly, I nodded.

"Do you want to taste me?"

Irene had told me about this. It was something men loved and she had enjoyed doing it.

But was that too much too soon?

"I'm not sure."

His smile eased my nerves. "Then we don't have to do that." I felt his hand slide down my back and land on my backside. "Straddle me but face the window."

With as much grace as I could manage, I sat up and moved my legs so they were on either side of his torso. It felt silly and I didn't understand why he wanted me to face away from him.

His cool hands grabbed my exposed thighs. "Move yourself backwards."

I looked at the lack of free space left between my backside and his head. "But then I'll be..."

"That's the aim of this, *pajarita*. You are going to sit on my face."

"Oh!"

The hands still on my thighs gave them a playful slap. "Come on, the night is waning."

He asked me to do this, so despite feeling like I was about to smother him, I placed my exposed core right above his mouth. His hands helped guide me into the perfect position.

Then his tongue licked down my center.

A soft moan flowed out of me as I leaned forward. My face was only a few inches away from his renewed arousal.

I couldn't see what Matias was doing, but I felt him lick every inch of me before focusing on my bundle of nerves. It wouldn't take me long to reach that pleasurable peak he had sent me to twice now.

I wanted him to feel that again. I wanted him to remember how good I made him feel.

With more confidence this time, I undid the buttons of his pants.

He pulled away to quickly say, "Isabelle, you don't have to."

I looked behind to see him staring at me over the curve of my backside. "I want to."

There was a twinkle of adoration in his eyes. "Then I won't stop you."

"Good." Smiling, I turned back to my task. I pushed his pants and undergarment down just enough for his arousal to be freed once more.

Irene had told me how to satisfy a man with my mouth. She expected that I would use her advice on Ashley. But choosing to let Matias be the first man I did this with felt exhilarating. I would remember this moment and this night any time I did this again.

It would be my secret way of still being free even when I was trapped.

All the muscles in Matias's stomach were tense. I peppered them with kisses as I made my way down to his cock. With a swift motion, I took as much of him in my mouth as I could.

Matias resumed his work on my sex. I tried to match the rhythm I bobbed my head with how he stroked his tongue against me. It was hard to maintain my movements. I wanted to stop everytime the pleasure I was receiving became too much. All of my moans turned into hums against him.

This time there were no ripples or sudden waves. This time I felt the gradual build up with each flick of his tongue. I could tell I was just about to climax but then he switched up the way he was moving.

Freeing my mouth, I demanded, "Do what you were doing before."

"*Claro*." I swore I felt him smile against me before he went back to the circling motion he had been doing.

"Yessss," The word was all I could manage before I put him back in my mouth.

The rush of pleasure hit me just a few licks later. I felt myself pulse around his tongue. The whole time, I kept moving my mouth up and down his shaft.

"Isabelle," He tapped my thigh so I paused to look at him. "I'm close. Let me finish on your slip."

I shook my head, "I want to taste all of you too." Irene had told me what would happen at the end of this so I was prepared. I wanted to prove to Matias that I could handle it.

"You are nothing like what I expected."

With a coy smile, I resumed working him with my mouth. He was right that he was close. It was just a few more moments before I felt the hot rush of his release hit my tongue. It was salty and tangy but it wasn't terrible.

When he was finished, I quickly hopped out of bed to finish off the glass of water. "I can get more if you need some as well."

"I'll be fine."

Nodding, I moved back into the spot I had been occupying by his side. This night could not have gone better. I was able to experience things I had always wanted to try but with someone I was genuinely attracted to. As I settled against Matias, I wondered what he was thinking. Did he feel like this deal was worth it? I wanted to ask but was afraid of hearing the wrong answer.

Instead we laid there in a content silence. I could feel my eyes getting heavy but I didn't want to miss a second of this experience.

Abruptly, Matias took a deep breath, then announced. "I must leave now."

Reluctantly, I pulled away from him. He quickly hopped off the bed and began dressing himself. I couldn't help but protest, "You promised a night."

"I did." He pointed at the clock. "And it is currently the morning."

I looked and saw it was just a few minutes before four o'clock. "So it is. I would like you to stay longer but I won't beg you."

He smiled like he was genuinely sorry. "I would stay but I must leave before the sun rises."

"I understand." The daylight would illuminate what we had done and make it easier for him to get caught. He needed to slip out now in the dead of night. "What about your carriage? Do you intend to walk home?"

"Some fresh air will help me clear my head."

I tried not to sound upset as I repeated, "Clear your head?"

"That's not-" Matias laid back on the bed, careful to dangle his boots off the edge. "I do wish I could stay longer. You have just made me the luckiest man here tonight."

I tried to joke to hide the pain that was suddenly moving through me, "I'm sure you say that to all the women who have taken you up on this deal."

His tone was serious as he stated, "I don't."

"Well," I said what I needed to say instead of what I wanted to say. "You must be on your way."

Matias's face softened, "I really must, and you must be tired."

I nodded. My body was spent but my mind was racing.

His voice felt both far away and in my ear at the same time. "You must be about to close your eyes."

"I suppose..." There was fogginess starting to blur the edges of my vision. Matias's lips curved into a sweet smile.

His voice sounded like music as he whispered, "Sleep now, Isabelle. When you wake, you'll have no memory of me or our magical night together."

I sat straight up. "I will never forget this night."

His eyes went wide for just a second, before settling back into a relaxed gaze. The fog started to creep back in. "No, *pajarita,* you must forget all about me."

With a shake of my head the fog was completely gone now. Clarity was sorting my racing thoughts. "What do you mean I must forget you? I will never forget this."

"I only mean you must not tell anyone about this night. It must be like it never happened."

I swallowed to keep myself from saying something rash. He was right of course. I couldn't breathe even a hint of this to anyone. So I nodded and whispered, "I understand."

His finger gently lifted my chin so our eyes met. The fog started to come back as his dark eyes stared into mine like they were trying to look past me. There was no emotion in the stoic panes of his face. His features were starting to blur. I was more tired than I realized. But I wouldn't let sleep ruin this. With a more assertive shake of my head, the fog disappeared. Calmly, I repeated, "I understand."

"Good." He cleared his throat and jumped up off the bed. His hands went into his hair, "I just, I don't want anything bad happening to you because of me. This night was meant to be a good memory for both of us."

"Let me escort you out of the house."

"No need," He motioned towards the window. "I can go out this way."

"It is a far drop down to the ground."

"I'll manage."

And because I didn't know what else to say, I told him, "Thank you...for all of it."

He backed away towards the window. "For all of what?"

I smiled while hot tears started to pool in my eyes. I hadn't expected to be this upset at his departure. It was a condition of the deal we had made. But that didn't lessen the sting I felt in my chest.

As Matias continued to back up towards the window, I tore my gaze away. My sight was starting to blur from the tears I was refusing to let fall. I shook my head to remind myself not to give in and cry. My eyes caught sight of something black laid on my vanity chair. "Oh!" I cried out as I stood up to grab the jacket.

But Matias was already gone.

When I went to the window to see if I could maybe catch him in his climb down the side of the house, he was nowhere to be found.

Six

Matias

As soon as my feet touched the grass underneath Isabelle's window, I sprinted away from the house. The need to get out of Alexandria as soon as physically possible pushed me forward. I went as fast as my legs could carry me back to the cemetery I was using for respite and cover from the sun.

This had so much potential to end terribly.

Isabelle would remember who I was when she woke in the morning. I couldn't compel her to forget; no matter how much I tried, I couldn't make her forget about me.

That hasn't happened since I figured out *how* to make others forget all about me.

It didn't take long for me to run through the woods that bordered Isabelle's home, cut through the town square, then past the church into the cemetery. To avoid the giant iron gate squeaking, I leapt over it then continued on my trajectory.

No one would have been able to see me as I went, but I noticed that there wasn't another soul out at this time of night. Last night the town was quiet but I managed to catch a few stragglers coming home from the bar. This morning there was no one. I wondered if it was because of the lavish party the Hallers had thrown. It did look like everyone who was anyone was at that house.

I was too frazzled to hunt even if I had run into a human. Blood would help me keep up my frantic pace, but I couldn't risk the time it would take to do all that. I should have snuck a drink from Isabelle.

I almost did. There were so many chances to knick her with one of my fangs and just taste her blood. She wouldn't have been able to tell. I would have been expertly careful with her delicate skin.

Those tempting thoughts slowed my pace. Perhaps I could go back for a quick taste of her on my way out of town?

No, I needed to focus all my thoughts into fleeing this place before the sun rose.

With supernatural ease, I flung open the stone door to the mausoleum. It just as easily closed behind me as I stepped in the darkness.

It only took a moment for my eyes to adjust to the lack of light. Heightened senses allowed me to see in the dark, but it wasn't instantaneous.

Everything looked just as I had left it when I set out tonight. The coffin was in the middle of the room. Its evicted occupant lay in a pile in the corner. I didn't even bother lighting the torch that hung on the wall. In the darkness I saw how clearly tonight had been a mistake.

"*Mierda!*"

The shout escaped me and echoed in the small space.

My fingers raked through my already mussed hair. Even with my lack of reflection, I knew Isabelle's fingers had sent my curls flying in different directions. She had undone more than my hair.

My feet instinctively started pacing around the room trying to rid myself of this anxious energy. "Why the hell hadn't it worked?" I asked out loud to help my mind focus. I knew when we danced that she was fighting my compulsion, but that wasn't rare. People usually fought having their mind taken over.

But she was able to shake me off completely.

That had never happened to me before and I didn't realize it until it was too late.

My lust for her distracted me before I fully realized what was happening. She would remember everything and that could put her life in danger.

How could I have been so careless? The whole time we were dancing, I wanted nothing more than to whisk her away and get into trouble with her. Those blue eyes had pulled me in from the moment I locked onto them. They reminded me of the color of the Tenerife Sea over in Spain, something I desperately missed.

When she said we could only dance, that nothing more could come from our meeting, I tried to leave her alone. None of the other women who flirted with me brought out the same reaction as she did. Then that buffoon walked in and I instantly knew he was the reason Isabelle wouldn't go further than dancing with me. They were together, though Isabelle acted like she preferred it when he wasn't there.

I should have just left the party then. I had already made sure everyone I spoke to or interacted with would forget me. After so many months of using my gift, it only took seconds to plant the compulsion in their minds. She was the only loose end to tie up. That's what I told myself last night. I had to stay and make sure she forgot about me and our dance.

So I waited and watched her. All these other women were throwing themselves at me, but I had to be hooked by the one woman who was unavailable. I saw her as a challenge and I hadn't felt that rush since I had escaped my imprisonment.

Women had never been a challenge when I was human. It had been a few weeks since I had tried to seduce anyone, but it had only become easier now that I could compel anyone to do what I wished. I quickly figured out that she was so hesitant to do more than dance because she was promised to another. But that had never stopped a woman that I had wanted before.

I wanted her because I couldn't have her.

When she led the buffoon out into the garden, I followed. I hid in the shadows and I listened to what he was threatening to do to her.

He wouldn't have been able to hear how her pulse sped up or smell how her body panicked. I wanted to kill him in front of her to give her a way out of this life her body was violently protesting against, but I didn't. I listened to her come up with an excuse to get away from him.

I followed her just to make sure she made it to her room. I hadn't planned on saying anything, but I couldn't help myself. I had to see if she was going to be alright. The relationship she was forced into was taking its toll on her. The vibrant face that blushed when we had danced was sunken with worry. She needed a night that was just about her, a pleasure I would happily give.

Feeling her was worth it, because it was supposed to be a memory only I would have. It would keep me company as I continued looking for answers about what happened to my family while I was imprisoned.

It had been so long since a woman had made me feel like Isabelle did. The other women I took to bed while I traveled were a means to an end, but not with her. For some reason, perhaps because of her situation, it all felt different. The other women had practically thrown themselves at me when I offered my deal to them. She hadn't reacted the way I expected her to.

Nothing about her was what I expected. I had just wanted a night of pure pleasure, something I hadn't had in a very long time.

Which made the fact that I couldn't erase her memory of me all the more dangerous.

Because if the Lord of Shadows was tracking me down, he could find Isabelle and torture her until she revealed what she knew about me. Not that she knew much, but it wouldn't matter to him. He would torture whatever information he could out of her and then he would suck her dry. She would be killed because of me.

"No." I shook my head as I sat on the edge of the coffin. "No, that's irrational." Before I let my wild thoughts run, I recited the mantra *mi mama* always repeated. "*Tranquilo y piensa.*"

As I took deep breaths my thoughts sorted themselves out.

I hadn't seen any signs the Lord of Shadows was hunting me since I escaped his prison months ago.

If he was trying to find me, he would have gone to my family home in Florida and found the same dead end that I did.

From there he would have to look for people who knew what happened to my father and sisters, but even I couldn't find them.

Then he would have to follow my father's old business connections up the coast, which would bring him to Alexandria.

But he would never be able to figure out I was here because I erased everyone's memories along the way. Everyone I had interacted with from the moment I escaped had been compelled to forget all about me. I made sure of it. No one remembered me.

But Isabelle would.

"*Mierda!*" I stood up and flung the lid off the coffin.

The wood hit the ground with a loud boom that echoed. When the sound stopped, I asked myself. "Perhaps I could stick around for a few more days and make sure she is safe?"

And risk getting caught myself? That would be even more foolish.

I needed to leave.

Now.

Isabelle was a smart girl. She would hide all evidence that we had spent a night together. Nothing would happen to her as long as I left now. Her buffoon was a man with money and connections. He could keep her safe better than I could. All I would bring was more danger to her life.

I turned to the hook on the wall where I had hung my suit jacket. But it was empty.

I only had a few items of clothing so it wasn't like it could get lost.

"Where the hell–" My mind wound backwards to remember where I last had the jacket on. It was in Isabelle's room before I took it off and placed it on her vanity chair.

And then I had been so distracted by leaving her room as quickly as possible that I had forgotten it.

"*Carajo!*"

I needed to get that jacket back. Tucked inside the pocket was all my money and the only picture I had of my mother. How could I leave something so important behind?

What a huge mistake this night was.

"No, no," I spoke out loud to stop that train of thought. She wasn't a mistake. It was my own fault this was blowing up in my face. But I would make it right.

I shoved the mausoleum door back open and was greeted by the first rays of the sun peaking over the trees.

Had that much time passed already? In my panicked state the hours had felt like minutes.

I had no choice but to wait until the sun was back down to go retrieve my jacket from Isabelle's room. Then I could get the hell out of here.

Seven

Isabelle

The sun rose far too early the next morning. It felt like I had barely slept even though I fell into a deep slumber almost as soon as Matias had left and I returned to my bed. I had made sure any evidence of what happened was thrown away underneath a dress I hadn't worn in years so it would look like I was just tossing out old clothes.

At first, I thought last night had been a very intense, realistic dream. It had been too good to be true. I turned, still under the covers, to see Matias's jacket still hung up on my vanity chair.

It wasn't a dream.

"Isabelle!" Irene was calling my name over and over. The voice was getting louder as she approached the door. Immediately, I stashed Matias's forgotten jacket under the pile of clothes. I quickly threw on a robe, barely covering myself before Irene burst through the door.

"Sister!" She cried out as soon as her eyes locked on me.

"Yes?"

"I had the most amazing evening!" She flopped down onto the bed with a soft thud.

"That pleases me to hear." Which was the truth. I was happy that Irene got to enjoy her night. Even though I knew the truth about Ashley paying Roger to marry Irene, she seemed so happy. I couldn't ruin it for her.

"After you left Roger and I danced the rest of the night! As the night wound down, Roger and I snuck out to the garden and..." Irene wiggled her eyebrows.

My eyes widened, "You didn't!"

"We just kissed!" Irene played with the hem of her robe's sleeve. "But that kiss was just a preview of the other things I imagine his lips can do."

Blush lit up my own face, and not because of how boldly Irene was speaking. We openly discussed pleasures like this before. I blushed thinking about what I had done just a few hours ago with a man that was not who I was intended to marry. Matias would never give me a diamond, the only thing I would ever have from him was a pleasurable memory.

She continued, "Imagine, you marry Ashley and I marry Roger then we have to move to Washington! We could be socialites! Invited to all the parties!"

"That would be wonderful."

"We could have our babies together, and take strolls through parks together. It *would* be wonderful!"

It took all my energy to match Irene's excitement. "Yes, it would."

"Will you talk to Ashley? I want to know if Roger feels the same as I do. I feel like he does. He clearly showed his interest in me when we were alone, but I'm worried he'll find out about what happened and change his mind like all the others."

"I'll speak to Ashley at church today."

"Church!" My sister sprang up from the bed. "I need to prepare myself! Do you think Roger will be at church?"

"I'm not sure. If he is staying with Ashley then he should be there."

"Then I need to look my best!"

Irene ran from the room. I sank back into the bed staring at the ceiling thinking about how wonderful my own night had been. I expected to feel regret or anxiety about what I had done with Matias last night, but I didn't. I felt the warmth of pleasure seeping out from my core and into the rest of my body.

Last night was a secret I would keep with me for the rest of my days. My own scandalous memory, something I would never and could never share. Laying back on the bed, I closed my eyes, and started imagining Matias's hands and mouth on my body again.

"Miss Isabelle?" Mary's voice ripped me from my fantasy.

"Yes?"

"May I come in?"

"Just a moment!"

I made sure my robe was covering me before I told Mary to enter.

Her eyes scanned my body, "Are you feeling well?"

"Yes, Mary." I sat up to reassure her I was. "I'll be ready for church soon."

A wrinkly smile lit up her face as she approached me, "You seem..."

I tried to stay relaxed as she eyed me. There was no way she could know what I did last night. Even if she suspected something, Mary wouldn't tell. But I didn't want to admit what I did. I wanted to house this secret within myself.

Her eyes looked around the room and landed on the pile of clothes that hid my ruined slip and Matias's jacket. The black sleeve was poking out but surely that wouldn't give anything away?

Her eyes scanned me as she finished her sentence. "You seem tired."

"I am. I had trouble sleeping last night. Too much wine gave me a headache."

She winked, "That's why I always tell you girls to be careful."

I nodded.

"I'll be helping Irene if you need me."

"Thank you, Mary."

As soon as the door was shut, I sprang out of bed and found a better place to hide the jacket.

* * *

The church bells rang out ten times to signal the hour. We joined the huddle of people filing into the old wooden building. The church was one of the first places built when Alexandria was founded. My father's ancestors had lended their hands to the construction of it in the eighteenth century. We attended Sunday services every week.

As I looked around, I saw the same faces that had been happily drinking and dancing the night before now looked worn and long as they trudged into church.

My family took our usual pew just two rows back from the pulpit. We all smiled and waved at the people coming in and sitting around us. I heard the familiar voice of Mr. Middleton as he greeted my father. "An excellent evening as always, Haller. You two know how to throw a party."

"It is all Marg's hard work." My father wrapped an arm around my mother. "Surprised you are up and about this morning after how red you were last night."

"Can't miss a single service." Mr. Middleton smiled at my father.

"Of course." He gave him a playful pat on the shoulder. I was tempted to ask about Matias, but there were too many ears around to risk it.

Ashley was filing into the other side of the pew with his mother, father, younger brothers, and Roger. Our families greeted each other before all sitting down. Roger maneuvered himself so he was sitting with Irene.

Ashley was impossibly close to me, encroaching on my space. "Your father told me last night that I was to come over for lunch today. A special meal is being prepared."

"I can't imagine why." The words were dry.

His hand slid into mine before he flipped it over to look at my bare ring finger. With a tight squeeze he commanded, "You need to work on acting surprised."

With a fake smile, I replied, "I will."

There was no other choice but to go along with what Ashley wanted. Slipping back into that fake version of myself would make everything moving forward easier.

At least I had enjoyed one night of freedom.

Ashley leaned into me as Pastor Stevens began speaking. He led us through hymns before giving the same lecture about the sin of drinking that we hear every year after my parents' Autumnal Ball. Everyone in the church who had been at the party tried to hide their grins and giggles for the sake of Pastor Stevens. It's hard to hide sins in a town this small, putting them out in the open makes us all accomplices.

I tuned him out and focused on Ashley's clammy hand holding mine. It was nothing like the cool, soft touches Matias had used last night.

Would I be comparing Ashley's touches to Matias for the rest of our days? Ashley was like the sun, constant and a bit oppressive at times. Matias was a lightning strike that hit me just once but scarred me in a way that I would never recover from.

Ashley jerked me up as everyone began to stand at once. We sang along to the next hymn then finished the service and began making our way around to speak with anyone we hadn't talked to on our way in.

Ashley broke off to speak with one of the neighboring farmers, while my father finished joking with Mr. Middleton. After they shook hands, my father started leading us all out of our pew.

As I filed past, I carefully got his attention. "Pardon me, Mr. Middleton."

"Isabelle," He stopped just outside the pew. "What can I help you with?"

I took a step away from the pew so we had a bit more privacy. "I'm sorry to bother you, I just want to inquire about Mr. Ciervo. Did he leave town already?" I told myself the only reason I was asking about him was because I needed to return his jacket.

Mr. Middleton made a face. "Who?"

"Matias Ciervo. You brought him to the party last night."

"I haven't seen Matias Ciervo in over a decade.When I last heard from his father, he was in Spain."

"Spain? No, he was here, staying at your home."

He chuckled, "Isabelle, I think I would know if a man like Matias Ciervo was in my home."

I didn't understand if he was lying or just making some cruel joke. "What do you mean?"

"He has an effect on others, especially the women he interacts with. He wouldn't be able to get in or out of that place without my maids gossiping about him. You must've heard one of them speaking about when he visited with his family so long ago. Even then, he was a problem."

"A problem?"

"My dear, I do not believe such topics are appropriate for your delicate ears, but, yes, he was caught in many..." he coughed as he found the words, "compromising positions with some young ladies who were employed by me. It was one of the things that led his father to send him to Spain."

"Oh," My eyes suddenly couldn't focus on anything. I took a step back from Mr. Middleton. He clearly remembered things much differently than I did. Last night he had spoken so highly of Matias, perhaps something had changed between them this morning. "Yes, I had a bit too much to drink last night and I must've misheard some gossip."

"It happens to the best of us." Mr. Middleton gave me a reassuring smile. "Drink plenty of water and rest today."

"Of course. Good day, sir." I nodded. He seemed to buy the lie I had spun him, but I didn't understand why I needed to lie. I was asking him about someone he claimed to be friends with. Someone who almost everyone at this church had seen last night. Perhaps it was just Mr. Middleton's memory failing him now?

"There you are." Ashley wrapped a possessive arm around my waist and pulled me away from Mr. Middleton. "Your parents are outside waiting for you."

Ashley would remember Matias. He had been irate after he found out I danced with someone else. But bringing that back up would only bring back that rage.

Silently, I let Ashley lead me outside the church.

On clear Sundays, my family liked to walk to and from church. Ashley wanted to walk with us but his mother insisted that he come home with his family. With a quick kiss we said our goodbyes. Ashley had to practically drag Roger away from Irene.

We started walking back towards our house, my parents ahead of us talking and looking back at me every few minutes. It was easy to gather that they were discussing the impending proposal.

"Irene," I whispered as I snuck my arm around hers and pulled her close. "Can I ask you something?"

"Anything!" She grinned, leaning in closer.

"Do you remember that handsome stranger last night?"

"Roger?"

"No, the one before Roger."

She scoffed, "There was no one before Roger."

"No, there was this man you wanted to dance with but he asked me to dance instead-"

"You danced with someone else?"

"Lower your voice!" I waited to see if my parents would react to her outburst, but they continued walking. "Yes, you remember, don't you?"

"No." Irene's face pinched into a scowl. "No, and you should pray that no one remembers because if Ashley finds out then..." She shuddered.

"I know." Had Irene drunk so much last night that she had forgotten all about Matias? She cried over him and made a scene in the library because I danced with him. There was no way Irene would just let that fizzle out and pretend she couldn't remember.

Irene whispered, "Did you really dance with a stranger?"

"No, he asked me to but I said no." The lie felt bitter on my tongue.

Eight

Isabelle

Back at the house, I practically ran into my room and locked the door behind me. Using the excuse that I wanted to change into the perfect outfit for the proposal, I had all the privacy I needed. And what I needed was to assure myself that what I remembered actually happened.

With a deep breath to steady myself, I approached my wardrobe. Before church I had hidden Matias's forgotten jacket in there tucked underneath a pile of nightgowns in one of the drawers. I ensured that none of the black fabric was poking out.

I took it out of its hiding spot and laid the jacket out on my bed. It smelt like him, subtle spice and whiskey. The proof was still here.

My fingers slipped into the jacket pockets. I found a clip of money and a picture of a woman and a young boy. The young boy was probably Matias, they seemed to have the same shaped eyes, and I assumed the woman was his mother.

There was just over one hundred dollars in the money clip, which he certainly would notice was missing. There was nothing that gave me a clue of how to get this jacket and the contents back to its owner. He would have to come back for these things.

The thought of seeing him again refreshed the memories of our night.

What if he came by the house today asking for it back? What would happen if I saw him during the day? Would it be obvious something had happened between us?

I was getting ahead of myself. If Matias really needed this jacket, he would come back for it, otherwise, it wouldn't matter.

Just to be safe, I set the money and the picture in my nightstand drawer before stashing the jacket back in my wardrobe. Once everything was safely hidden, I started to get myself ready for the inevitable.

* * *

A soft knock on my door brought my attention away from my reflection in the mirror. I had been sitting there brushing the same section of hair over and over again as I relived last night with Matias.

"Miss Isabelle?" Mary's soft voice came from the otherside of the door.

"One moment!" I called back, getting up to unlock the door.

Mary shuffled in once the door was open. "You locked your door?"

"Just needed some privacy."

"Ah," She waddled over to the wardrobe. "This is a big day for you."

"It is."

Mary looked me up and down. "You're not dressed yet?"

My hands went to my slip. Almost identical to the one I had tossed after what happened last night. Smoothing out the silk, I shook my head. "No, no, my mind went to other places while I was dressing."

I hoped she would fill in the blanks and assume I was thinking about Ashley.

"What's troubling you?"

I straightened my back, "It is just a big day, as you said."

"Irene and your parents look more excited than you do."

"They aren't the ones getting engaged today."

"No," She sighed, "But they shouldn't be the happiest people today. I know this isn't what you wanted, but perhaps you could learn to make the best of it? Mister Ashley's money could afford you your own personal library."

"Mary, are you suggesting I get married just for books?"

"I'm sure you can find other ways to entertain yourself with someone that handsome, but yes, the books would fill the other twenty-three hours of your day."

We shared a laugh that helped ease the tension I had been feeling.

"Now," She moved to my wardrobe. "What will you be wearing for this momentous occasion?"

"You pick, Mary. I'd rather not make any more decisions today."

"You won't have me around to pick for you much longer." She started sorting through my dresses. "Soon you'll be in a house with your husband and someone else will be helping you get ready."

"Don't say that." I meant to make it sound like a jest but the words came out sad.

"Perhaps once Irene is married as well, I can come visit you girls."

"I would love that."

"Good," Her smile didn't reach her eyes as she turned around holding a pale pink dress. "This one is what I always imagined you wearing."

"Then I shall wear it today."

Mary helped open up the buttons on the back of the dress before lifting it up over my head. She pulled it down, adjusting as she went, and then started doing the buttons back up. I pulled at the white lace that trimmed the cap sleeves and bust before slipping on the matching shoes. Finally, Mary flared out the skirt before spinning me around to look in the mirror.

The pink of the dress brought out the pink in my cheeks. The bodice was tight enough to show my curves, but softened them so I looked more modest with a flared skirt. My auburn curls flowed down my shoulder and onto my back. I looked like a young woman who was going somewhere special.

Mary started, "Well my dear-"

"Isabelle!" Irene burst into the room, her smile turning into awe. "Well, don't you just look like an angel!"

"Thank you, sister."

"Ashley has arrived and he brought Roger! They are waiting for us in the garden." Her excitement was making her voice squeaky. She looked at me then down at herself. Her light blue dress was a compliment to mine. The silhouettes were similar, but Irene's had longer sleeves and the dress was dotted with pearls instead of lace. "Perhaps I should change."

"No!" I shouted.

"You look lovely, Miss Irene." Mary smiled.

"Are you certain? I feel like you look better than I do."

"Let your sister look the best today." Mary chided. "You look better every other time."

Irene took a deep breath. "Ready, sister?"

No.

Instead of admitting how I really felt, I nodded before taking Irene's hand and walking out.

The sun had warmed the fall air, so I was glad I wore a dress with shorter sleeves as we sat in the garden. Despite sitting at a table under the shade of an oak tree, I could feel a drop of sweat sliding down my back. The flowers in the garden created a sweet cacophony of scents. Fall hadn't begun to wilt the plants and trees yet.

We had made it through most of the lunch with Irene dominating the conversation, which I didn't mind. She shamelessly flirted with Roger, grinning and giggling at everything he said. As overt as Irene was, Roger seemed to be lapping up her attention like a cat does with milk.

Once we were officially done with the meal, Ashley took my hand in his. "Walk with me."

My stomach sank; the lunch I had just finished threatened to make its way back up my throat. I did my best to bury the sick feeling to reply, "Of course."

"Excuse us." Ashley said to Irene and Roger, but they were too far gone to notice us. My sister was offering her new beau a piece of cake from her fork.

Ashley took my hand in his, laying it in the crook of his arm. "They seem to be getting along perfectly."

"Yes," I felt conflicted at this. All Irene had wanted for the last decade was to find someone to love and marry her. Here was the perfect man for the task and yet I was bitter at their union because it meant I could no longer put off my own. "Despite being persuaded to go along with this, he does seem to enjoy her."

"He does." Ashley's chest puffed with pride. "He admitted to me that he finds her *entertaining*."

"Good." Was all I could manage to respond.

We kept walking, Ashley pulling me along every time I slowed my pace. It was my last attempt to prolong what I had been avoiding for years. The slower we walked, the longer it would take to get where I was certain he was taking me.

Ashley's hand landed on my lower back to forcefully guide me towards the willow tree. It was my favorite spot on my family's land. Tucked beneath the thick limbs and branches, I used to read for hours, until I grew too tall to comfortably fit up there. It was where Ashley had proposed over a decade ago. I knew he would take me back there for this moment.

The silence was buzzing between us. I didn't want to ease it. I wanted this to feel awkward now. Maybe he would change his mind? Maybe he would realize that I wasn't a good match for him after all?

Right in front of the willow, Ashley pulled my arm to stop me.

"Izzy," He sucked in a deep breath.

"Yes?"

His hands grabbed onto mine. "Do you remember what I said to you all those years ago?"

"That you would marry me so I couldn't run away from you during hide-and-seek ever again."

"I believe I added that I would treat you like a princess from those books you were always reading."

I looked down at the ground to avoid showing too strong of a reaction. The memory of that day was not a fond one for me. I had taken Ashley's vow that day as a joke, but what I didn't know at that time was he went and told my parents that I had agreed to marry him. That set us on the path we've been walking since we were eight.

"I have loved you since we were children. I know you didn't realize it when you were young, but you have always been the one that I was going to marry. You are going to make a perfect wife and a loving mother to all the babies we are going to have. Now that nothing else can stop me," Ashley bent down so he was on one knee. "Will you marry me?"

My stomach flipped. Tears started to fall before I could stop them. I smiled so they looked like happy tears when I answered, "Yes."

He slipped the ring with a diamond bigger than an acorn onto my finger before pulling me in for a sloppy kiss. The size of the rock dwarfed my hand. It took up the entire space between my knuckles. The weight of this ring was unbearable.

* * *

"Congratulations!" A chorus of synchronized voices rang out as we approached.

My parents had joined Irene and Roger outside by the garden table. I went through the motions of showing them my ring. Roger and my father gave Ashley approving pats on the back while my mother and Irene practically drooled over the size of the diamond. My sister turned to Roger and told him, "You'll have to out do that."

Roger snuck a wink at Ashley. My family saw it as a joke but I recognized that Ashley would b e the one paying for Irene's engagement ring. Ashley would be funding their entire life so that he could have me as his wife.

Champagne was passed around as my mother asked, "So when would you like the wedding?"

"We spoke about it already and we want to be wed as soon as possible!" Ashley pulled me in tight as he lied. I knew I would have to accept the proposal, but I was hoping I could put off the wedding as long as possible.

My mother lit up, "I can have it all arranged in a month!"

I choked on the sip of champagne I had just taken. "That soon? I expected this would take half a year at least."

"Oh, Isabelle, I have been planning your wedding since you were a child! I have every detail already decided, we just needed a date and now we have one!"

"A month. But that's..." My mind floundered for an excuse. "So close to Irene's birthday!"

"I don't mind sharing!" Irene beamed at me. "As long as I have my party before your wedding."

My mother looked down as she thought, "If Irene's birthday is the twentieth then we can do the wedding on the twenty-third, which should be a Saturday!"

"I don't want to share our wedding weekend with Irene's birthday. Perhaps we should wait a little longer?"

"Nonsense!" Irene shook her head. "I want nothing more than to see you married!"

"Cheers to that!" Ashley shouted and everyone but me raised their glasses.

There were no more excuses to give. No more reasons to push this back. Other than I just didn't want this, any of this, there was nothing else I could say to stop it.

Ashley and my mother eagerly started discussing the guest list while Irene and Roger wandered off to whisper together.

"Father," I went to where he had taken a seat on the garden bench. He had been quiet while everything was happening, which was unlike him since he always had an opinion on everything. "What do you think of all this?"

Without looking up from his glass, he answered, "I think it's fine."

"But it's too soon."

He shrugged, "It's what Ashley wants."

"It's not what I want."

He turned his gaze to me. "That doesn't matter."

"Why don't the feelings I have about my own wedding matter?"

"Ashley is taking you without a dowry so he can demand whatever he wants and your mother and I will oblige."

"Give him my dowry and push the wedding off-"

"There is no dowry for you now."

"What?" I whispered in disbelief.

"Ashley agreed long ago to take you without one. So we only have one for Irene."

"So then pay him now-"

"There is nothing with which to pay him." His expression hardened. "You are being an ungrateful brat. That man," he pointed at my now official fiancé, "has done so much for this family. He wants you without any financial gain from it. He's just bought a house for you and is going to give you everything we have ever dreamed of. I couldn't have bargained a better deal if I tried. So you will do whatever he wants and whatever your mother says. Irene will need all the help she can get to be an appealing match for someone. You are sorted and this matter is done. Am I understood?"

"Yes, father."

Nine

Isabelle

After celebrating the official engagement, Ashley was finally leaving to return to his own home. Everyone said their goodbyes and left us alone just outside the door. Roger was waiting in the carriage, having promised Irene he would come visit again as soon as he could and write to her every day.

Ashley lifted my hand so he could examine the ring. "Just a few more weeks until I can take you away with me."

"Could we possibly postpone the wedding?"

"Why?" His grip on my hand tightened.

A dry swallow burned my throat as I lied. "I always wanted a spring wedding."

"Well, I want to be married as soon as possible."

"Could we perhaps-"

"We've waited long enough, Izzy."

"We only just got engaged today."

Ashley scoffed, "If that's what you believe then what was the point of the last fifteen years?"

It was getting harder to mask the panic in my voice. "Please, I just want a little more time-"

"For what?"

"For whatever I would like."

Ashley grabbed my arm, harder than I expected him to. "You are about to ruin the happiest day of my life. Do not continue with this."

"Ashley..."

"We will be married as soon as I want and you will be bearing my child shortly thereafter. I don't want to hear anymore of this nonsense about you needing more time. From now on, you're on my time."

But everything had already been on his time. He had already been controlling so many aspects of my life and he assumed he would just be able to continue to control me. I saw no other option but to let him.

"I'm sorry, I'm just...I haven't been feeling myself since the other night."

Ashley sighed and the tension in his body seemed to dissipate. Carefully, he pulled me into him so our bodies were flushed together. I tried to pass the uncomfortable shudder off as pleasure. "I'll expect to see *my* Izzy when I return this weekend."

"She'll be here." I gave him the best smile I could muster. With a quick peck on the lips, Ashley turned and left.

I ran straight to my room and removed the ring before flinging it on my bed. How could something so small feel so heavy?

Tears that had been kept hidden all day immediately started flowing. My whole body felt like it was melting as I fell onto the bed. The edge of the giant diamond cut into the exposed flesh of my arm. With a growl, I took the ring and slammed it onto my nightstand. I wanted to throw it out the window, but that would only infuriate Ashley.

For the rest of my life I would be doing everything I could to keep Ashley's temperament calm. Everything I had done to try to avoid this outcome didn't matter now. I was getting married in a month.

I cried myself to sleep.

* * *

When I woke up, my room was completely dark. My hands cautiously searched out the gas lamp on my nightstand, turning it on so I could make out what time it was. The clock said just after midnight.

The diamond ring lit up despite the faint light. The glare was harsh to my sensitive eyes. To avoid having to look at the ring, I placed it inside the drawer.

My head was still groggy with sleep but I realized I was still in my dress. The corset had shifted while I had slept, so it was pinching into my sides. As quick as I could, I stripped it off and changed into a nightgown then crawled back into bed.

I tossed and turned, unable to shake visions of how Ashley would threaten and manipulate me until I died. I imagined raising a little boy, who looked just like Ashley as a child, bossing me around. I practically heard Ashley's voice boasting, "He gets that from his father." Everyone in the imaginary scene laughed as I faded away.

Wine would help these ominous visions become more and more muddled until sleep could take me again. Wine usually helped me sleep, even if there were some repercussions from it in the morning, it was worth it tonight.

My legs felt heavy as I snuck down to the kitchen. The whole house was quiet, and felt like it had been for a while. I knew this stillness wouldn't last. Soon, people would be running around getting everything ready for Irene's birthday party and my wedding.

I expected to have to go down to the wine cellar, but there was an opened bottle of merlot left on the counter. It must have been from the dinner I had slept through. The bottle was basically full, probably opened by my mother then taken away by my father. After opening it myself, I threw the cork out. It would take all of this to get me back to sleep.

Slowly I walked back to my room, savoring the quiet and the wine. My time left in my childhood home was now limited. Life with Ashley in Washington would be vastly different, but if he traveled for business, perhaps I could find ways to enjoy myself while he was gone?

The wine was warming my cheeks as I went up the stairs. I hadn't seen the house I would be living in yet. I'd let Irene come and decorate it. She cared more about those things than I did. All I wanted was a library. As long as I had that, I could tolerate living with Ashley.

I paused at Irene's door. She would be married soon enough and we could keep each other company. This *whole* arrangement wasn't terrible.

A stifled laugh escaped me as I started walking back to my room. It was terrible. I was going to be shackled to someone who just wanted to control every aspect of my life. I looked at the almost empty bottle of wine. There were going to be many more bottles emptied to help numb me going forward.

"Cheers." I whispered to myself before finishing off the last sip. I placed the empty bottle on the floor by my door. Mary would grab it in the morning.

"*Mierda!*"

The word leaked out into the hallway from behind my bedroom door.

I instantly recognized Matias's voice even if it was a harsh whisper.

My heart felt a jolt and my cheeks flushed as just the sound of his voice brought back the memory of his hands exploring me. He must have returned for his jacket and was unable to find the spot where I had tucked it into my wardrobe. My lips curled into a sneaky smile.

I coughed loudly before slowly turning the doorknob so I didn't startle him. There was a soft rustling sound but I didn't see anything as my eyes adjusted to the very dim lighting in my room.

Pretending to yawn, I moved sleepily to the wardrobe, using my body to shield the jacket as I took it out. My eyes just barely noticed Matias hiding in the shadows of the far corner of my room, but I did my best to ignore him. I turned and made it look like I was getting into bed. Then, I paused.

I thought about bringing the jacket into bed with me to see if he would try to pry it out of my fingers. I thought about throwing the jacket out of the window and seeing if he would jump out after it. But none of those felt like the best way to handle this.

Slowly, I turned to where he was attempting to hide in the shadows and held the jacket up. "Looking for something?"

Matias stepped into the light. His lips were curled into a grin but his nostrils were flared. "Yes, actually, thank you for finding my jacket."

"You left it here."

"I did." His chest heaved with a light laugh. "Now if you would just hand it over to me, I will be on my way."

"If you want it back, you need to explain something to me."

He stiffened as his face fell, "What would that be?"

"Why am I the only one that remembers you?"

The grin that split his face was hiding something. "Isabelle, we had a very memorable night."

"That's not what I meant." I huffed. "I asked Mr. Middleton, the man who brought you to the party, and he said the last time he saw you was over a decade ago."

"Well, the memories of old men can't always be trusted."

My annoyance was leaking into my voice. "Yes, but when I tried to talk to my sister about you, she had no memory of you either."

He was trying too hard to act relaxed now. "She was upset that I did not dance with her, of course she wouldn't want to speak about that."

"You don't know my sister. She would have used the slight against her as ammunition to guilt me into doing favors for her for weeks."

"Perhaps-"

"No one remembers you except me. I almost thought I had gone mad until I came home this morning from church and your jacket was still where I hid it."

Matias just looked at me with a blank face.

"Explain yourself. Why am I the only one who remembers you?"

He shrugged, "How could that be possible?"

I had given some thought to what might have happened. "You could have drugged everyone at the party while we were..." My eyes scanned his covered body, remembering how he felt next to me. I shifted on my feet, suddenly feeling too warm. "Occupied. The drug made them forget things."

A smirk curled his lips, "Then that's what happened."

I scoffed. "What drug could do that?"

"Clearly some kind of drug if you were able to concoct this theory."

"You are agreeing with me too easily for this to be the truth."

"The truth is subjective, Isabelle." He held out his hand. "Now, my jacket please."

I rolled my eyes before throwing the jacket at him. He quickly slipped on over his more casual shirt and pants before checking the pockets. When he realized they were empty, his eyes flicked to mine.

"What is the matter?" I crossed my arms. My nightgown kept me mostly covered but there was enough skin exposed to distract him. Those brown eyes went to my chest before they came back to mine.

"Where are the contents of my pockets?"

I feigned ignorance, "What do you mean?"

"You know exactly what I mean."

"Oh, you mean the money and the photograph?"

His hands came out of his pockets curled in tight fists. He nodded and took a step towards me.

"They are hidden somewhere in the house." I motioned to the door. "I will retrieve them for you when you tell me the real reason why I am the only one who can remember last night."

Matias rushed around me, heading for the door.

"You'll never find them without me. Or my father and his shotgun will find you first. So just tell me what happened last night."

He looked back at the door, fingers running through his hair as he thought. I wanted my hands back in those dark curls while his head was between my thighs.

After a few beats, he turned back to face me. "You are correct about what happened last night. I drugged everyone."

"Why?" This wasn't making sense.

"So I could rob the rich guests at the party," He threw his arms out at his sides. "But I got carried away with you and now here we are."

I didn't quite believe him. A thief wouldn't have spent as much time with me as he had last night. A thief wouldn't drug an entire party just to steal things when they could have just robbed the empty houses of the people at the party. No one had reported anything missing either. I wanted to press him further. "You were here to rob everyone, but weren't able to?"

He nodded as he ran his fingers through his dark brown, curly hair.

"Do you make a habit of bedding women and then stealing from their homes?"

"When I am able to successfully accomplish it, *si*, I do."

"Why?"

"*Por que?* I need money. Desperate women in loveless marriages tend to be very easily manipulated. I gain access to their rooms and take their valuables before leaving."

"Then you think I am desperate?"

"No." He softened when he said this. "No, you are the exception, not the rule."

My anger was gone now that he was speaking to me as if I was a wounded animal. I shuffled to my nightstand, opened the drawer, and then pulled the false bottom that hid my diary along with his photograph and money. I took his belongings out before turning to him. "Here."

Cautiously, he took them from my hand. "Thank you."

"Who is that a picture of?"

I watched him look down at the worn image. "*Mi mama* and I. It was taken when I was ten."

"You always carry a picture of her?"

Matias pocketed the picture and money. "Yes, that's all I have left of her."

"My condolences."

He gave a curt nod then hesitated as his gaze darted between me, the floor, and the window. I expected him to leave then but he just stood there.

To end the silence, I asked, "Why do you need money so desperately?"

"I'm looking for answers to what happened to my family while I was incar-" He shook his head, "In Spain. The money is meant to make traveling around easier. Trains are faster than carriages. So even though I don't enjoy stealing, I do it out of desperation."

"I'd be desperate to get back to my family too."

"It's been-" He let out a shaky breath, "Tortuous."

I motioned to his pockets. "Is that all the money you have?"

"Yes," His smirk was sweet as he admitted, "Not a very good thief."

I saw the faint outline of a wild plan and blurted out, "If I give you money, can I come with you?"

His face fell in shock. "You want to come with me?"

"Yes," I took a step closer to him. "You said it yourself, I am trapped here. I don't want to marry Ashley. I don't want to be stuck in Alexandria."

"Isabelle..."

"You can just get me out of the state and then we can go our separate ways. I just need your help to get out. I won't make it far at all by myself but I can pay our way. We can hop on a train in the morning. I just...I just need your help."

"I think you have drunk a bit too much to be thinking clearly."

"No," I dared to take another step closer. "No, I tried so many things to prevent this marriage from happening but all that won't work any longer. I need a new plan. I need you."

"I can't." He shook his head and took a step back from me.

"Why not? I'll pay you for your troubles."

"It's not about the money."

"But it is, you just said it. Whatever else you need, I'll figure it out, I'll-"

He pointed a finger at me. "You can't." He turned his finger towards himself. "I can't." That same finger jerked back and forth. "We can't."

"Matias, please..."

"Do you want me to just escort you out of your home and take you somewhere else?" I nodded. "*Pajarita*, people will come looking for you. Your father and your fiancé will hunt you down."

"Which is exactly why I need your help. I've never really left this town but you have traveled and could guide me. We could pass for a couple and no one would look twice at us."

"It won't work."

"Why not?"

He sighed, his eyes pleading with me to drop this outlandish request. "For many reasons."

"Explain them-"

"*Por favor*," His words were sharp but then he softened, "Please, stop. I already feel terrible enough."

I considered his words and while they were true, they still stung. Warm tears were pooling in my eyes, but I still refused to let Matias see me cry. Instead, I scoffed. "I was a fool to think I could trust you. Last night should have never happened."

His face fell to the ground. "I don't regret it." He looked back up at me. "As much as I would enjoy your company, I can't take you with me."

I took a deep breath to push down the sob that was rising up my throat. "You have your things back. It's time you left."

I saw his hand lift towards me. For a wine-fueled, hopeful moment, I thought he was reconsidering. I must have looked pathetic enough. But his hand fell to his side.

He sucked his bottom lip into his mouth and nodded. "Goodbye, *pajarita*. I'm sorry I couldn't help you."

Matias paused for a response and when he realized it wouldn't come, he went to the window, hopped over the edge, and climbed down.

Then I let the tears fall.

Ten

Matias

I almost accepted Isabelle's offer. The ease her money would be able to afford me was so tempting. At least, that's what I told myself as I sprinted away from her house. It was the money I wanted, not her.

Even as I thought it, I couldn't believe the lie. I wanted her. I wanted to help take her away from the life she didn't want and give her the one she did. Which is why I had to say no. I couldn't give her the life she wanted, not anymore.

The curse of immortality would allow me to live forever with the guilt of leaving her tonight. She had done her best not to cry, but I could tell by how her heart sped up that she wasn't in control of her emotions. The only time her heart calmed was when she asked me to help her. It beat that way last night as I held her.

Now that I knew how miserable she was, I felt even more guilty. But what could I do? Taking her with me would never work. Besides the obvious risks, I wasn't even sure where I was going next or how long this quest for answers would take me.

I hung my head as I stalked into the bar that was just on the edge of town. It was practically empty at this hour, but there were a few potential victims that I could choose from when the time came.

After ordering a whiskey neat, I went to the corner to sulk. Every-time someone popped up from their seat, I assessed how drunk they were. Blood mixed with alcohol burned going down, but it was an easy kill to make and I needed easy tonight.

The sip of whiskey did nothing to ease the knot stuck in my throat. I was just drinking it to fit in at the bar.

Too many emotions had run through my body in the last twenty-four hours. I hadn't felt this human in so long. Isabelle was bringing my humanity back to the surface after I had buried it down inside myself. It would take some depravity to push all that softness back down.

So when the woman who looked old enough to be my mother stumbled off her bar stool, I threw the rest of the whiskey back and discreetly followed her out the door. Her footsteps were uneven as she started walking left then jerked herself right as if she suddenly remembered where she was going. For a moment I stopped following her, thinking that she could live through this night and maybe turn her life around for the better.

But it was just a moment.

Once we were far enough away from the bar and I knew we were alone, I sped up until I was right behind her. My hands grabbed her body to pull her into the shadows.

Before she could even scream for help, my teeth were on her throat. My bite was sloppy, piercing her skin too deep and the blood gushed out faster than I could suck it down. With each gulp, I drained the tangy, coppery, and bitter tasting blood from her. It ran down my throat, through my veins, and the warm feeling spread all through my body. My arms tightened around her as I sucked, squeezing her small frame until nothing was left.

Normally once I drained someone, I would lick the wounds, letting my saliva heal the cuts, before laying them down in a way that suggested they just died from drinking too much. But I had made a mess with this woman. Blood had dripped down her neck and onto her gray dress, leaving a stain that crept down her chest and onto the skirts. Instead of healing the bites, I dragged my teeth against her skin to make the wound look like it was done by a blade.

As I laid her against the wall, I surveyed my cover up. It barely looked like the cut of a knife, but it would work. There was no other logical explanation. No one would ever suggest that this woman was killed by a vampire.

The naivety of humans is what monsters like myself relied on. An entire supernatural world was pulsing right under them, but they were too wrapped up in their own bullshit to notice. I used to be one of these ignorant humans until the truth was forced onto me.

With blood in my stomach, an ache in my heart, and a throb in my brain, I took off running South and away from Alexandria.

Eleven

Isabelle

The only subject of every conversation all week had been the wedding. I made sure I had my ring on when I was outside of my room, but once I was alone again, I would tear it off like it was burning my skin. It was starting to leave a faint indentation around my finger.

While I was stuck listening to everyone make plans about me, I would spin the ring around my finger. Irene would interject and whine about planning her birthday party, so my mother would just oblige her request then return to her piles of papers and letters that were guiding her preparations for my fast approaching nuptials.

It felt more like my mother was planning her dream wedding instead of mine. But I didn't care enough to protest any of her suggestions. I gave her honest opinions when she asked me about colors, food, and guests, but she would just tell me that wouldn't work and go with whatever she wanted anyways.

It was just easier to let her have her way.

It was easier to let everyone around me have their way.

No one was listening to me anyways.

News of a few dead bodies showing up in the seedier areas of town did distract us for a bit, until my father dismissed my mother's worries.

"But it's just been women that are attacked." She pleaded over breakfast Saturday morning. "Three so far and not a single arrest yet. What if I or the girls are harmed on our way to see Anne and her new baby today?"

"Did you plan on stopping by a bar late at night? Or offering up one of our daughter's for a bit of money?"

"Of course not!" She gawked.

"Then you shouldn't have anything to worry about. Whoever this killer is, he is picking on prostitutes leaving bars late at night. Which none of you should be doing." My father grumbled as he continued reading his paper. "If it will ease your worry, I could come along, though I would rather do anything else."

"No," Mother turned back to her breakfast. She hated to make father do anything he didn't willingly agree to. "No, just perhaps another man with us on the coach?"

He nodded, a signal to cease discussing this subject.

I agreed with him that we had nothing to worry about. While it was upsetting that women were being murdered, Irene and I would not be easy targets for this killer.

As we piled into the carriage after breakfast, my mother joked, "You'll take one look at that beautiful gift from God and then you won't be groaning about Ashley wanting to marry you so soon!"

"Mother!" I huffed while she and Irene giggled.

"Relax, Isabelle." Irene smacked my leg. Even through my skirts, her slap stung. "I warned Ashley that he could be married first, but I would need to have the first grandchild. As the oldest sister it is my right."

"Then perhaps you should remind him of this." I scowled at her.

Mother smiled, "I just want a grandbaby. I do not care who gives it to me."

"Roger and I shouldn't be too far behind you." Irene winked at me and I did my best to smile at her.

Even if this match had begun because of Ashley's influence, the way her face lit up each morning when a letter from Roger arrived made me so happy for her. After everything, she deserved happiness.

Which is why I was going to make this marriage work with Ashley. If he was going to fund Irene's happiness, then that would make me happy. I would have to make this marriage work. There was no other way.

Mother's grumbling brought me back to the conversation in the carriage, "While I do hope Roger proposes soon, but we shall have to wait a moment before we throw another wedding, Irene. Let us get through all the holidays before we finance another celebration this grand."

"What about a winter wedding? I could wear a luxurious fur with my dress!" Irene's face lit up at the thought.

"No, no, you will wait until at least the spring." Mother smoothed her skirts before looking at me.

"Oh and then you and I can be pregnant together!" She squealed, "Please do your best not to be pregnant before then so we can share this together!"

Mother shared her enthusiasm, "I love this idea!"

"But I thought you wanted grandchildren right away?" My tone was combative.

"I changed my mind. Am I not allowed to change my mind?"

The unintended reminder of the fate I currently suffered was not lost on me; I certainly wasn't allowed to change my own mind about anything but this wasn't the time for the argument.

The carriage was slowing as we arrived at our cousin's home. Once it had come to a complete stop, we sat there until the driver opened the door.

Mother went first, then Irene, and finally I joined them on the gravel in front of the steps. The house was smaller than ours, but still grand. Anne had married a man that came from a wealthy family back in France. His family had come over shortly after the French Revolution to start over. Despite not having roots in this country as deep as my own family, the Duprees treated my cousin so well, and her husband, Pierre, was a good man.

He came out of the wide door to greet us himself. "Welcome Hallers!" His bright smile lit up his face, despite how dark the bags under his eyes were. "I was delighted to hear that you ladies would be visiting us today."

"We wouldn't miss a chance to celebrate little Pierre for the world!" My mother allowed him to kiss both of her cheeks before she motioned for the driver to hand over the basket that had been in the carriage. "This is for you all. Some things I found useful when I was in your position not so long ago."

"You shouldn't have." Pierre took the basket before giving my mother another hug.

"It was the least we could do. Now," my mother clapped her hands, "let me see that baby!"

Pierre led us into the warm house and up the stairs to a large bedroom. Lying in the middle, holding a squirming baby to her chest, was my cousin. When she saw us walk in, her eyes grew wide. "Pierre," She tried to cover herself. "I'm not-"

"Hush," My mother moved around Pierre to lean over Anne. "What a mother does to take care of her children is nothing to be ashamed of." She started shushing and rubbing the baby's head. "And it's nothing I didn't see of you growing up and running around the creek."

Anne blushed as she patted the baby. "Thank you for coming, Aunt Margaret. My mother was here, but she went home to change her clothes."

"Which is exactly why I am here." My mother motioned for Anne to give her the baby. She carefully passed the bundle over then fixed her gown to cover herself back up. The baby immediately started to cry out as he moved further away from his mother. "Hush, your great aunt is here." My mother cooed, cradling the baby.

"Pierre Lafayette Dupree the 4th," His father informed us. "He has quite the legacy to live up to."

Little Pierre was still crying and squirming in my mother's arms.

"Perhaps I should try to feed him more." Anne started to get out of bed.

"No!" My mother commanded and she shrunk back into the bed, "You need rest." She sniffed the air. "He just needs to be freshened up. Irene," She motioned to her with her head. "You come with me and practice. Pierre, where are his cloths?"

"Right this way!" He led my mother and an overly eager Irene out of the room.

I turned back to Anne, who was anxiously smoothing the blanket over her lap. When our eyes locked, she laughed. "Everyone forgets about me as soon as they see my baby."

"A crime." Her body shook with a light laugh as I sat on the edge of the bed. Anne and I were always closer with each other than the rest of our cousins. Perhaps it was because we were so close in age, her only a few weeks older than I, but we always felt an understanding of each other. "How're you?"

Anne scoffed, "Wrecked."

"What do you mean?"

"I'm exhausted, Isabelle. I labored with him for over a week."

"They said you had him yesterday."

"Friday was when he finally came out, but my body started trying to push him out last weekend. That's why we didn't come to your parents' party." She frowned, "It felt like I was being split in half. I've never hurt like that before. Never. And I knew it would hurt, everyone told me it would. The prize at the end of the pain was this beautiful boy. But..." She messed with the blanket again. "Nevermind."

"You know I won't judge you, Anne, tell me."

Her lip trembled as she fought back tears, "All he does is cry. I can't feed him right. I told my mother and she just keeps trying different ways to get him to feed. She says babies know what to do so if something is wrong then it's my fault. And I'm so tired, as soon as I am able to rest, he cries. He needs *me*." Her hand went to her chest as she winced. "No one else can ease his needs. Pierre tries to hold him, but even he gets frustrated and hands him back to me."

"Pierre seems so in love with the boy."

"He is," The tears were flowing. "He is so in love with him but I don't feel that. I don't love this thing that keeps taking and taking from me. God, I sound like a monster. But I just can't keep being drained like this."

"You're not a monster," I patted her hand. "You just went through something traumatic."

"That's not what everyone else says."

My mother's voice was leaking into the room through the hallways. Anne started to wipe away her tears, gripping my hand in hers. "Put this off as long as you can, Isabelle. I thought I was ready, but I wasn't. No one is. You just need to put off having children as long as you can. It's not..." She cut herself off as my mother walked in, Irene following behind her holding the baby.

"He is perfect." My sister gushed looking at my cousin.

"He is." Anne made it look like she had been crying tears of pride at Irene's comment instead of the anguish I had just seen on her face.

Irene passed the bundled up baby to me. "Just imagine it, sister. We could do this together."

I tried to reconcile what Anne had just told me with the fantasy that Irene wanted.

I couldn't.

I didn't want to be the crumbled shell of a woman that Anne was now. She had always been so full of life and laughter. The woman before me looked like she wanted to melt into the bed and never get up. I didn't want to feel like she felt towards someone she was supposed to love, toward her own child. I wasn't ready. And now I wasn't sure if I would ever be.

Ashley needed to understand this. If we were going to make the marriage work, he needed to concede to me on this. I had to speak to him tonight when he came over for dinner.

"I am going to try to rest." Anne cleared her throat as she reached out for her baby. I gently placed him back in his mother's arms where he visibly relaxed. "I can't handle visitors for too long, but please come back again soon."

My mother nodded with understanding before we all shared quick goodbyes.

* * *

Dinner that night with Ashley was winding down, when he asked to take a walk with me. He had spent the whole evening discussing the plans my mother had made and working out how each thing would be paid for with my father.

Ashley was paying for almost everything this wedding needed. My father kept offering but Ashley would just insist that there wasn't a price too grand if it meant my happiness. I had to smile at him when he said that.

He thought it was endearing, but I was mocking the idea that he could just buy my happiness.

Ashley excused us when he was ready, taking my arm to lead me away from my family. Silently we walked towards the gardens. The moon was high in the sky, and the sun was long gone.

"Gorgeous." Ashley whispered next to me.

"Yes, it is a lovely night." I shivered as the crisp fall air wrapped around us.

"Not the night," I looked up to find him staring at me. "You are gorgeous, like a statue in a museum."

"Thank you." I tried to make myself blush, but it couldn't be forced.

"Just a few more weeks now." His arms snaked around my waist, pulling me into him until our hips touched. "Then I can take you home with me as my wife."

"A wonderful thought."

"That's all I can think about." His nose slid up against my neck. "My mind races with the ways I'll take you once you are mine."

I hummed in agreement, trying to make my body react positively. Perhaps if I faked happiness long enough, it would become my reality?

Ashley's hand slid further down, grabbing the flesh below my waist. "Have you thought of me? Only me?"

"Of course." The lie rolled quickly off my tongue. "I think about you every night."

Ashley nodded before touching his forehead to mine. "I hope we make our son on our wedding night."

"About that..." I took a step back so I could look into his eyes. He was already scowling down at me. "I was hoping we could wait until at least the spring."

Through gritted teeth he asked, "Why?"

"Irene is hoping we can be pregnant together and she has to wait until the spring to marry Roger."

"I don't give a damn what Irene wants. *You* are to be my wife, not her."

"Well, I would also like to wait."

His grip tightened on my hips. "No."

"Ashley, please, I saw Anne today and she was miserable."

"Anne has always been miserable."

"I think Anne was the least miserable of us all. She said to wait to have children, that she wished she had waited. If we just wait, we could travel together, we could-"

Ashley cut me off, "I don't want to travel with you. I want to start a family with you. A family you also said you wanted."

"I never said that. You never asked if I wanted children. You just assumed-"

"Stop." He shook his head to emphasize the word.

"I'll give you children if you let me decide when."

"I don't need you to decide." He snorted, "I want children now, and I am the one who controls that."

I scoffed, "What do you mean?"

"I mean," His gaze darkened in a sinister way, "You can't really stop me if I want to get you pregnant."

Quickly, I backed away from him. "Don't you dare do that to me. I'll, I'll kill you if you touch me like that."

He matched each step I took away from him, "Did you just threaten me?"

My back hit the brick wall, the rough texture coming through the thin fabric of my dress. Ashley caged my head in with his arms and planted a leg on either side of mine. I tried to push him away, but he was too strong. "Ashley, stop..."

"Stop what?" His words were a harsh whisper. "Stop trying to give you a perfect life? Stop trying to get your whore of a sister situated as well? Stop paying off your father's debts?"

"Paying off father's debts?"

He sneered down at me. "The poor old fool thinks he's so clever. He asks me to take money from an investment account and send it to 'business acquaintances'. What he doesn't know is there is no investment account for him. I took the money there and reinvested it elsewhere. I just pay off his debts from my account. And based on where the money goes, he seems to have terrible luck betting on horses."

Breathing was becoming difficult. "I had no idea."

"Because I handled everything. I always handle everything." He leaned in so I could feel his warm breath tickle my ear. "I don't mind. I like being the one in charge. And I'll keep helping your family. All I ask is that you just do exactly what I tell you without complaining."

"But Ashley-"

He used one hand to grab my jaw. "That sounds like the start of a complaint."

Would he hit me? Ashley had been violent before but it was always towards other men. I had never seen him strike a woman, but as his future wife, maybe he felt like he could hit me. My voice was shaky as I croaked out, "You're scaring me."

His body shook with a sigh. Then he let his hands fall back to my waist. "I didn't want to scare you, but if this is how I get you to comply," He squeezed my hips until I winced. "Then this is how our interactions will be until your attitude improves."

I just needed him to leave and get as far away as possible. The sooner I had some distance, the sooner I could figure out what to do. "I'll be better. I promise."

"I want to believe you." He pressed a gentle kiss to my forehead. "I'll be back again in a few days. If you are acting like my future wife, I'll give your consideration to postpone children more thought."

"And if I'm not up to your standards?"

He straightened but didn't move away from me. "My love for you has limits, Izzy, do not let me reach them."

I swallowed back my tears, "I understand."

Ashley bent down and kissed me possessively. When he was done, he looked into my eyes, "You can be exactly who I want you to be. I've seen you do it before."

"I'll do it." With a bit more bite than I intended, I added, "For my family, I'll do it."

Ashley shook his head. "No, not for them. The help I give them is inconsequential. I want you to do this for me. I'm going to be your family."

I nodded.

Playing my part, I walked him out the front door, then eagerly kissed him goodbye. My heart was thudding as I ran back to my room and locked the door.

Panic took over.

Twelve

Isabelle

The suitcase on my bed was almost full. I told myself that I would only take what I could fit in one bag, more than that would slow me down, and I needed to put distance between myself and Alexandria as quickly as possible.

"Nightgowns." I thought out loud as I turned to open the drawer in my wardrobe. "How many should I bring?" My hands grabbed the top two white satin gowns from the stack. "I'll have to make this work."

"Going somewhere?"

My heart leapt as I let out a gasp. Slowly, I turned around to face the one who had just asked me a question. Matias was in front of the window, eyeing me up and down. My voice was shaky when I asked, "What are you doing here?"

He tsked then smirked, "You answer me first."

"I'm leaving." The nightgowns I held were tossed into the suitcase.

He cleared his throat but I refused to look at him. "For your honeymoon with the buffoon?"

"No." I scoffed. "I'm not going anywhere with him."

Matias took another step towards me. "Then why are you packing? Did something happen?"

My hands gripped the edges of the suitcase but I didn't shut it. "I'm running away."

"Running away? *Pajarita*, you can't just-"

Anger forced my gaze on him. "Why are you even here? Our deal was for a single night, yet you have come to my room thrice now. Why? What could you possibly want from me now?"

He took another cautious step towards me. "I saw in the newspaper that women were being killed and I was worried something might have happened to you."

I rolled my eyes, "Whoever that killer is, he is attacking prostitutes out late at night. Even though I indulged myself with you in the dead of night, I assure you I am not desperately wandering the streets looking for more."

"That's not," He groaned, "That's not what I meant. I know you aren't running around whoring yourself out."

I snapped, "So then why do you care? Why did you feel the need to check on me?"

"I'm...I'm not sure. But I wasn't able to shake the feeling that something was wrong so I decided to come and see you."

His honesty softened me. I looked back up at him as he walked closer and leaned up against the bedpost.

"Now tell me, what happened to make you want to run?"

A tear slipped down my cheek. Quickly, I wiped it away and refused to let anymore tears escape. "I can't marry him. I can't stay here." I let myself plop down on the bed. Matias put himself in front of me and gently lifted my face until I was looking back up at him.

"What did he do to you?"

"What hasn't he done?" I swallowed as those whiskey brown eyes went wide. "He hasn't raised his hand to me or forced me to sleep with him, but I know he will. He's said he will. I just need to leave. Will you, could you help me?"

Matias sighed, "Isabelle..."

"Please..."

He lifted his hand and it gently stroked up my cheek with his thumb. "I want to *pero* it's impossible for me to help you."

A harsh laugh bubbled out of me. "I should've known better than to ask again." Abruptly, I stood up forcing him to take a step back. "Why did you even come back here?"

"I came to see that you were well and that you suffered no consequences for what we did together."

"Then you can leave here now with a clear conscience." My tone was becoming combative. "No one has discovered our indiscretion and no one ever will once I leave."

I turned away from him to fix my suitcase but Matias spun me back around to face him. "You can't just run away, Isabelle. It's not safe for you to be alone in the world."

"Better alone than with him."

His grip on my arms tightened, but in a concerned way. "You don't understand. There are monsters out there that prey on humans like you."

"Monsters?"

His throat worked on a swallow, "Like me."

"Do you mean thieves?"

Matias shook his head but didn't elaborate further.

He wasn't making any sense. I sensed his desperation for me to just take his word and refuse to leave but I couldn't. He owed me an explanation. "Then what are you warning me about? Men like you who bed random women they meet at parties?"

I saw the conflict in his eyes. After a long pause he admitted, "I'm no longer a man."

My eyes roamed his body. He looked like a man. A very handsome one at that. How was it possible that he wasn't one? I dared to ask, "If you are not a man, then what are you?"

He grimaced, "You won't believe me."

I raised my eyebrows, "Will this better explain how I am still the only one who remembers you?"

He slowly nodded.

"Then tell me. What are you?"

Matias ran his hand down his face. I held my breath as I waited for him to speak. Just as I started to open my mouth to fill the uncomfortable silence that was building between us he blurted out, "I am a vampire."

A laugh escaped, the sound filling my ears as I realized how horribly I had just reacted to this admission that clearly pained him. He winced and took a step away from me.

I matched his step, "Prove it."

There was a flicker of surprise before Matias scanned the room. His eyes fell on my desk. He carefully stepped around me, grabbed the letter opener in one hand and used it to cut a thin slice across his palm. Blood immediately seeped from the wound and dripped onto the carpet under the desk.

I cried out, grabbing up the skirt of my dress as I ran over to him. My intention was to use the fabric to soak up the blood from the cut but he held up his uninjured hand. "Watch."

As I pulled his cut hand towards me, the skin he had just split was connecting itself back together. Once the skin was sealed again, I used the bit of my dress to wipe away the excess blood. There was no trace of the wound on his palm.

"And now another one of your dresses is ruined." Matias was grinning when I looked up at him.

I should have panicked or screamed or done anything to get this monster away from me. A part of me did feel the shiver of recognized danger travel down my spine, but a bigger part of me was suddenly an insatiable void of curiosity. If he had wanted to hurt me, he could have done it the first time he had me alone. He could have harmed me to get his money and photo back.

I needed answers and I would only get those if I allowed him to stay. My voice was barely louder than my pounding heart as I asked, "How?"

He shrugged, "Part of the curse of being a vampire."

"You cannot die?"

"I never really had the rules of this all explained to me, but from what I understand I cannot be cut or marred or broken, unless someone uses silver against me. I can only die if someone cuts off my head or I am left to burn in the sun. In exchange for this, I have to drink blood to live. Air, food, and water do nothing to sustain me now. All the curse needs is blood."

"This curse is also why no one but me remembers you?"

"Yes, when I was turned, I gained the ability to make humans forget they ever saw me. It has worked on everyone I have come across up until I met you."

My curiosity peaked. "And why didn't it work on me?"

"I'm not sure."

I sat back down on the bed, "When were you turned into a vampire?"

His face fell as joined me. "About ten years ago, but that's not important. I only told you what I am so you understand why I can't help you run. There are limitations to what I can do. I can only travel at night, for one."

He wanted to help me. I could work with that. "I don't mind traveling at night."

"There are other risks, things you can't understand."

"I think I've done a wonderful job of understanding things so far."

"You wouldn't be safe with me."

"Why not? You just told me you are a supernatural monster. What could be more dangerous than you?"

"Other vampires, particularly that one who tortured me for the last decade."

I deflated at the anguish in his voice. "Oh," My arms wrapped protectively around me. "Am I in danger?"

"No, *bueno,* I don't think so. I escaped months ago and I haven't seen any sign of him but he's out there, somewhere. If he *is* looking for me and finds us together, he would do terrible and inhumane things to you just to hurt me and he would enjoy every second of it. I can't put you in danger like that, so you cannot come with me, *pajarita*."

"But what about everyone else you've been with? Are they not in danger as well?"

"I erased all of their memories. And I've never gone back to a place once I've left. It's how I cover my tracks, just in case he or any vampire hunters are looking for me."

"So you risked all of this to come and check on me?"

His grin showed his dimples, as he looked me up and down. "It was worth the risk."

My whole face heated with blush.

"It was worth the potential danger to see you blush again."

The heat spread to my whole body. There was a tension building between us that had started the first night we were together. I could work with that. "What if you just got me out of Virginia? Then I could travel alone and-"

"A woman like you wandering around alone isn't any safer."

"Then take me with you," I locked onto his brown eyes. "Please, Matias. I feel safe with you, despite," I breathed, "what you are. I need you, your help. Will you just help me think of a plan to escape?"

Matias shut his eyes as he drew in a deep breath. I prepared myself for another rejection. It was a lot for me to ask of him, but I needed to try. If he was willing to risk potentially being found, then I meant more to him than I initially thought. That had to mean something. To help force an answer from him, I added, "There are *other* ways to get out of this engagement, but I'd rather not do something so drastic."

His eyes went wide. "You will take your own life to avoid marriage?"

I nodded.

"*Mierda. No puedo creer lo que estoy haciendo.*" He breathed out the words before opening his eyes. I didn't understand what he was saying in Spanish but he was going to tell me he couldn't help me. This was such a foolish plan. Asking a supernatural creature for help escaping an unwanted marriage was so ridiculous, I almost laughed as the realization ran through my thoughts.

Those whiskey colored eyes scanned my face for any hesitation, but instead of cowering, I lifted my chin. His shoulders slumped in defeat. "*Bueno.* I'll help you escape."

Without thinking, I threw my arms tight around his neck. "Thank you!"

His arms covered my body as he squeezed me back. As I pulled away, I gently kissed his cheek. It was meant to show my appreciation that he agreed to something he so clearly was against. Instead, the feeling of his smooth skin against my lips brought up flashbacks of how the rest of his skin felt against mine. But there wasn't any time to explore those feelings now. I had to be out of here as soon as possible. "Let me finish packing and then we can be on our way."

"No, no, no." His arms kept me held in place. His eyes flickered between my lips and my own harsh gaze. For a moment, I thought he was going to kiss me. His voice was stern as he declared, "We aren't leaving tonight."

I pulled as far away from him as I could, "Why not?"

"If we just leave now, your father and fiancé will chase us."

"So what do you propose we do?" Again, he looked down at my lips. There was a struggle happening in his eyes when they went back up to mine. His fingers squeezed around my waist before he released me from his hold. Reluctantly, I sat back down on the bed, but turned so I was facing him.

Matias ran his fingers through his hair, "We need a plan. A way to let you leave without anyone raising suspicion."

"If I had a plan like that I wouldn't need you."

He grinned and showed his dimples, "Watch yourself, *pajarita.*"

"What does that even mean? *Pajarita?*" I completely messed up the way the r was meant to sound.

"*Pajarita.*" He repeated, the word rolling effortlessly off his tongue. "It means little bird."

"Little bird?" No one had called anything about me 'little' in a very long time.

"Because," Those tans hands motioned to the room. "Of this lovely cage you are kept in."

"Ah," I nervously played with the hem of my dress. "Good thing you are going to help me escape."

"Yes, but we need to be smart about it. We get you out of here, make sure no one follows us, and that you'll be safe to live out your days as you wish."

For a few moments we both sat in silence. Two heads were always better than just one. Together we would think of some way for me to get out. My eyes fell onto the shelves full of books. What better inspiration than already thought out escape plans. I scanned the titles then blurted out, "What if we faked my death?"

Matias followed my eyes to the bound copy of the play. "Like *Romeo and Juliet*?"

"Yes, but with much less woe."

He smiled at my joke. "I might be able to work with that." Matias stood and started pacing around the room as his rambling thoughts came out in mumbles.

He seemed so human. It was hard to remember that he was a vampire, unless I looked closely at how controlled his movements were. The books I had read featuring those creatures made them seem like monsters. Matias was nothing like that. It wouldn't be that much different being a vampire, would it? "What if you turn me into a vampire?"

He stopped pacing, slowly turned his body, and stared at me. His breathing stalled completely before he stated, "No."

"Why not? It would be perfect. I could appear dead, and then you could come get me from wherever my family buries my body. It could be just like *Romeo and Juliet*. You said all I need is blood, which I could get once you rescue me and then-"

"Isabelle, *pajarita*, no I cannot turn you."

"Cannot or will not?"

"Oh, I can do it. I know how it was done to me. What I can't do is rob you of your life. That's exactly what you're trying to run away from."

"No, I am running away from my choices being taken away from me. I'm choosing you and I'm choosing to turn."

He threw his hands up. "You don't even understand what you are asking for."

"Immortality in exchange for drinking blood? Sounds like a fair exchange."

He towered above me, "And do you think murder is fair? Because that is how you would get the blood needed to sustain your life." A mix of anger and regret swirled in his eyes. It looked like they his pupils were dilating, the black taking over the brown of his iris. "Do you think never seeing your family again is fair? Because you could never come back here and see your sister again once you are turned. You won't be able to do anything human ever again."

My voice was calm as I replied, "But it would be my choice."

Matias's mouth formed an 'O' before he hung his head. "I didn't get this choice." That conflicted gaze flicked back up to mine. "So I will give it to you." My mouth curled into a triumphant grin. "But, you will take your time with this decision."

"The wedding is meant to be in three weeks. It needs to be done before then."

"*Bueno,* it will be." My heart skipped when he said that and he paused like he heard the missed beat. "In that time I want to convince you not to turn and we can think of another plan. *Pero* this is your choice to make."

"Thank you." I had to bite my lip to stop my spreading smile.

Matias reached up and used his thumb to free my lip. "Don't thank me yet, Isabelle. I've done nothing."

"You've done more than you realize. I was feeling hopeless before you arrived here tonight."

He shook his head, "Hope is all I can give you right now." Matias flashed one of his dimpled smiles. There was a feeling building between us that was familiar to how our first night together felt. It was an eager anxiety knowing something irrevocable was about to begin. He tucked a loose curl behind my ear, "Now go to bed."

My hand grabbed onto his wrist, "You're leaving so soon?"

"*Si, pajarita, pero* I'll come back. We need to sort out this plan."

"Could we not sort it out tonight?"

"If I am going to spend the next few weeks with you, I need to go get my things in Richmond and tie up some loose ends. I hadn't planned on staying longer than tonight."

"Oh," I looked away from him but didn't let go of his wrist. "I understand."

His thumb gently stroked my cheek, "Just stay here and stay safe and I'll come for you."

"Promise."

"*Juro*, I swear it."

I leaned into his soft, cool hand on my cheek. My face suddenly felt hot with blush as I let out a shaky breath. Nothing about this night had gone the way I expected it to. I never imagined I would see Matias again. His touches were only meant to be memories. Now that I was feeling them again, I wanted more.

But did he want more? Our original deal was only for a night. This new arrangement didn't change that, did it?

He leaned down.

My lips parted in anticipation.

His lips landed on the top of my head in a sweet kiss. "Goodnight Isabelle."

A simple goodnight wasn't what I wanted, which is why it was for the best. As flat as I could, I answered him. "Goodnight Matias."

He gave my cheek one more soft stroke before letting go. Already, I missed his cool touch.

I watched him walk towards the window, and hop onto the ledge. He gave me one last look, shook his head, cursed in Spanish, and then leapt down to the ground.

Instinctively, I jumped up and ran over to the window, convinced he had somehow hurt himself. But when I looked down, I saw him smiling up at me. With a final wink, he took off into the night.

Thirteen

Matias

I couldn't believe I just agreed to help Isabelle escape her marriage.

But I refused to just leave her to manage on her own. She was so frazzled and her heart was beating so fast I could hear it from outside. I seriously thought something had happened to her as I scaled up the house and leapt through her window.

I thought maybe he had found her.

Which was a ludicrous thought. At no point in the last few months had I worried like this about being found by him. But then again, this was the first time in the last few months I worried about someone other than myself or finding my sisters.

When I was at the bar in Richmond and read about the women being murdered, my immediate thought was that a vampire was behind it all. I could only account for the one life I had taken. The other two could have been victims of any other vampire, or perhaps another human, but I wasn't able to shake this nagging feeling that I needed to go check on Isabelle.

I needed to see that she was well with my own two eyes.

I ran all the way back up here to Alexandria. It took me all night and all my power to sprint back up here and I barely made it back into the mausoleum that I had been hiding in before the sun started peeking up over the horizon.

I hadn't been able to sleep at all. I spent the whole day pacing back and forth, deciding if I should even go see her. If I saw she was fine, then I would leave her alone, but if something was wrong, then I felt like it was my duty to fix it.

The way her heart raced when she saw me made my brain fuzzy. If she had the same senses I did, she would have known how difficult it was to control myself around her. She was a scared bird fluttering around the room as she gathered her things. The need to save her was driving all my actions.

I just didn't realize it would end with me agreeing to help her run away and potentially turn her into a vampire.

That was the last thing I wanted for her. She was so full of life, so full of potential. Turning her into a vampire felt like she was replacing one set of shackles for another.

But she was right when she said it was her choice.

What she didn't choose was to take on the burdens that I owned. I needed to figure out a safe place to take her, whether she turned or not. Once she was settled, I could continue looking for my sisters. I wouldn't force her onto that so far futile quest.

So as I ran, I decided that I needed to keep space between us, despite that being the last thing I wanted. It would be necessary to keep her safe. I wouldn't risk her life.

She wouldn't be the first woman whose life had tragically ended because of choices I made. That realization stung my heart. Every woman whose life became entangled with mine seemed to meet a tragic end, and it was always because I was being selfish. I couldn't be selfish in this. I wouldn't add her to the list of women I had ruined.

It had been so long since I cared for another like this and the feeling made my chest ache. For a moment, I almost turned around and went right back to her. But I needed to get back to Richmond to make sure no one remembered seeing me. I hadn't been able to erase anyone's minds because I left in such a rush. She was driving me to careless distraction, though I admittedly welcomed it from her.

First, I needed blood. That would fuel me enough to sprint back down South to handle everything.

There weren't many people on the streets tonight. The whispers of some madman running around with a knife could be heard as I passed by a group of young women risking death to earn a few dollars. They smiled at me and I smiled back to put them at ease.

I needed a quick kill, someone who would fill me up so I could run all night.

My feet carried me back to the bar I had frequented before. I didn't want to drink from a drunkard, but I was getting desperate to get on the road as quickly as possible. The sooner I went down to Richmond, the sooner I could get back to Isabelle.

I stopped walking when I realized where that train of thought had gone. "*Mierda.*" The curse slipped out as I ran my hand over my face. I wouldn't be able to fight my feelings for her much longer.

A shout rang out behind me. It was quickly followed by a squeaky scream. I turned just in time to see a burly man dragging a small boy into the alley.

After a quick glance to see that no one else was going to help the boy, I silently snuck after them.

The man had the boy pressed up against the wall and his large frame was blocking whatever he was doing. Before the man could sense me, I snaked my arm around his neck and dragged him backwards. He tried to buck me off of him, but I was stronger. I wasn't a small man. Even when I was human, there were very few times I lost in a fight. But now I was stronger than any human I encountered. It made killing so easy, almost too easy.

I applied pressure to his neck until the man went limp in my arms.

My gaze flicked to the boy, who was staring at me with wide brown eyes. "What are you doing out so late?" I asked, though I could guess the answer.

"Got nowhere else to go."

I dropped the man onto the ground and carefully walked closer to the boy. "Why not? Where are your parents"

"My parents are dead."

I reached into my pocket and grabbed a few of the bills I kept stored in there. "Take this." The boy's small, dirty hands wrapped around the money. "Get yourself some food and a bed somewhere."

The boy sniffled, "Th-thank you."

"Don't thank me." I held his gaze until his eyes glazed over. "Just forget you ever saw me and that this happened."

The boy nodded before sprinting out of the alley.

I turned my attention back to the unconscious man lying on the ground. A quick sniff of him let me know that he hadn't been drinking tonight. The realization that he was sober while hurting that little boy made my stomach turn more than alcohol mixed with blood would have.

My fingers wound into his hair as I pulled him up, leaning his back against my chest. The movement started to bring him back to consciousness and he groaned when I nudged his head to one side.

He grunted when my fangs sank into the thick flesh of his neck.

I made the bite as painful as possible, knowing he could still feel everything I was doing to him. He had tried to hurt an innocent boy tonight. He was going to use his strength and power to ruin that boy's life, but he hadn't planned on running into something stronger and more powerful. I savored the thought of this predator becoming prey as I sucked his blood down my throat in deep, long pulls.

His body involuntarily started convulsing as I reached the end of his blood supply. I tightened my hold on him and kept sucking until literally nothing else came out of this pathetic waste of a human.

I ripped my fangs out so hard that it tore his skin then threw his body into the wall. It hit the bricks with a hard thud before falling in an unnatural way onto the ground. The mark I made looked like another knife wound, and I hoped they would assume he was another victim of the deranged killer on the loose.

With my stomach now full, I took off sprinting back to Richmond.

Fourteen

Isabelle

"Surprise!" Ashley's smiling face beamed at me from where he stood in front of the church doors.

"You said you wouldn't be here!" I threw my arms around his neck and pretended I was hugging Matias. I would touch and tease him like I would if it was Matias standing in front of me instead of him. It was easy to interact with Ashley now that I knew we wouldn't end up married.

He stiffened but squeezed me back. "I'm leaving right after the service. Just wanted one more chance to check on you before I'm away for five days."

"I'm happy you decided to stay."

His eyebrows furrowed, "You are?"

"I am." I smiled as convincingly as I could. It was getting easier to force a smile. This was just temporary.

Ashley let me go from the embrace but adjusted my arm so it was wrapped around his. He exchanged pleasantries with my parents but Irene had already run off to greet Roger.

With my arm still around Ashley's, he led us into the church. We went around the room saying hello and making small talk with other people from the town. We were the epitome of a perfect couple.

Ashley slid into the pew next to me and I let my hand rest on his thigh. He smirked as he placed his arm over my shoulders. Our bodies molded into each other and it felt familiar, like putting on an old pair of slippers. I knew that some part of me cared for Ashley. How could I not after how long I had known him? But I couldn't reconcile the feelings with the kind of man he had become. His behavior last night was just a glimpse of the kind of control he planned to use on me.

"You seem to be doing better since our talk." He whispered as the preacher called for everyone to take their seats.

"I was overly anxious about everything, but it's settled now."

His wet lips pressed a kiss to my cheek.

The preacher led us through the service, and the whole time I touched Ashley. I held his hand while we prayed. I even rubbed my foot on his. It all seemed to convince him that everything was back on track with us.

But despite trying to focus on making Ashley feel wanted, my mind drifted back to Matias. Had he made it back to Richmond alright? How soon would he be back? Normally, traveling to Richmond by carriage took several hours. I hadn't seen a carriage when he left, so did that mean he was walking? How long would that take a vampire who could move supernaturally fast?

Ashley would be gone until Friday evening. I hoped that Matias would return before then and it wasn't just because of our deal.

After the service ended, Ashley walked out with my family. He fit so seamlessly into my life because of the space that he had been carving for over a decade. Roger took Irene off to the side to say their goodbyes as Ashley and I followed.

The sooner I started, the sooner these forced interactions with Ashley would be done. He looked down at me to ask, "What'll you do while I'm gone?"

"I'll miss you."

"I know," His arms pulled me into him. "But soon we won't have to part like this. Soon you'll be in Washington with me."

"That is the plan."

He leaned down and kissed me hard. I tried to pretend it was Matias, but everything about Ashley felt too different. His shoulders were wider, his lips were thinner, and the sounds he made as our mouths moved together were making my skin crawl. I pushed my revolution down to help convince him that everything between us was fine. I didn't want him to have any reason to suspect anything.

I went through the usual routine we had when kissing. It was mostly letting Ashley control the pace and length of each kiss. Letting him lead was just easier.

Irene coughed, before snarkily jeering. "Save something for your wedding night."

I pulled away from Ashley then shot her a look.

"She's just jealous." Ashley chuckled then kissed my cheek. "Keep getting everything ready for the wedding. We'll finalize plans when I come for dinner on Friday."

"Wonderful."

His gaze lowered expectantly.

"I love you." The lie slipped off my tongue easily.

His blue eyes were lit with nothing but satisfaction, as he replied, "I love you too, *my* Izzy."

* * *

After church, I listened to Irene go on and on about Roger. She was more than smitten with him. She was obsessed and he seemed to be reciprocating the feeling.

Would Roger still marry her if I ran?

"Irene,"

She stopped pacing around my room and looked at me sitting at my desk. "Yes?"

"Do you know, well have you and Roger discussed when he would propose?"

Her brown eyes lit up, "He let it slip he wants to propose on my birthday."

"Perfect!" I practically jumped up to hug her. If Roger proposed on Irene's birthday, then I could turn and run away before the wedding. This still risked Roger backing out of the engagement, but from everything Irene had confessed to me, he would marry her regardless of Ashley's money. And if everyone thought I was dead, how could Ashley hold that against my sister?

This plan would have to work. Irene would need someone to help her after my untimely departure. Roger would be the perfect support system and distraction for her once I was gone.

She kept listing off the things she loved about her potential fiancé and I listened as intently as I could. Once I was turned, I wouldn't ever be able to hear her ramble on about anything ever again. Soaking in her words now helped ease the guilt I was starting to feel about the deal.

Overall, the deal I had made with Matias still felt right in the light of day. Once I was alone again, I started to think about how it would be to be immortal, to be a vampire. I went through my books to find every text that mentioned the supernatural monsters. I had read and then reread Bram Stoker's *Dracula* so many times that I felt like I knew what I was getting myself into but I went searching to see if any other writers had the same or conflicting information.

My fingers raced along the leather bound novels and stories as I ran through my mind to think who could have written a poem about a vampire. I grabbed John Palodori's *Vampyre* and Heinrich August Ossenfelder's poem *The Vampire*. When I saw the name, Lord Byron, I remembered his poem *The Giaour*.

Gathering up all the texts on vampires that I could find, I spread them out on my desk. Then I grabbed a pen and paper to start making notes of what each text said vampires could and couldn't do. From that list, I started writing down questions for Matias:

Could I not go into the sun at all?

How many days can I go without drinking blood?

What other supernatural gifts will I acquire?

Does the transformation hurt?

The last question was the most important to me. I knew turning into a creature like a vampire wouldn't be an enjoyable experience, but I didn't know to what extent I would be in pain.

It wouldn't deter me from making this change, but I did need to ask. Knowing would make this transformation easier.

I understood why he said I needed time now.

I waited up as late as I could for him to come, but eventually sleep took me.

Fifteen

Isabelle

Matias had my back flushed against his bare chest. Without any clothing to act as a barrier between us, I could feel the coarse hairs along his legs, chest, and arms tickling me. His skin was so cool against mine, causing goosebumps to erupt all over. The contrasting warmth of his breath tickled the sensitive skin of my neck.

"Matias?" My voice sounded so far away as I begged him.

"*Si, pajarita?*" Matias's lips gently pressed against my pulse.

"Please."

"Please?" He asked against the shell of my ear as his fingers traced a line up my torso. His other arm hooked around my waist. My hands found purchase on his thick forearm.

"Please...bite me."

The same fingers that moved up my body stopped on my chin. Slowly, he twisted my head until my neck was exposed to him.

His whole body shook with a growl that rattled through me. I felt the sharp pain of his fangs piercing my skin. My nails dug into the flesh of his arm. As I cried out, my hips surged away from his.

And then I bolted upright in bed.

My fingers went up to my neck, feeling only smooth skin. "It was just a dream." I swallowed down shaky breaths. "Just a dream."

"What dream?" My sister's voice made me jump.

"What the hell, Irene?!" My hands grabbed the blanket out of instinct. "What're you doing in here?"

"I came to see if you were awake!" She took a seat on my bed.

"Well, now I am."

"What was your dream about?"

"Oh," I waved my hand. "Just a nightmare."

"Who is Matias?"

"Pardon?" I tried to hide how my heart started thumping loudly.

"You called out for him in your sleep." Irene closed her eyes and started thrashing, imitating my voice as she said, "Matias? Please. Please!"

"Irene!" I threw a pillow at her.

When it hit her head, she rolled back giggling. "I'm sure Ashley would love to hear all about this Matias of your dreams."

"It's just a character from a book I read."

"You and your books." She rolled her eyes.

"Men in books are much better than men in real life." I hoped my joke would help sell the lie.

"I prefer my men to be real." Irene hopped up off the bed. "Now get ready! We're wedding dress shopping for you, and possibly me today!"

"For you?"

"If we're going into Washington to look for dresses, I'm not going to just sit there!"

"Right." I rolled my eyes and Irene threw the pillow back at me.

"Get dressed!" She squealed and ran away before I could retaliate.

* * *

The carriage ride to Washington was long and dull. The sun was hidden behind thick clouds that threatened rain the whole time. As we hobbled along the road, my eyes started getting heavy. My mother was going over plans for shopping and lunch. When necessary, I would respond with a 'Yes, ma'am' but for most of the ride I was quiet.

Irene kept filling any silence with her ideas of what to do in Washington, meeting up with Roger tomorrow, and how excited she was for both her birthday party and the wedding.

I could feel my eyes shutting but couldn't force them back open anymore. My mind was showing me images of Matias from my dream.

From far away I heard her mother cry, "Isabelle!"

I shot back up and looked around. Irene was grinning like a cat as she announced, "She's dreaming about some man in a book."

Mother gave me a look of confusion mixed with concern. "Is that so?"

"Yes," I yawned, trying to shake the sleep off but could feel it lingering in my body. "I apologize. I didn't get much rest last night. I was trying to finish the book I was reading."

"Well, I had hoped that you would be more excited about dress shopping."

"Yes," I sat up straighter. "I am ecstatic. I have an idea of what kind of dress I would like. Something simple, but elegant."

"Bore-ring." Irene jeered.

The air in the carriage began to feel heavy and smelled of a mixture between the sting of smoke and the heaviness of rain. Irene stuck her head to the window and was staring out at the sprawling city.

The carriage roved through the streets, past monuments and buildings with giant white columns separated by manicured green grass. Every time I came into Washington, I was awed at how the planners of this city were able to arrange it all together. The further into the city the carriage went, the tighter together the buildings became until they were pressed right up against each other. This is where all of the newest goods were taken, and this was the best place to buy a wedding dress. One that would never be worn, but my mother didn't know that.

"Almost there!" My mother cheered as we rounded onto a busy street. Women were pushing baby carriages, or walking in pairs and laughing. Men were walking in a rush from one place to the next, while some were standing on the street having animated conversations. The storefronts did their best to stand out from each other, despite all being the same shade of bright red brick.

I loved this electric feeling of being in the city. I just hated the reason we were here.

Within a few minutes, the carriage slowed to a stop. Irene practically jumped out when the driver opened the door, my mother following her and I exited last. The overcast sky was threatening to rain, but it wouldn't matter. We would be inside all day.

"Come along, girls." Mother walked into the shop directly in front of us. As we entered, we were swept into a room with dress forms covered in white silk. Each dress was more elaborate and ornate than the last. They had every imaginable white wedding dress from modest to the more low cut and even some dresses that would not require a corset underneath. A row of three gowns were on mannequins in front of me and my fingers dared to touch the lace lining the top of the middle dress. "They're all so beautiful."

"Take your pick, darling!"

I turned to face her, "Mother, I-"

She gracefully took my hands in hers, "I have waited for this day just as long as you have. Pick the dress you want, no matter the cost." Did my mother not know about my father's money troubles? Or did Ashley tell her he would cover this wedding expense as well?

"Isabelle," Irene whined from the side. "This is a dream. Pick out a dress or I will pick one out for you!"

There was no point in arguing or trying to put this off. I needed my mother to think this wedding was going to happen, and part of that deception was getting a dress. Perhaps I could bring it with me when I went with Matias? I could wear it for him.

I shook my head at that train of thought. Matias wasn't helping me because I was going to become his bride. He was helping me because I threatened to end my own life if he didn't. I preyed on the guilt he felt but he would only be burdened by my presence for a bit. We would have to go our separate ways once I was safely stashed away.

Perhaps they would bury me in this dress? That would be so poetic. It would be the death of the terrible arrangement I had been forced into with Ashley. When I rose from the dead, I would be able to do whatever I wanted for the rest of eternity. With the morbid idea that I was picking out my funeral gown, I looked back at the rows of dresses.

A lace covered white satin gown stood out to me. I turned to the shop attendant, "Could I try that one, please?"

The woman, who looked about the same age as my mother, nodded and went over to grab it off the mannequin. "Follow me."

I followed the attendant behind a thick, burgundy, velvet curtain, which she quickly closed. The dress was hung on a rod that went across the wall. "Alright, dear, let's get you out of this." I quickly unbuttoned my navy blue day dress and slipped it off my body.

I wasn't standing in just my undergarments for long. The attendant grabbed the satin wedding dress, then brought it over my head so I could slide my arms in. Once the arms were in place, she carefully rolled the fabric down the length of my torso and then let it flare out over my legs. I stared at myself in the mirror as she did up the buttons in the back.

"I'll have to add a bit more fabric to it." She huffed before looking at my eyes in the mirror. "You have more to work with than the average woman." Her sharp eyes looked at my chest.

I nodded, feeling her breathe out a sigh on my still exposed back. She continued to make small adjustments and tweaks to how the fabric hugged and then draped over my body.

"This will still give you an idea of what the dress will look like."

The dress looked stunning, even without the top being tightened across my chest and neck. The layers of lace over the satin hit my curves in a way that made my waist feel small. The pure ivory color made my auburn hair and freckles pop out against my skin. I looked the part of a blushing, innocent bride.

My skin suddenly heated in all the places the dress was touching me. The rising wave of panic was making it harder to breathe, but I swallowed it. I had to. If I panicked now, then my mother would know something was wrong and I needed her to believe everything was right.

The attendant shoved the curtain back. I carefully walked the few steps out to see my mother and sister sitting on a plush couch.

"Isabelle!" They both cooed when I stopped in front of them. There was a mirror set up so I could look at myself while they looked at me. The attendant explained the alterations we would need to make as I stared at my reflection.

I took a deep breath to help settle the rising nausea. I needed to get out of this dress now. This was making the wedding feel more real. I could now picture what I would look like walking down the aisle towards Ashley. That vision swirled up more panic. My voice shook as I declared, "I think this is it."

Irene's mouth gaped. "The first one?"

"Same arrangement I have with Ashley." I forced a smile. "The one and only." Even mother laughed at that joke.

"Well," She said when she finished laughing. "We have all this time before lunch."

Irene's eyes lit up and she waved another attendant over to start gathering dresses to try on.

I shuffled back to the fitting room to get out of the dress. The relief I felt when I took the dress off was noticeable to my attendant, who shook her head as she took the gown away and left me to dress.

My day dress was almost all the way back on, but the zipper snagged on something and I couldn't close it all the way.

Irene's voice called out as she approached. "You may not have taken your time finding a dress, but I shall!"

"Irene," I hissed, pulling the curtain back just enough to poke my head out. "Can you help me with my dress?"

She snuck behind the curtain and helped me fix the zipper. "What'll you do without me? You and Ashley will be all alone in the city until I can join you, and with how much he works, you'll have nothing but your books to keep you company!" Irene's eyes found mine in the mirror as she patted my back.

"Sister…"

Her face paled. I only used that endearment when I was about to be serious with her.

I hadn't planned to tell her anything, but I couldn't allow her to keep picturing a future that she would never get to have. That would break her heart more than it would break mine. My voice was as quiet as I could make it as I said, "I have something I must confess to you."

Her jaw dropped before she started, "Isabelle, if you and Ashley already-"

"NO!" I shrieked then went quiet again, "No, no it is not that."

Irene waited with her mouth hanging open.

"I, well…I do not think I can go through with this marriage."

"I beg your pardon?"

"I am not going to marry Ashley."

She laughed.

"Irene," Her face fell at my serious tone. "You know I have never wanted to marry him."

"Is there someone else?"

I swallowed, "No."

"So you would rather be alone than marry Ashley?"

Slowly, I nodded.

"Why?"

"He's threatened me."

"And?"

"And?" I hissed back. "That should be reason enough not to-"

"Has he hit you?"

I reeled back. "No, but-"

"Has he told you what you need to do to appease him?"

"You cannot-"

She shook her head. "Why can't you just do what he wants? He is going to give you a perfect life."

I scoffed, "At what cost?"

"Pay the cost!" Her voice rose. We looked around to make sure we were still alone. When we were certain, she continued, "You pay the cost, Isabelle. You do whatever it takes to keep him happy and keep him around. If he leaves you, what will you have? *Nothing*." She spat the last word. "He has all the power. Men always have all the power." She took a deep breath and squared her shoulders. "Take it from me, you should make choices that make your life easier. Ashley is the easiest path. Just do what he wants."

"I thought you would understand. You've always known how I truly felt about him."

"And I thought you understood your place in all this." Irene shook her head again. "You have to marry him. There is no way around it. Father agreed because Ashley is going to take you without a dowry and mother has already planned the wedding. You need his money. Just go through with it and start taking lovers like all the other women do."

"That's not what I want."

"Well," She grabbed the edge of the curtain. "We never really get what we want." She started to leave.

"Irene!"

With her hand holding the half-opened curtain, she paused, waiting to see what I had to say.

"You won't tell him, will you?"

Irene took a deep breath. "No, Isabelle, I will keep your secret. I need you married so I can get the dowry and marry Roger. So I won't tell Ashley, but you should."

"I have and he didn't listen. I asked for more time and he didn't care."

Her face softened, "Just marry him and then fix these issues between you. Life will be better for us all that way."

Irene let herself out of the fitting room.

Sixteen

Matias

Finishing up things in Richmond took a little longer than I had anticipated. I had to make sure no one remembered me, especially the little boy I helped before I left. This level of caution had kept me safe since my escape, and I couldn't let my guard down now.

While on route back from Richmond, I stopped by the Hugh Mercer Apothecary Shop. They had just opened for the morning and the sun hadn't fully started spreading its rays out so it was safe for me to make this detour. I wanted to know if there was any kind of herb or concoction that could mimic the look of death. The older man behind the counter laughed before realizing I was serious.

"No, son." He sighed. "Unless you want to actually kill them, there is nothing that could do that."

"What about nightshade? Or perhaps a low dose of opium?"

He eyed me a bit suspiciously while he advised me. "The risk is too high. I'm not even sure what dosage you would need to almost kill a person."

I thanked him for his help then left to find shelter from the sun. The whole time I hid, I thought about other ways we could sneak Isabelle out without provoking her fiancé and father to come after us. Nothing I could fathom worked better than just turning her into a vampire.

After what I experienced, I couldn't understand why someone would willingly choose this. I had promised her that she could decide her fate. But I never promised her I wouldn't try to sway her in a different direction.

Once the sun had set and I felt it was safe to travel again, I started the journey back up to Alexandria. My goal now was to convince Isabelle not to turn. If she let go of that plan, perhaps together we could think of another way to avoid her impending marriage. She was smart, seemingly smarter than me. Surely there was some other way to achieve the same goal without risking her life in any way.

Slowly, I made my way to her house. It was late at night but there were still the few debaucherous wretches who thrived in the night lining the streets. The world was quiet at this time. The quiet eased my nerves as I approached her house.

I was nervous to see her again because the more time I spent with her, the stronger my desire for her grew. She was consuming all of my thoughts. I was reworking my plan around her. This couldn't happen. Despite how much I wanted to keep her around, I needed to let her explore life unburdened by a man. And I needed to see if I could find any of my sisters. That was my whole purpose for coming to Alexandria in the first place.

Isabelle's house was dark as I approached it.

It was a sprawling brick mansion, bigger than my father's estate in Florida. This house was built from money that had come from generations of wealth. My father's rum business was fruitful, but it had nothing on the wealth that families in this part of the country brought over from England.

The whole house was wrapped in a porch and four giant white columns stood out against the front. Two wings split off from the center of the house, one side holding Isabelle and her sister's rooms, the other wing housed her parents.

Her window was cracked open but there wasn't any light spilling out into the night. The last few times I had visited her, there had been the soft glow of a candle or a gas lamp.

Perhaps she had fallen asleep?

The bricks that made up the house also made it easy to climb. So many bricks stuck out just far enough for my fingertips to grip them. I used that to hoist myself up until I could grab the window sill. Launching myself through the window was the easiest part of this whole endeavor. I had always been 'un toro,' as *mi mama* said, bulky but strong. Moving my body was easier now that I was a vampire. One of the few benefits of turning.

I used to climb in and out of my family home in Florida using the branches of an orange tree. I smiled to think how easy it would be to get away with childish stunts like that now. What I would give to go back to that time in my life. What I would give just to see one of my six sisters again.

I shook my head to stop the spiraling of my thoughts. Time was impossible to get back. I needed to focus on the present. And without any more helpful information about what happened to my sisters after my father died, I would never find them. Isabelle could help me with that. I hadn't brought it up yet, but that was something else we could discuss.

Silence and darkness greeted me as I climbed over the ledge of her window.

"Huh." I muttered to myself. My whole body felt weighted down, like my heart had just dropped down into my stomach. It wasn't often that disappointment surprised me like this.

I had expected her to be here.

Being able to see in the dark was another supernatural advantage. I looked at the clothes lying on her unmade bed from when I assumed she dressed earlier in the day. The other times I had visited her at night, everything was put back in its place, so she hadn't returned since she had left. But where had she gone?

I looked around the room for clues. If she was going to return soon, I could wait for her.

I wanted to wait for her.

Another shake of my head to push away the unwanted thoughts. I couldn't want her. She needed to stay human, and far away from me.

"Where did you go, *pajarita*?" I asked out loud as I studied the discarded dresses that led me to believe she went somewhere for just the day. I dared a peak in her wardrobe and nothing else had been packed or moved. The suitcase that she had been filling last time I was here was back in its spot at the bottom of the wardrobe, surrounded by shoes.

So she wasn't going to be gone much longer.

I sighed before sitting down on the edge of her bed. Was that too forward of me?

Ay Dio, I had tasted her in this bed. She had touched me in this bed. My mind brought up the memories of her that I had been replaying over and over again as I went to sleep each morning. I could hear her moans as she let my fingers and tongue explore the untouched parts of her. I could feel her writhing atop these pale pink sheets like it was happening in real time. I could see the way her face crinkled and then smoothed as her body finally let her pleasure flood her.

It made me ache for her to be here with me.

I popped back up off the bed and started slowly walking towards the bookshelf against the far wall. A book could distract me while I waited.

As my eyes quickly scanned the shelves, I noticed she had all my favorites: 20,000 *Leagues Under the Sea*, *Frankenstein*, *The Three Musketeers*, and *Don Quixote*.

My fingers felt the spine of *Frankenstein*. It was a well-loved copy of the book. Tenderly, I removed it from the shelf and opened it to see that it was an original printing, just like the one I once had back in Florida.

Carefully, I flipped through the pages. The book naturally fell open to a page that Isabelle must have looked at many times. It was the beginning of chapter sixteen, when the Creature is questioning why Frankenstein didn't just kill him after seeing how appalling he was.

I often wondered the same thing about my own sire. Why didn't the Lord of Shadows just kill me? Surely my death was a more fitting penance for the crime I had committed rather than torturing me.

Though, from my perspective, everything I had done over a decade ago was self-defense. Obviously,the Lord of Shadows didn't feel the same. I had murdered his partner. He would always see me as the villain.

The pages of the book slammed together with a loud thud. I winced at my lack of restraint and checked the book was unmarred before returning it to its spot on the shelf. So much for using reading as a distraction.

The desk next to the bookshelf held a short stack of paper, some pens and ink, all perfectly arranged and untouched. I could leave her a note and try to come back again tomorrow. But what else did I have to do with my night? I didn't need to hunt. I had already arranged my things back in the mausoleum before I came here. Isabelle was the only task that was left outstanding.

Quietly, I walked back to her bed and sat down, picking up the small clock she kept on her nightstand. It was getting close to midnight. Where the hell was she?

My ears picked up the sound of footsteps rushing towards the door and the distinct click of a lock being opened by a key.

"*Mierda.*" I cursed quietly before jerking down to the floor. The only place I could think to hide was under the bed, so I rolled myself into the tight space.

Someone left the door cracked open as they huffed towards the bed. A woman's voice was grumbling, "Sent someone to tell me they wouldn't be coming home when they could've just come home." All I could hear was the rustling of fabric as the woman took her time hanging and returning the dresses to the wardrobe, muttering to herself about how she had other things to look after instead of cleaning two rooms.

I thought about coming out of my hiding spot to ask this person about where Isabelle was and when she would return. My body started to roll out when I heard the woman mutter, "But soon she'll be gone, and I know I'll miss her messes when she leaves."

I froze. She was referring to Isabelle marrying and moving in with the buffoon. Hearing someone else say it out loud made my fists clench. Did no one else know how vehemently Isabelle didn't want to marry? Was I the only one who knew she would take her own life if she had to marry him?

The sheets above me started to move and the one corner that had been hanging far off the edge of the bed was pulled up. If I revealed myself and she screamed, it would alert others and I didn't want to erase the memories of everyone in this house. It would be easier to just stay hidden.

"Alright, that should be the last of it." The woman's voice started to move away from me. The door creaked closed then I heard the lock click back into place.

After a few more breaths, I rolled back out from my hiding spot. The bed was free of clothes and perfectly made.

My blood was rushing through me as I ran a hand through my hair. Why was I so frazzled? Sneaking in and out of places was something I had done while I was still human. If anything, being a vampire was making this easier now.

It must be the room. Being back in this room, especially without its occupant, was making this whole situation feel odd.

If I saw Isabelle now, I wasn't sure if I would actually try to convince her to stay human. I would scoop her up in my arms and just run away with her. We would flee this place and the terrible feeling it was putting in my gut.

Instead of staying here and waiting, risking ruining everything I was trying to accomplish, I quietly snuck towards the door.

Right before I turned to climb down, a steady breeze floated through the window, moving my curls and rustling the loose papers on her desk.

Against my better instincts, I jumped back down off the window ledge then went to the desk. The pen moved at the same pace as my racing thoughts. I looked down to reread what I had written:

Pajarita,

I had expected you to be waiting for me, so imagine my surprise when I arrived at a very inappropriate hour for guests and you were not in your bed. I can't think of what you could've been doing that is more enjoyable than plotting with me. You'll have to tell me when I come by tomorrow.

Please be waiting for me this time,

M

That was all wrong. Well, it was how I rightly felt, but I couldn't leave her a note like that. It would give her the wrong impression of what this arrangement between us was. I crumpled the paper up and stuck it in my jacket pocket before grabbing a fresh sheet.

Pajarita,

You weren't home when I stopped by. We can discuss the terms of our deal tomorrow night.

Stay safe,

M

I was satisfied with this letter, as cold as it was. My eyes scanned the dark room for the perfect spot to leave the note. I settled on her nightstand, tucked underneath the gas lamp. She would see it when she arrived home, whenever that would be.

Back to the window I went, ready to descend, but my body hesitated again with a reluctance to actually leave. My brain and my heart raged in a quick war, but my heart lost.

I leapt from the window.

Seventeen

Isabelle

The paper felt smooth under my fingertips as I rubbed it in my pocket. I hadn't dared to leave it in my room, just in case the wrong pair of eyes fell on it. It had been in my possession since the moment I found it when we arrived home this morning. After spending the entire day in Washington, my mother thought it would be a wonderful idea to visit her cousin who lived just outside the city since it was on the way home. Dinner turned into dessert, which turned into drinks, which turned into an offer to just spend the night because of how late it was.

If I had known last night was the night Matias would be returning, I would have protested staying, or asked my mother to just let me go home without her. My heart had sunk when I saw the note waiting on my nightstand for me this morning. I had missed a chance to discuss our plan.

I had missed *him*.

And that thought had nagged me all day long, like a fly buzzing right behind my ear.

I missed him.

But it didn't matter, he didn't want anything to do with me beyond our deal. Once he fulfilled that, he would leave me. There was no point getting attached to someone who didn't want to be tethered.

"Are you alright?" Irene's voice brought me back to the hallway, just outside her door. "You have barely said a word all day."

I shook my head, removing my hand from my pocket. "Still tired from yesterday, that's all."

"Sister," She cleared her throat, "About what I said in the dress shop, I know it's been hard for you-"

"No, you're right." I feigned resignation. "I need to marry Ashley. Everything will be better if I just go along with what's planned. I can sort out my feelings later."

Irene's shoulders relaxed, "I hoped you would see it this way! I promise, I want you to be happy, but I don't want you to ruin your life either."

"This is why I need you, sister." I wrapped her in a hug.

"I need you too," She hugged me tightly. "Which is why you need to marry Ashley. I need you close to me." She took my hands in hers. "Get a good night's sleep. Tomorrow we have much to do to prepare for the party and the wedding!"

"Yes, goodnight!"

"Goodnight!" Irene turned and went into her room.

My hand instinctively went back into my pocket to touch the note, as if it could've somehow disappeared from its hiding place. I hurried to my room and locked the door behind me, then took out the note and read it again.

It didn't say much, which made me wonder.

Looking over at the gas lamp, I debated burning the note. If anyone else saw what was written, it wouldn't be hard to use it to incriminate me of having an inappropriate relationship with another man.

Slowly, I tipped the edge of the note into the flame. Immediately the fire ate up the paper and I dropped it before it could burn my fingers. The smell of burnt paper hit my nose. I had wanted to hold onto the note a bit longer, but I needed to get rid of any evidence that could give away what I was planning.

A few hurried steps brought me in front of my wardrobe where I slipped out of my dress. I grabbed my nightgown with the intention to dress for bed and then worried that would be too...odd? Matias had already seen me in my nightgown, but in those interactions, I hadn't expected him to arrive. Now that I knew he was visiting, what would be acceptable to wear?

"Isabelle."

I shrieked at the sudden sound of Matias's deep voice, barely covering myself with the silky white fabric. He wore a crooked smile that exposed one dimple along with the same clothes I had seen him in last time.

"You-you're," In a panic, I pulled the wardrobe door around my naked body. With the little bit of privacy that afforded me, I quickly slipped into the nightgown. I poked my head around the door, refusing to show him how affected my body was. "You're not supposed to be here yet!"

A mix of a growl and a chuckle hit my ear as he started to walk towards me. "It's almost eleven at night. Most people are in bed by this hour."

The lamplight lit up the planes of his tan face as he closed the distance between us. His strong hand grabbed the edge of the wardrobe door and pushed it away, so there was nothing but air separating our bodies.

"I was getting dressed for bed." It was meant to sound annoyed, but it sounded more breathy.

"My apologies for interrupting." His whiskey brown eyes scanned my figure. "And as much as it pains me to ask this of you, I need you to put on more clothes."

"Why?"

"I'm going to show you how vampires live."

My eyes went wide as a smile erupted on my face. I spun around and threw a long black coat over my nightgown.

"No, *pajarita*, you're not meant to be excited." He ran his fingers through his curly hair. "This is to show you why you shouldn't want to turn so we can figure out something else."

"We'll see about that." In my excitement, I struggled to slip my feet into the black boots I had just grabbed.

"Allow me, *por favor*."

And before I could protest, Matias dipped onto one knee. Those whiskey brown eyes locked onto mine as his strong hand slid down my calf and lifted it up. He lined the tips of my toes with the opening of the boot. Carefully, he guided my foot into the black leather boot.

Once that was done, he perched my now covered foot on his thigh. He kept his eyes on mine as he secured each buckle. His cool touch lingered on the bare skin above the top of my boot before he gently lowered that foot to the ground.

He repeated the same slow process with my other boot, taking his time, and never taking his eyes off my face.

Watching him, bent down in front of me, made me remember the last time his mouth had been that close to the most sensitive part of me.

"I can hear your heart speeding up." His eyes locked onto mine.

Once he brought my attention to it, my heart skipped a beat. "Just excited to go out with you." I shook my head to try to stave off the blushing as he rose to his full height. He towered above me, even with the added lift of the heeled boots. "I mean go out together, oh, you know what I mean." My face felt hot from how hard I was blushing.

Matias took my hand and pulled me towards the window, "Come now."

My eyebrows shot up, "Do you intend for me to climb down the same way you leave?"

"Yes?"

"I can't," I huffed and Matias let go of my hand. "I've tried before. It's impossible for me to sneak out this way."

"*Pero* you've never tried with a vampire."

"You can take the window, I'll sneak out my way."

"What's your way?"

This time I grabbed his hand, "Follow me."

Sneaking out through the kitchens was always the easiest way in or out of my house. Irene had used this door when she would meet up with her lover years ago. I myself had used it only a few times just to sneak out and sit in my favorite tree at night.

The door could only open from the inside. Once the door knob met the lock, it wouldn't be able to open without a key. Irene had fashioned a small piece of metal to fit in the space between the knob and the lock so it would still be able to open when she returned. It was brilliant of her to come up with this, but I often wondered if she hadn't figured this out, what would or wouldn't have happened?

The hallways were quiet and the kitchen was dark, almost too dark to see. There was barely any space between our bodies as he followed my lead.

The only sound I heard was my controlled breathing trying to slow down my racing heart. It was the combination of Matias's closeness with sneaking out that was causing such a surge in me. I wasn't paying attention to where I was walking and my foot snagged on the one floorboard that was permanently popping up.

I felt myself start to fall forward but I never hit the floor. Matias has somehow maneuvered himself in front of me. My body fell onto his but he didn't even falter as my weight hit him. I knew he was strong and fast, but I had never seen it.

He tsked and put me back on my feet before whispering, "Careful, *pajarita.*"

I nodded and he smiled before moving out of the way so I could take the lead again. We made it to the red kitchen door without another incident.

I could feel his eyes on me as I knelt down, feeling blindly for the scrap of metal that was stashed in the small gap between the cabinet and the wall. Once I had it, I opened the door. Moonlight spilled it and lit up his inquisitive face. I nodded for him to come out.

He obeyed but continued to watch as I slipped the piece of metal into the lock. Slowly, I closed the door and let out a breath of relief when I didn't hear the click of the lock catching.

We set off into the cool, fall night. Matias took the lead.

"That is quite a trick." He said once we were in the woods surrounding my house.

"Irene actually came up with it."

"Your sister?"

I nodded.

He let out a light laugh, "I only met her the night of the party, but she doesn't seem like she could think of something like that."

"You'd be surprised what Irene can do when she sets her mind to it."

"I would be."

I cleared my throat before asking, "Where are we going?"

"Three guesses."

I scanned the trees as I thought. Based on the direction we were heading, there were only a few places I felt a vampire would be taking me. "The cemetery?"

The moonlight illuminated his gorgeous smile. "*Muy bien, amor.*"

"Pardon?"

"Yes," He held out his hand to guide me over a thick branch in our path. I took his hand and felt his cool palm against mine. "We are going to the cemetery."

"For?"

He didn't drop my hand even after we cleared the root. "I want to show you what life would be like once you turn. I'm hoping you'll see this isn't the best option."

"Have you thought of other options?"

He sighed, "I thought maybe nightshade or opium. In small doses, it wouldn't kill you but make you sick enough you would appear dead.

But even if I could get my hands on either of those, I'm not sure how little to give you. And I won't risk your life when I'm trying to save it."

"Save it?" I stopped walking so he had to look back at me.

He shook his head and pulled me to start walking next to him. "You shouldn't want this life, Isabelle. You'll die and become a monster like me."

"But I'll be free and I'll get to be immortal, and strong, and powerful-"

"At the expense of drinking blood."

"You seem to manage."

"I didn't get a choice. When I was turned, I was starved until I was forced to kill." Matias breathed out as he looked up at the night sky. We had cleared the woods, and were walking along the moonlit streets on the outskirts of town. I kept my eyes on his face, contorting as it worked through a rapid series of emotions. His throat bobbed with a swallow. "Once you get a taste of human blood, especially in those first few months, it's all consuming. You kill and feed indiscriminately."

"I see..."

"Are you going to be able to live knowing you're taking lives?"

"How do you live with it?"

He chuckled, "I wasn't exactly a pillar of morality before I was turned."

The looming gates of the cemetery were finally in our vision. "So you kill people to live?"

"I do, but I try to pick people who deserve it."

"Deserve it?"

"They are doing evil things themselves or are wasting the life they have been given."

The morality of what he was doing was not black and white. In order to survive as a vampire, I would need blood too. Could I kill people who deserved it like Matias did? "Couldn't I just drink animal blood?"

He shrugged, "It's disgusting."

"I see." I took a moment before asking, "How often would I need to kill?"

"A person every few days."

I would have to kill so many people to satisfy my vampiric appetite. My mind was trying to rationalize it as hunting, as a necessary evil, as something that would help rid the world of dangerous people, but my thoughts still circled back to one word: murder.

Could I be a murderer?

"You'd need a lot of blood when you first change." Matias continued, our steps starting to crunch the gravel path that led into the cemetery. "You'll be ravenous, insatiable even."

We paused as he reached out, his strong hand grabbing one of the metal rods that made up the gate, and effortlessly pushing it forward. The gate creaked sharply as it opened. I walked in front, wincing at the harsh sound. Matias followed before shutting the gate behind him with another loud creak.

He continued explaining as we walked, "And you'll have to avoid the sun, which is why I sleep in a coffin."

"Because you'd burst into flames?"

"No," Half his lip curled into a grin, "No, your skin will burn slowly, like you're being cooked alive and it'll weaken all of your abilities."

"So the books got that wrong." My eyes started scanning the headstones shaped like crosses, blocks with rounded edges, and perfect rectangles. Even in the moonlight, I could see the grays, whites, and blacks from the different materials each headstone was made of. Some had moss growing from neglect, some were brand new and shining. There were all types of flowers placed at the different graves, but roses seemed to be the most popular choice.

What flowers would Irene lay at my empty grave?

"Yes," Matias's deep voice brought my gaze to him. "The sun is not the worst of our fears."

"What is?"

"Well, mine is eventually being found by the Lord of Shadows." He expertly weaved us around the graves. "But I suppose for others, it would be vampire hunters. They know how to expertly kill us."

"How often do you run into them?"

"I haven't yet, but I heard all about them when I was imprisoned." He stopped in front of the stone door that sealed the mausoleum. The building had columns on each corner, and the otherwise smooth surface had an ornately carved lion in the center of the door. "Here we are." Without taking his eyes off me, Matias pushed the solid stone door back. "Welcome to my temporary home." And he pulled me over the threshold.

In a whisper, I declared, "I can't see a thing in here." There was no need to whisper, but I felt awkward speaking loudly in the pitch black space.

"*Un momento.*" Matias huffed, and I felt the swift breeze as he moved around me. There was the scrape of a matchstick striking, and I watched the small flame move to touch a torch. Immediately the top of the torch caught fire, and a soft glow filled the small space. The walls were lined with squares and plaques bearing people's names. If I looked closely, I'm sure I would've recognized families from town. But all my eyes could focus on was the large wooden coffin that was taking up most of the space in the middle of the floor.

Suddenly, Matias was behind me, "I need to make sure there is no chance of the sun or anyone else finding me while I sleep during the day. It's taken some trial and error, but a coffin inside a place like this has worked out the best."

"No one comes in here?"

"No one can open the door without making a lot of noise. If that were to happen, I would just erase their memories of me and run to the shade."

"You sleep in this coffin?"

"I do." He gently placed a hand on my lower back and nudged me closer. "You would have to as well."

"Could we both fit in there?"

"No," His breathy laugh filled my ear. "You would have your own."

"Oh..."

"Go on, try it out."

I shook my head.

"C'mon, *pajarita*." Matias walked around me to stand in front of the coffin. With one fluid motion, he lifted the lid off and leaned it up against the wall. "You want to turn into a vampire, this is part of it."

My heart started beating so hard I could feel it pounding against my chest. As I stared down at that empty coffin, a vine of fear started creeping up my spine. My breath hitched in my throat. I couldn't think of how to make a sentence flow together, my thoughts were all crashing into each other.

A coffin is where I would spend my immortal days. I would be dead, but alive somehow. Did I really want that?

"Go on," Matias closed the distance between our bodies. "You said you wanted this. What's stopping you?"

"It's just, I didn't, I don't..."

His words were silky as he whispered, "Are you afraid, Isabelle?" A finger brushed the loose auburn curls behind my shoulder. He lowered his lips so they were hovering just above my pulse. "You're alone in a confined space with a monster." His arms wrapped around my waist and jerked me into him so my chest was pressed up against his. "It would be so easy to just bite down into your beautiful neck," His cool lips brushed against my skin. "Then suck all the delicious blood out of your tantalizing body, and leave your corpse here where no one could find you." My whole being shook when I felt the light scrape of his fangs against my pulse.

A dry swallow worked through my throat. That vine of fear started to tighten, but the way Matias was holding me forced another emotion to overpower that. If he had wanted me dead, there had been better opportunities. And Matias didn't seem like the type to play with his food. This was all his way of trying to get me to change my mind. But that wasn't going to happen, because sleeping in a coffin and drinking blood seemed inconsequential when I could spend more time in Matias's arms.

No, spend more time just doing whatever I wanted to do. I was doing this so I could make my own choices. All of this needed to be my choice.

Instead of shrinking away, I grabbed onto the lapels of his jacket. "Sounds like an enjoyable way to die."

Matias grinned against my cheek, "You never react the way I expect you to."

"Sorry to disappoint."

He pulled back to meet my eyes, "Nothing about you is disappointing." I watched his brown eyes flick down to my lips and then back up to my eyes. "Go on. Get in."

His hold on me loosened. I turned my whole body to face the coffin. Matias had just told me that I wasn't a disappointment to him and I didn't want to start now. I wanted him to think I was brave, that I could handle living as a vampire.

After taking a deep breath, I put one foot and then the other into the coffin. With as much grace as I could, I lowered my body down until I was laying in the coffin looking up at Matias.

His face was blank.

"Care to join?" I joked, moving over as much as I could in the confined space.

After blinking a few times, he shook his head. "No, no, you've proved yourself. Now," He extended his arm. "Let's try something else."

I grabbed onto his tan hand and let him effortlessly pull me up. Our bodies ended up flushed together. "What are we trying next?"

"You're going hunting with me."

Eighteen

Matias

"Hunting?" I could hear the slight waver in Isabelle's voice.

"*Si*," She put some space between our bodies. "I told you, I am going to show you what being a vampire is like. This is part of it."

"Of course." She tried to keep her voice steady but I heard how her heartbeat was picking up. It had been slightly raised the whole time we were together. The moment I mentioned hunting, beating spiked.

I turned and opened the stone door. Isabelle went out into the night first. Hopefully the fresh, cool air would help calm her nerves.

After we both exited the mausoleum, I slid the stone back into place. Isabelle stood there in the moonlight scanning the sky. Her heart was slowing down and beating at a normal pace.

When I came to stand next to her, she asked, "What else will change about me when I turn?"

I wrapped my hand around hers. "Everything." We slowly started walking out of the cemetery. "You'll die and then come back with all your senses heightened. You'll be faster, stronger, harder to kill but it's not impossible."

"And I won't age?"

"No, from the moment you turn, everything about your appearance and form will stay the same."

"That sounds wonderful, looking twenty-three forever. How were you when you turned?"

"I was twenty-five."

"And you can't change your appearance at all? Does your hair grow? Can you grow a beard?"

"No," I laughed at her line of questions because of how innocent they were. "I didn't have one when I was turned, so I'll never be able to grow one."

"This is how you looked a decade ago?"

I nodded.

"What have you been doing all this time?"

"A story for another time. It'll only depress you, though maybe it would make you reconsider-"

Her voice was firm. "I'm not going to reconsider."

"We'll see what you think after you help me pick someone to kill."

Her heart rate spiked again. I should have started the night with hunting. This would convince her not to become like me.

"I won't change my mind." She sounded like she was convincing herself more than me.

"Are you always this stubborn?"

"Irene would say yes."

"Surely you don't want to leave your dear sister behind to mourn you."

"No," She sighed. "That's the one thing I have been struggling with."

I tightened my hand around hers. "It doesn't have to be a struggle."

"It does." She pulled her hand away. "But I can't marry a man who will hurt me just to make my sister happy."

"No, you won't marry him."

Her eyes lit up as she looked at me. "Thank you."

"For what?"

"Being the only one who wants to help me avoid marriage."

"That I don't understand, *pajarita*. Your family has to know that you don't want this marriage for valid reasons."

"They do." She sighed. "But they don't care. There are too many other factors. Until you can whisk me away, I'm just going through the motions making it seem like this wedding will happen. My mother took my sister and I to look at dresses yesterday and Irene spent more time trying on gowns than I did."

"Did you find a dress?"

"I just picked the first one I tried on." She flicked her gaze up to me, "I won't end up wearing it."

I shook my head. "When is the wedding meant to be?"

"October twenty-third. Irene's birthday party is on the twentieth and since everyone will be in town for the wedding, her party is becoming a grander spectacle than my parents originally planned."

"So tell me, *pajarita*, when did you plan on having me turn you? Because once I turn you, you won't be able to see your family ever again."

She scrunched her lips as she thought. "Could you do it the night before the wedding? I still want to be at Irene's birthday."

"One last party?" My chuckle was half-hearted.

"Something like that."

The lights and voices coming from the bar on the edge of town were getting closer. I stopped while we were still covered by the woods. Isabelle stood next to me, expectantly studying my face.

"We're going into the bar." I pointed to the brick building about thirty feet away. "You are going to pick a person to kill. You'll watch as I drain the blood from them and leave their corpse to be found tomorrow morning."

Her eyes frantically flitted between the bar and myself.

"Unless, you don't want to-"

"I want to."

It was my turn to stare expectantly at her.

She took a deep breath and continued. "I want to turn. I don't want to kill, but I want the freedom turning will allow me. If you can do it, then I can."

"*Bueno.*" I took her shaking hand in mine. There was no resistance as I started to pull her towards the bar. The grass under our feet turned into packed down dirt.

"Matias," She whispered just before we were exposed by the street-light.

I spun to look at her, expecting to hear that she changed her mind.

"If someone recognizes me, can you erase their memory of seeing me?"

Not what I wanted to hear, but it was clever of her to think of that. "*Si, pajarita.* No one will know you were here."

She squeezed my hand to signal she was ready. Together we walked into the bar I had frequented just the few nights I had been in Alexandria. I made sure to erase everyone's memory of me. The man behind the bar was the same one I had seen the other nights I had been here, but he looked at me like it was the first time someone like me had come into his establishment.

Isabelle kept her head down as we moved towards a table in a dark corner.

"I'll go get drinks." She sat down, but I remained standing. The sounds of people talking, laughing, and a few voices singing filled the space around us.

"Can you drink?"

"*Si, pero* the alcohol doesn't affect me."

"That's a shame."

I lifted my shoulder in a shrug. "I don't miss it. I mostly buy drinks so I blend in with the rest of the patrons."

She nodded before reaching into her pocket. "Here." Her fingers brushed against my skin as she placed a few dollars in my hand. "For all the trouble I'm putting you through, I should at least pay for your drink you won't enjoy."

"No," I put the money back in her hand and made her fingers close around it. "It is no trouble."

"But-"

The loud laugh carried across the bar. Isabelle froze. Her breathing stopped. I even heard her heart skip a beat.

"*Pajarita*, what is it?"

She didn't move her body but her eyes tracked where the laughter had come from. My gaze followed the same path and landed on none other than her buffoon.

He was sitting at a table all the way on the other side of the bar with a woman perched on his lap. Her hair was a shade darker than Isabelle's and the curls were less defined, but she looked so much like the woman who was sitting in front of me. They both had pale skin, soft features, and curves that corsets were made to emphasize.

"*Mierda*." I said out loud as Isabelle silently watched her buffoon slip his hand under the tattered skirt of the woman. What the buffoon was doing was in the same vein as what I had done with Isabelle, but something about where he was and how publicly he was touching this woman made it worse. Before I did something drastic, like march over there and rip his arms off, we needed to leave. "*Vámonos.*"

Carefully, I grabbed onto Isabelle's arm and pulled her up from the table. Using my body to shield her from the buffoon, we left the bar. She was silently staring at the ground until we were back in the woods.

"I..." She started, shook her head, then continued. "I'm sorry I can't help you hunt. At least not there."

"No, we're done for tonight. Let's get you home."

"I'm not trying to get out of this test." There was a bit of panic in her voice.

"I know." My hand on her arm slid down until I could weave my fingers into hers. I gave her hand an encouraging squeeze as we started walking back to her house. "I can go back and kill him for you."

The side of her mouth lifted. "I would love that, but not yet."

"You just caught him cheating on you."

"I know about that already."

"You do?"

She nodded. "Well, I never knew for certain, but I always suspected it. After he left to go study business, whenever he came home, he kissed me differently. Like he was learning more than balancing accounts and ledgers while he was at university. When I asked him about it, he would deny it, but I knew in my gut he was with other women."

"And did that upset you?"

She shook her head. "I don't love him. I barely care for him outside of the friendship we had as children. After seeing what love did to my sister, I was content with the marriage Ashley and I would have. It wasn't one built on love or even lust. I would never get my heart broken this way." A long sigh left her. "He just wants me because he can make me marry him. I'm the only girl who has never been charmed by him. I often implored him to just marry one of the girls who so desperately wanted him but he wouldn't have it. He said I was the only one for him. And until tonight, I had never seen him with another."

"I'm sorry you had to see that."

"Don't be." She sighed. "I'm just thankful he didn't catch us. He would have killed me."

A flash of red rage clouded my vision."He could've tried."

"Promise me you won't go back and kill him."

I stopped walking so she was forced to turn and look at me. "Why?"

"I need Ashley alive until certain arrangements are set in place. Then you can kill him."

"Would these arrangements be before or after you turn?"

"After."

I dropped her hand. "Care to elaborate?"

She hesitated, letting her weight shift from one foot to the next, then stated, "He is paying a friend to marry my sister and handling my father's debts. That's why I need to fake my death. I'm worried if I just run, he'll stop helping my family out of spite."

Just when I thought I couldn't hate him more than I already did. I knew he was a terrible man. He reeked of pretentiousness and violence, walking around her family's home like he already owned it. But to hear the extent of how he was manipulating Isabelle and controlling her family heightened my rage. I had done terrible things in my past but none of them were done with this kind of malicious intent.

I took a breath to steady my voice before telling her, "*Escucha*, listen, I will do whatever you want. I don't want you to turn and become a monster like me, but I won't trap you with a different kind of monster either. We'll figure this out together."

She nodded and took my hand in hers. We walked in silence the rest of the way to her house. The whole time I felt this urge to just take her far away from here. I could get her somewhere safe where that buffoon could never find her. This situation was too complicated for a solution as simple as that. Turning her was still the only option that worked. And I needed to make sure she understood the extent of what she was agreeing to by coming with me.

But not tonight. After what she just witnessed, that conversation could wait until tomorrow.

We snuck back into her house the same way we left. Isabelle tucked that scrap piece of metal back into its hiding spot before silently leading me back to her room.

Her whole body relaxed once we were safe behind her locked door.

"Do you, would you like to stay?" Her fingers went to idly play with the button on her jacket.

"I would like to but I should go. You had quite a night and we could both use some rest."

"Oh," Her eyes went to the floor.

Gently, I used my finger to lift her chin. Her blue eyes were swirling with a mix of emotions. "I'll return tomorrow night. I'll try to come as soon as the sun is down."

"Come closer to the time you came tonight. I can't guarantee I'll be done pretending to care until then."

"*Si, amor,* I will."

"Perfect." She let out a breath and leaned into me.

I started to lean back into her. It felt so right, especially after what happened tonight, to kiss her soft, pink lips. The desire surged through me as I closed the space between our bodies and wrapped my arms around her waist. I felt her fingers run up my chest and grip the lapels of my jacket. Her eyes closed and her mouth parted in anticipation of a kiss.

After what we both saw, Isabelle might want just more than a kiss. If she didn't intend to marry the buffoon, then we wouldn't need to worry about her purity. I didn't think I would be able to control myself if Isabelle allowed me access to her body again. I wanted to touch her gorgeous curves again so badly the need was pushing every other rational thought away. I wanted her but not like this. Not without her knowing what tethering herself to me would entail.

"I can't." I whispered just before our lips touched.

Her eyes shot back open. "Why not?"

"I don't think I'll be able to stop." I barely brushed my lips across hers. "The next time I kiss you, I want it to be when you are ready to fully accept this deal. When you know everything and still choose it."

"Understood." She breathed the word into me.

"I will return tomorrow night." Her teeth tugged on her bottom lip and my thumb snuck up to release it. "Stay safe until then."

"I will."

I didn't let her go right away. For another long moment, I just held her close to me.

Finally, I let her go from my embrace and without another word, I dashed towards the window. I tried to twist my body so I wouldn't have to see Isabelle again before I started to climb down, but it was impossible. My eyes tracked her standing there, arms wrapped around herself, that damn lip back between her teeth, looking at me like she was watching a boat leave port.

"Goodnight, Isabelle."

"Goodnight, Matias." Her voice followed me as I disappeared over the ledge of the window and started climbing down the wall. Once my feet hit the grass, I looked back up to see her hanging out the window meekly waving down at me.

My heart leapt from my chest as I waved back.

Before I listened to my mind screaming at me to climb back up into her room, I stalked into the woods. My feet found the familiar path that led into town. I needed to shed this feeling that Isabelle had left me with: that I had just left a part of myself in that room with her.

I missed her.

And if she decided not to turn I would be so relieved but so disappointed. I wanted to keep her by my side for the rest of eternity. I wanted to make her laugh in one moment and have her crying out my name in the next.

Tonight was meant to convince her not to want this life, but it had the opposite effect.

She wanted this.

She wanted me.

And I wanted her too.

I shook my head and ran my fingers through my already tousled hair. This was not supposed to happen. I only wanted her for a night, and now I was about to bind her to me forever.

But the dread I expected to feel wasn't there. In the past, when women had tried to talk to me about marriage, there was this gnawing feeling in my chest that would propel me to get as far away from that person as possible.

That feeling wasn't there. I felt content, calm, and ready.

If she would have me.

Nineteen

Isabelle

When I woke up the next morning, there was an unexpected pulse of giddiness through me because Matias would be returning again tonight.

It drove me to distraction as my mother and sister went over menus and plans for the birthday party and wedding. I nodded every time I was asked for input on anything. It didn't matter. This wedding wasn't going to happen. All of my mother and sister's labors were for nothing.

There was a mix of grief swirling with the giddiness. An eternal life as a vampire looked so fantastical, despite what Matias had shown me. I could truly go anywhere and do anything I wanted for multiple lifetimes. This wild thought brought a smile to my face as I imagined visiting all the places I had read about in books. I would have to visit them during the night, but I could still see them with my own two eyes. No more pictures or drawings of the wonders in the world. I would have my own memories of them.

Missing out on the special events and moments a mortal life would give me was making my heart ache. I didn't want to leave my sister, or my parents. Despite the urge to sneak away and start reading every time my sister and mother gossiped through the day, I tried to soak in the moments I had left with them.

Maybe I could return after a few years had passed? I could visit Irene and see how her life was shaping out, if she and Roger were happy. I could probably convince her that I was a ghost haunting her. She would be scared at first, but I'm sure I could sway her to not be. Irene would appreciate it if I showed her attention from beyond the grave.

My mother was in the middle of explaining why we hated an aunt who was coming to the wedding when my father interrupted, "A visitor is here to see you." He winked when he looked at me. There was only one man who could visit me during the day.

Ashley was here, unexpectedly.

But perhaps I should have anticipated this since I knew he was in town early.

Irene giggled as I stood, doing my best to look excited. The thought that I should just pretend it was actually Matias flashed through my mind and suddenly my smile felt more genuine.

I followed my father to the front of the house, where Ashley was standing up straight, his hands clasped behind his back. "Thank you, Mr. Haller."

My father eagerly asked, "You'll be joining us for dinner?"

"Actually, I was hoping to take Izzy out for the evening." Ashley's gaze was fixed on me. "If you'd have me."

"I have nothing else to do." The words didn't match my smile.

"I suppose now that you are engaged, that would be more than alright. Just have her home at a decent hour." My father walked back towards my mother and sister.

Once we were alone, Ashley took a step closer to me.

"This is an unexpected surprise." I took a step back. "You weren't meant to visit until Saturday."

"I finished work early and was desperate to see you."

"Only me?"

He didn't catch what I meant as he answered, "Well mother wanted me to bring you to the house for dinner but I refused. I want you all to myself."

"I'm not dressed-"

"Go change."

I couldn't hide my scowl at his tone.

"Please," He whispered into my ear.

"I'll be a moment."

"I'll wait."

I nodded before slowly walking to my room. Irene's quick steps started behind me when I passed her room. "Where are you going?"

"To dinner with Ashley."

"Alone?"

I shrugged as I opened my bedroom door. "Father agreed to it."

"Where?"

"Not sure."

"Oh!" Irene squealed then raced around me to my wardrobe. "What shall you wear?"

"You pick." I knew it would make her happy and I didn't care what I wore tonight. I just needed Ashley to think I cared.

"This one!" She grabbed the one yellow dress that I owned, a gift from our mother, but I had never worn.

Without a word, I took the dress from her.

"But..." She turned around while I started to change, "You hate that dress. I grabbed it in jest."

"Oh," I let the word hang between us as I turned to her so she could fasten the buttons in the back.

"Are you sure you're alright?"

"Just nervous about dinner with Ashley." That wasn't a total lie. I was nervous because I needed Ashley to be pleased with my performance so he didn't follow through on his threats.

"Well," Irene finished the buttons and spun me around. "You do look lovely in this shade. Ashley will love it."

And he did. From the moment he helped me into the carriage, he seemed convinced that I was going to be the perfect, agreeable, submissive wife.

The whiskey Ashlry ordered with dinner was the same one we had snuck from my father's bar when we were thirteen. He brought it up and reminded me that was the night he dared to kiss me for the first time. Even though I told him I didn't want to kiss him.

There were very few important moments of my life that didn't involve Ashley. He forced his way into my life constantly.

But I didn't let my hostility towards him show. He wouldn't be able to force his way into my immortal life. I kept reminding myself of that when I wanted to say something that would annoy or enrage him. I spent most of dinner just drinking my wine while he went on and on about business and his plans for us. Dinner passed by in a blur.

When the carriage pulled up in front of my house, I faked a yawn. "I'm exhausted."

"All we did was eat." He laughed as a hand reached out to me.

I took it and smiled, "And drink."

"That also requires little effort." His tall, broad form left the carriage first, then he easily helped me out.

We walked up to the door. I had just wrapped my hand around the door knob when he cleared his throat. I looked up at him. "Did you have something else planned?"

"I had hoped to spend a little more time with you tonight."

"Oh," My attempt at flirty came off dry.

"Invite me in, Izzy." The tone of his voice was right on the edge of annoyed.

There was no way to avoid bringing him in the house, but once there I could work the situation so I didn't do anything with him. I would just have to play this whole thing carefully.

I swallowed but tried to hide it with a quick smile. "Would you like to come in?"

Ashley opened the door and let himself into my house.

* * *

It was quiet.

We hadn't come home that late, the grandfather clock in the foyer reading just after ten o'clock. My parents would be in their bed, but this was the calmest the house had been since the engagement. I didn't even hear Irene's voice echoing anywhere in the house.

"Where did you want to go?" I offered, "The library?"

He shook his head. The grip his hand had on mine tightened as he led me up the stairs. He was taking me to my room.

"Ashley, perhaps-"

"Shhh," He scowled. "You'll wake the house."

I thought of doing just that. If I screamed someone would come out to see what was happening. Unless Ashley had paid them not to.

As we passed Irene's door, I thought of accidentally tripping or bumping into something to make noise. But the way Ashley was pulling me behind him, there was no way I could try something like that.

I would have to handle this once we were in my room.

Ashley opened the door then strolled inside with an earned famil-iarity. He waited until I was in the room then locked the door behind us.

He sat down on the bed and stared at me expectantly. I sat down next to him just shy of actually having our bodies touch. We had been in this position before and he'd never taken advantage of me.

"Are you planning on bringing all those books with you?" Ashley motioned to the shelves.

"Of course!"

"But I already have all these books. Why would you need more?"

"You should know better than anyone that I would need to bring these with me."

He nodded, "But will they be in our bedroom?"

Our bedroom. I tried to make my shiver of disgust into a shiver of pleasure. "If it's to be our bedroom, then yes, I would like them in there."

"Alright, if it'll make you happy."

"It will."

Ashley started to lean in closer. Panic was seeping into my blood and making my heart race. Perhaps I could just kiss him enough to satisfy whatever this was then send him home? The thought of kissing him made the wine in my stomach swirl with disgust. He wasn't the one I wanted to be kissing now.

But it was unavoidable at this moment.

I tilted my head to try to make this kiss believable.

My eyes instinctively flicked over to the movement I saw in my window.

Matias was silently pulling himself up onto the ledge.

Twenty

Matias

I heard their voices before I saw them. I almost climbed back down and waited in the shadows until the buffoon left her room, but there was no chance in hell I was going to let him have alone time with her.

Without making noise, I hoisted the top half of my body over the window's ledge and locked eyes with Isabelle. I saw the flash of excitement followed by panic in her eyes.

The buffoon started to turn around to see what she was looking at.

I jumped up so I was perched on the window and ready for whatever he would try. I wanted him to try something. I know Isabelle needed him alive but his death was going to be so satisfying.

Isabelle's hands grabbed the sides of his head and turned his attention back towards her. She kissed him with such sudden force that I heard their teeth clack together.

It didn't stop the buffoon though. Instead he pulled her closer to him, enjoying this moment they were having.

Her blue eyes popped open and she scowled at me while continuing to kiss him. I smirked as I slowly, quietly started stalking towards her.

I didn't think it was possible, but her eyes went wider the closer I came to her bed. Her already racing heartbeat went frantic. The thought of her blood pumping wildly through her body distracted me. Just before I reached the edge of her bed, I turned and headed towards her bathroom. She groaned but turned the sound into something that sounded more like a moan.

I knew it was fake. I knew everything about this kiss was fake but I still wanted to rip the buffoon away from her and kiss her the way she deserved to be kissed.

Her eyebrows crinkled in a plea for me to hide myself so she could stop kissing the buffoon. I nodded before tucking myself into her bathroom. My body was pressed against the door so I could hear everything, including how fast her heart was still beating.

"Damn, Izzy." His voice sounded strained.

"Just a few more weeks." Isabelle giggled and I heard the bed rustle. "Stop now." The playful tone in her voice was gone. "It's getting late."

"It's just two more weeks. What difference does two more weeks make?"

"It makes a difference to God."

"Is he in this room right now?"

My hand was clenched around the doorknob. I had to fight the urge to throw the door open and handle the buffoon myself. Isabelle's voice was confident as she stated, "We're waiting until our wedding night. Isn't that part of why you want me? You told my sister I was the good chaste one who was worthy of marriage."

The buffoon grunted. "Two more weeks then."

I heard their kiss this time. An audible snarl slipped past my lips.

Isabelle gasped, "Ashley!"

"I won't have to stop myself once you're my wife."

The metal of the doorknob was denting from how hard I was gripping it.

Isabelle's voice calmly stated, "Let me walk you to the door."

There was some shuffling before I heard the door creak open and then shut.

When I went to open the bathroom door, I pulled the doorknob out completely. The grasp on my control wasn't as secure as I had thought. I shrugged as I tried to shove the doorknob back together. It barely held so I left the door cracked before taking a spot on Isabelle's bed, facing the door.

I only had to wait a few minutes before she came back, making sure the door was locked behind her. Isabelle's face was flushed with embarrassment and her hands were on her hips. "What are you doing here already?"

My eyebrow shot up, "Would you like me to leave?"

"No, just don't do that again." Her quick steps brought her right in front of me, but she stopped just outside of my reach.

"I could just kill him now."

She groaned, "No."

"But he touched you when you didn't want it?"

"I have to convince him that I do want it. He needs to think everything is fine so my sudden death won't stop him from helping my family."

"Fine." I huffed.

"Are you-" her mouth stretched into a smirk. "Are you mad I kissed him?"

I tsked, "Please, that was not a kiss."

"Yes it was!"

"Pressing your lips on his does not make it a kiss."

"Oh, yes," She rolled her blue eyes, "I forgot you are the expert."

Before I realized what I was doing, one hand grabbed her waist while the other wound into her hair and I pulled her flush against my chest. My lips found hers as a surprised squeak escaped her mouth. It had been an entire fortnight since I had last kissed her, but I remembered exactly how she felt: soft and welcoming.

Using the hand in her hair, I titled her head back so I could gain better access. Those full lips eagerly moved against mine, allowing my tongue to slip through the opening. When her hands slid up around my neck, I sucked her bottom lip between my teeth, careful that my fangs didn't pierce it. If I tasted her blood, I would lose the last bit of control I had over myself.

Finally, with one last soft peck, I pulled away. "That was a kiss."

Through soft breaths, she exclaimed, "Yes, it was."

Her eyes darted between my eyes and lips as I held her in my arms. She looked so eager for another kiss. I wanted to give her just that, but I hadn't come here tonight just to kiss her. I needed to tell her the truth about what I went through, and I couldn't let how much I enjoyed her warm, supple body against mine distract me from that. I tucked a curl behind her ear. "So, you still want to turn?"

She eagerly nodded.

"I need you to understand why I don't want you to choose this life."

Her shoulders slumped before she put some distance between our bodies. The absence of her warmth shook me, but I tried to act flippant.

"You're taking on more than you realize, *pajarita*."

She plopped onto her bed. "It's not going to change my mind. Turning me into a vampire before I get married is the best plan we have."

I held up a hand to stop her protesting, "*Por favor*, just allow me to tell you."

Isabelle's chest rose as she took a deep breath then settled herself against the pillows. "Ready when you are."

A hesitant smile forced its way to my face. I stood up, trying to avoid having to begin. "I've never told anyone this."

"You don't have to."

"No, you need to know what I've done, what could happen to you. It's...it's just hard putting it all into words. It's just been these awful pictures in my mind for so long that describing them," I shuddered as the words trailed off.

"Start at the beginning."

"Once upon a time?" A breathy laugh escaped me. "No, my life was typical for where I am from. I was born in Florida, but my parents are from Spain. My father worked in the rum importing business, and we lived very comfortably; not quite as grand as you," I threw my arms out, motioning to the house. "But I never wanted for anything."

I sighed, my feet started to move me in a short circuit in front of the bed. Isabelle's eyes tracked me the whole time. "As the first-born and only son, it was my obligation to take over my father's rum business. Every part of my life was preparing me for that. I had to be bilingual, an excellent reader, perfect at my calculations, and able to charm even the grumpiest of clients. I enjoyed it. These things all came so easily to me, and my parents were so proud of me. Life was great."

"I'm sorry." Isabelle's soft voice distracted me.

"Why are you apologizing?"

"Because you said it was, implying that this story is about to take a terrible turn."

"It is my own fault that my life turned out like this."

"How?"

A huff of breath left me, "I ruined everything. It started with my mother's death. I didn't handle it well. I started acting out, using other girls my age to distract me from my thoughts. My father didn't stop me or help me. As long as it didn't impact the business, he didn't care." I shook my head. "In a not surprising turn of events, it did impact the business. My father had a close business acquaintance, who specialized in wine. While my father and he discussed deals, I was left alone with this man's very young, very attractive, and very lonely wife."

I heard her suck in a breath.

"It started off innocently. We just talked, she complained about being left out of these meetings, about being married, things like that. I listened, which I think is ultimately what she wanted, just someone to listen to her. *Pero* she kissed me, and it all spiraled from there. It was too easy for us to be alone together. We would sneak off and be back in time so that my father and her husband would leave their meetings none the wiser."

"How old were you?"

"I was sixteen when this affair started."

Isabelle's eyes went wide. "And how old was she?"

"About a decade older."

"She preyed on you, Matias. This isn't your fault."

"It was, *amor*, because it was I that suggested she leave her husband for me. When she laughed in my face, I became very reckless. I wanted us to get caught. I figured that would force her to choose, because I couldn't let us be a secret anymore. *Pero* it wasn't her husband that caught us, it was my father. He caught us late one night after I had snuck out to see her and within a few hours I was on a ship to Spain. He needed that deal to keep the business afloat. I was going to ruin it so I had to be sent away until he could finalize everything."

"What happened to her?"

My shoulders lifted in a shrug. "I don't know. I never heard from her after I was sent to Spain. *Mi abuelita* picked me up at the docks. I had never met the woman before, but I recognized her immediately. She looked like my father with a wig on." Isabelle laughed at that and it brought a soft smile to my face. "She tried her best to straighten me out, but I was so angry and hurt that I kept doing whatever I wanted with any woman who was willing. Because I didn't learn my lesson, my father cut me off, but it didn't matter. I used all the training I had been given and started working at the embassy. Then things really got out of control."

My pacing feet slowed, "I'm not proud of how I acted during this time in my life. I know I hurt so many people, but I..."

She offered up, "You were just trying to hurt yourself."

"Something like that." I took a deep breath, "About ten years ago, I was out at a bar, and I saw this woman, unlike any that I had ever seen in America or Spain. It wasn't just that she was beautiful, she was entrancing, every man in that bar wanted to just be acknowledged by her." My mind recalled the way that woman had looked at me from across the room. It was like her eyes had their own magnetic force that pulled me in. Her dark curls fell around her pale skin that was barely covered by a tight red dress. She was the most gorgeous woman in the room. "And she picked me. Her eyes locked on mine, and for the rest of the night, I swear it's like she didn't blink. We danced, talked, drank, and at the end of the night, she grabbed my hand and pulled me to her lodgings."

A knot started to form in my throat. I coughed to clear it, but it didn't seem to help. "Once we were in her room, she started-well, she started to look at me the same way I had looked at my mother's cooking. I knew when she locked the door behind us, that it wasn't to keep anyone from coming in. She had locked the door to keep me from getting out. For hours she took my blood, slowly, drawing the whole ordeal out. She kept muttering about how 'he always hates it when I play with my food, but he's not here' and other weird things like that. I knew that if I didn't do something, I was going to die."

"But you didn't." Her voice sounded so hopeful.

"No, she eventually drifted off to sleep." The picture of that vampire lying on the couch, almost drunk off my blood as it dripped down her chin, popped into my mind. "I think she thought I was too weak or foolish to do anything. But somehow, I managed to get enough strength to pick up the shovel that sat with the tools for the fireplace. As silently as I could, I lifted it over her neck, and put all my weight into striking down." The phantom sound of her wet gurgled scream rang in my ear. "Her head rolled off her body, and I kicked it into the fireplace. *Mi abuelita* always told me that only fire can kill evil. I dragged her body off the couch and shoved as much of it as I could into the fireplace. Then everything went dark."

"Turning was the most agonizing thing I have ever experienced. No other physical torture inflicted on me hurt more than my entire body shutting down and dying. I was awake the whole time, my skin burning like I was being covered with hot coals, then I finally felt relief as an icy chill settled over me. Eventually I passed out from the pain. When I woke a few hours later, I immediately knew something was wrong. I tried to run out of the room I had been locked in, but as soon as the sun touched my skin it started to burn. I ran back inside trying to figure out what was happening to me. I realized that when I cut that vampire's head off, some of her blood had gotten into my mouth and since she had practically drained me dry right before that, it was enough to turn me into a vampire. "

Tears threatened to come as I started the next part of the story. "As soon as the sun set, I managed to make it back to *la casa de mi abuelita*. *Yo*-I wish I had gone literally anywhere else. Before I could even say a word to *mi abuelita* he arrived, his shadowy form becoming solid in the middle of the kitchen. I didn't know his title until later, *pero* I knew when I saw him that this was who the woman had been mumbling about. *Mi abuelita* fell over instantly, the shock of his arrival made her heart give out. He had literally formed from the shadows on the walls coming together."

"Because he's a vampire?"

"Because he controls shadows. He is them. When I was his prisoner, that's what all the guards called him, the Lord of Shadows. No one else is able to do what he does from what I heard."

"Like how you can erase memories?"

"*Si*, we each get a gift when we are turned."

"If you killed this woman who meant something to him, why didn't he kill you?"

The smile was an attempt to hide my pain. "So he could torture me instead"

She gasped.

"At least, that's what he told me as he dragged me behind him. He didn't realize I had been turned into a vampire, and since that had happened he couldn't just kill me. Instead, he was going to take me somewhere to serve out my punishment. He used some stone that allowed us to instantly be in a new place. One minute we were in Spain, and the next we were outside the doors of a giant stone building that didn't look like anything I had ever seen before. It was less decadent than a castle, but still loomed over us as he continued to drag me by my hair to a dungeon and into a cell."

"That's so...cruel. He killed your *abuelita* and then stole you away to be tortured."

"That's not even the worst part of the story."

Her face fell, but I continued, "All I felt at that point was overwhelming thirst, and I knew instinctively that it wasn't for water. He refused me any blood, not that I asked when he would come to check on me. I would just hide in the corner of my cell, hoping he would decide to just kill me."

I sighed, "A few days went by where he didn't come check on me. Instead he sent human guards to make sure I was still alive. When he returned, I noticed he had something slung over his shoulder. He opened the cell and threw a woman in there with me. 'She reeks of you.' He'd spat. 'Why do you think that is?' And I noticed, even in the faint candle light that it was Camila, a girl I had spent a few nights with months before then, and never spoken to again. My ears picked up her calm heartbeat, which I knew would change once she was conscious again, but I also could hear a faint, quick beating coming from below her heart. She was pregnant."

"No." The word was barely audible, I didn't think Isabelle even realized she had said it outloud.

"She was pregnant with my baby, and it had led the Lord of Shadows right to her. He said 'Since you are so willing to take a life, take the one you gave this woman.' I didn't know what he meant by that, but he didn't say anything else before he left. Camila woke up soon after." I shook at the memory of her sobs. "She was so scared, and I did my best to try to tell her it would be alright, that I would figure something out. The guards brought food in for her three times a day. At first, I tried to eat some of it, but it just made me sick. So she ate, and cried, and we tried to distract each other from the horrible situation I had put us in. Camila was a sweet girl, I knew that from the little time I had spent with her, and she did not deserve this. She was just a part of my punishment."

I paused, unsure how to start this next part. Isabelle's voice cut through my rushing thoughts, "What happened to her?"

"Well, I quickly figured out what role she was meant to serve in my torment. My thirst for blood grew by the minute, and it took everything in me to resist drinking from her. That's what he wanted. The Lord of Shadows wanted me to be responsible for the death of this innocent girl and my babe that she carried. But I refused. I managed about a fortnight. Long enough, that I could see the small bump of her stomach start to show." My breath stuttered. "She bit her lip. That's all it took, the single bead of blood from biting her lip while eating a crust of bread, and I was on top of her before she could even scream. My fangs sank so hard into her throat that I took out a chunk of flesh. I drained her blood in long, vicious pulls. Her heart stopped beating within a few minutes, and then the faint beating of the baby's heart ceased too. I...I killed them both."

"You were forced to, you-"

"Do not defend me." My words were soft, despite how harsh they felt coming out of my dry throat.

Isabelle leaned back into the pillows.

"When the Lord of Shadows discovered what I had finally done, he applauded me. Then the real torture started, but anything he did to me physically didn't matter anymore. My soul was gone the moment I took those lives."

"Then how did you escape?"

I finally sat back down on the bed. "As time went by, the Lord of Shadows came less frequently. Sometimes months would go by and I thought that maybe he had finally forgotten about me, but he would always turn up and give me just enough blood to keep me alive until he could torture me again. During those long stretches, I started talking to the human guards. Most of them were only there because of the money they were being given. They would talk to me, more to entertain themselves than to lift my spirits, but they still acknowledged my existence."

My lips curved into a smile at the next memory, "Then one day I joked to a guard that they must forget all about me once they leave here. The next day, he didn't show. No one came to check on me. For almost ten years, at least one set of eyes had come to make sure I was alive, *pero* not that night. So I told the joke to the guard who showed up for the next shift, and again he was absent. A frantic human came to check on me, but he wasn't a guard. He seemed like someone who worked for the Lord of Shadows in other ways. This human man accused me of compelling the guards. I didn't know what he meant. He said, 'You forced them to leave.' and I looked him in the eyes and stated, 'If I could convince them to leave, can I convince you to let me out?' And then he got this glazed look over his eyes and unlocked my cell. I bolted out of the door, shoving the human into the cell instead and locking him in. Then I ran and hid in the shadows of the woods surrounding the stone castle, putting as much distance between myself and it, not knowing when the Lord of Shadows would return. After hours of wandering, I got to a small dock, and snuck on board a ship. I had no money and didn't speak the language of wherever I was, but I was free." I looked at Isabelle, whose mouth was open and her eyes were wide. "And I've been running ever since."

"That's incredible." Her words were full of awe.

My fingers went into my hair. "No, no, it's not incredible. It's dangerous, so terribly dangerous. I have no idea where he is now or if he is hunting me. I haven't seen in the months I've been free, but I am always extra careful to erase everyone's memories. That's why I panicked when I couldn't erase yours. After what we did that first night, my scent would've been all over you. I tried to stay way but when I saw the women being murdered I came back to make sure you were safe. I was worried that my scent brought him here to you. I don't know if he is out there, but it's why I don't return to a place I have already been too. I can't risk him finding anyone who could lead him to me."

Isabelle popped up from the bed now, "Then why did you come back here? If you knew he could come for you, if he could smell you had been here, why did you return after the first night?"

"Because I'm selfish." The words came out louder than I intended. Isabelle stilled in front of me. "I'm so incredibly fucking selfish. I have been my whole life and not even this curse could change that. And it would be so selfish to ask you to come with me now, to become a monster like me, just because I want to keep you with me." The tears that were threatening to fall from her eyes stopped my angry rush of words.

She didn't let those tears fall as she asked, "Why did you agree to the deal?"

"I agreed to your deal because I couldn't let you kill yourself. I thought if I placated you, then you would come to the realization on your own that this could never work. You weren't supposed to want to become a vampire, but it seems everything I have done has only intrigued you more, and that was never my intention. I hoped together we could come up with another plan, another way to save your life, because I feel this need to protect you after how much of yourself you gave to me that first night. I never expected all of this to come from that first deal we made. I wanted this to work out to ease my own guilt but now," I sighed, "Now I've just made it worse. If you come with me, as a vampire or a human, your life will be in danger. No matter what we do, you lose."

I watched as those shiny blue eyes dropped to the floor. Her chin quivered, but she still didn't cry. "Then let me release you from the deal."

My whole body felt like it was sliding down, but I tried to stay calm as her gaze flicked back up to meet mine. Her confident voice continued, "I've been a spoiled brat, making you do something you didn't want to in the first place."

"Isabelle, *pajarita*, that isn't-"

"What you wanted? I know. You didn't want to help me. You just wanted a night with me, and I was trying to force more on you. I'm no better than Ashley. I'm not going to make you do anything you don't want, not after what you just told me you went through. So the deal is off."

"But you can't marry him, Isabelle."

She shrugged, "I'll figure it out. Irene has been saying marrying him is the easiest thing to do." The crack in her voice shattered my heart.

"Let me help." It was a desperate attempt to salvage what was between us. "Let me make sure you're safe. I truly don't think the Lord of Shadows will come here but let me make sure if he does I can lure him away."

"I think that you leaving now is the only thing that will keep me safe."

"I could help you get rid of the buffoon after you marry him?" I reached out for her.

She took a step back from me. Physically, there wasn't much space between us, but it felt impossible to cross. The sleeves of her canary yellow dress slipped off her shoulder as she crossed her arms. "I don't want you to keep worrying about me. I've burdened you enough already. I've handled Ashley my whole life. I can handle him for a bit longer."

"Isa-"

"I think it's best if you left now."

Without another word, I left her.

Twenty One

Isabelle

The tears I struggled to hold back finally fell after Matias left. And they fell again the next night, and the night after that.

Grief was the closest word I had to the way my body felt emptied. I lost my chance to easily get away from the life I never wanted. Despite spending every waking moment trying to think of a better plan, I couldn't figure anything out that would keep Ashley financially involved with my family without me having to marry him.

I would have to go through with this wedding.

I would have to let Ashley do more than kiss me. But every time I thought of being with Ashley intimately, my mind brought back up the memories of Matias.

Those memories made my heart ache.

It wasn't the loss of his help that I was mourning. Despite spending such a short amount of time together, I thoroughly enjoyed every interaction we had. Asking him to go away was difficult but it was for the best. He didn't need to worry about me when he had his own troubles to take care of.

He was free.

So why did it feel like my chest cracked in half?

The absence of Matias was like a death because it was final. Even though he couldn't die, this was the end of our deal. I had been tempted to go check the mausoleum we had visited. As I was getting ready to sneak out, I realized I wouldn't be able to open the giant stone door on my own. What good was going all the way over there just to find he was actually gone? That would only make the pain in my chest flare up again. He had left when I told him to and I knew he wouldn't come back. It wasn't safe for him to come back.

The only anger I felt about this whole deal was that he potentially endangered myself and my family. He claimed that it was safe, that he hadn't seen this Lord of Shadows, but the potential threat was still looming over me. I made sure to lock my window every night just in case.

A full body numbness filled me as I floated through my days just agreeing with my mother, Ashley, and Irene as they decided my future for me.

Any chance I could, I slipped away for some alone time. It was exhausting pretending and faking all day long. Even with wine to help improve my mood, I could feel myself floundering. Soon I would be drowning and then there would be nothing left of me.

* * *

A week after Matias had left, I saw a glimmer of hope.

I had excused myself after dinner was finished. I had drunk more than my usual two glasses of wine and fresh air sounded better than locking myself in my room.

As soon as the crisp, smoke scented air hit my nose I felt better. Since I had been locking my window, I hadn't been able to enjoy the chill of fall at night.

Despite goosebumps popping up on the exposed skin of my neck, I sat down and looked at the stars. Nights felt empty now without Matias's visits. I couldn't help but wonder what he was doing. Hunting? Bedding another woman?

That thought stung.

Booted footsteps started getting closer. I looked up to see Roger joining me on the back porch. "My sister allowed you a moment alone?"

He smiled, "She needed a moment."

"Ah," I understood that Irene needed to use the ladies room.

"Figured I'd come out for a smoke." He pulled a silver case out of his jacket pocket. "I didn't know you would be out here. I can go someplace else if-"

"No," I waved my hand. "I don't mind the smell."

He nodded, lighting a cigarette. After using a match to light the tip, the musky and rich smell of smoke filled the large space between us.

"Your father has an excellent product." Roger said after taking a long drag.

"So I've heard."

"You don't smoke?"

"No," I shook my head. "Irene and I feel sick if we inhale the smoke. Ashley loves it, which is why I'm used to the smell."

"Ah, that explains why your sister asked me not to smoke around her. It'll be hard to do in the winter but I don't want her to get sick."

"That's sweet of you." Ashley didn't change up his smoking habits after I told him it would make me sick. He always told me that I could leave the room he was in.

"I know we haven't spoken much." Roger started to take a step towards me but stayed where he was. I noticed he moved his hand so the smoke was as far away from me as possible. "I really do care about your sister. I plan to propose on her birthday. Your father already gave his blessing."

I flashed the first genuine smile in days. "That is wonderful! I know she cares deeply for you."

He took another long drag then cleared his throat. "Ashley told me you are aware of the deal he made with me regarding your sister."

My spine straightened, "He did."

"I want you to know that I am not pursuing Irene because of the money. I can still provide a comfortable life for her without Ashley's help, but he has promised to purchase a house for us and I would be a fool not to take a free house."

"He made it seem like you had nothing without him."

"I've had to work for everything I have but I can and will be the best provider for your sister."

Relief flooded my body. Roger didn't need Ashley as much as he claimed. I didn't need to stay here any longer. Irene would be taken care of. And if Ashley lied about how much Roger needed him, perhaps he was lying about my father's debts? It was worth the risk to finally be free of him. He was supposed to come visit tomorrow so I needed to act fast. I started to breathe easier. "I am so glad she found you. Even if the circumstances were not the purest, I know she'll be happy with you."

"I'll see to that."

There was a sudden knocking on the glass for the door that led to the porch. I looked around Roger who spun to see who knocked.

Irene's smiling face greeted us.

Roger dropped the cigarette and stomped it out with his boot. He motioned to the door, "Shall we?"

With the most enthusiasm I had in days, I followed Roger back into my house, a plan becoming clearer with each step I took.

Twenty Two

Isabelle

I started to pack a suitcase for the second time. The calm that was settling into my bones now wasn't there the last time I frantically packed to run away. This time, I felt solid in my choice to leave.

Looking over at my desk, I debated leaving a note explaining why I chose to run away in the middle of the night. But this wouldn't be a surprise or shock to anyone who knew the truth. Ashley could live with the lack of an explanation and the shame of having a runaway bride.

With that thought propelling me, I snuck out of my family home through the kitchen door.

The night was cool; one of the first fall nights that felt like winter was around the corner. A shiver went through me as I gripped the collar of my black jacket tighter with the hand not carrying my suitcase.

The train station was on the other side of town. The quickest way to get there was to just go straight through the busy center town square. The risk of being seen by anyone at this hour was worth it so I could put more distance between myself and my home.

The grass under my boots soon gave way to packed dirt as I approached the edges of the town square. There weren't many people milling around. A roar of laughter coming from the bar instinctively jerked my head in that direction. While I was distracted, my feet kept moving me forward right into the rigid body of a man.

His hands shot out to grab my arms and make sure I didn't fall.

"Apologies." I mumbled, trying to move out of his grip.

"Izzy?"

I froze at the sound of the familiar voice.

Ashley's grip on my arms tightened. "Izzy?" The surprise in his voice had been replaced with anger.

I couldn't look at him, even though I could feel his blue eyes boring holes into me. My gaze stayed focused on the ground as I was silent.

"What the hell are you doing out here late at night?" He took a step back putting some distance between our bodies. "And with a fucking suitcase? Are-are you-"

Breathing was becoming harder.

The hands on my arms squeezed, and it was like those hands were cutting off my air as they dug into my muscles. "Izzy," He hissed my name. "Look at me."

As if his words were magic, I obeyed his command.

Ashley's face had the classic signs of contained rage. His nostrils were flared, his lips were scrunched, and his face was flush. Perhaps that was from drinking, which would only make his temper worse. In his wide blue eyes I saw that restraint just waiting to be unhinged.

"Ashley," My words were soft. "You're hurting me."

He didn't loosen his grip. Instead, he pulled us off the street and into an alley where no one would witness whatever he was going to do to me.

"Where the fuck do you think you're going?" He wasn't yelling, but he didn't need to. The rage was rippling off him.

"I'm sorry," His hands finally let me go. I took just a small step back to give myself more room to breathe. "I just, I'm so scared, I can't-I can't marry you."

The clap of his palm smacking my face registered first. Then my head forcefully moved to the left, practically snapping my neck. When my hand went to cover the spot he had struck, that was when the sting of pain lit up the side of my face. The stinging kept growing as my brain started to piece together what happened.

Ashley slapped me.

"Did you even think of how this would look for your family? For mine? For *me*? A runaway bride?" Finally he yelled, "How fucking embarrassing!"

Hot tears were stinging the raw skin of my cheek. "I'm sorry! I tried to talk to you, but you weren't, you weren't listening to me!"

"Why the hell would I listen to you?"

"Because I'm meant to be your wife!"

"My wife!" His hands were grabbing my arms again. "My property! And you wanted to throw away all I am going to give you because I wasn't listening to you?"

"I...I'm..."

"Don't speak."

"Ashley, please, just listen to me now-"

Another slap, but this time, he delivered it to the other cheek.

I was silent after that.

"Is this what it takes to silence you? Will I have to beat the disobedience out of you?"

My blurry gaze was fixed on the ground.

"Let's go." Ashley kept one hand tight on my arm as he took the suitcase from me. With more force than was needed, he started pulling me behind him.

"Where are we going?"

"Back to your home. Let's see what your father thinks about this."

* * *

"Thank God you found her." My mother said before pursing her lips. "To think if she had been seen by anyone!"

"I don't think anyone saw her." Ashley reassured her from where he sat, perched above me. When we arrived, my father had met us at the door with a shotgun before ushering us into the library as Ashley quickly explained his side of what happened.

"What were *you* doing out at this hour?" Irene asked him from her seat next to us. She had heard the commotion and joined in on the interrogation.

"I don't think my actions are the ones being scrutinized currently." He spat back.

My sister opened her mouth to argue.

"Irene," My father held up a hand. "Right now, we need to focus on why your sister was running away, and nothing else."

"Yes," Mother turned to me. "What would compel you to do that?"

I didn't speak at first, expecting Ashley to speak for me like he had done since we arrived. When he didn't I started, "I-I'm not sure."

A silence filled the room.

When my mother realized I wouldn't elaborate she shrugged, "Pre-wedding jitters. I had them too, and your sister will have them as well."

My father raised an eyebrow. "But did you run?"

"I didn't get far before I turned around." She patted his arm before looking back at me. "And you would've turned around too, Isabelle. I know that."

"I would've." I nodded then looked up at Ashley. Lying would be the only way to fix this now and avoid being struck again. "I was about to when you found me."

Ashley didn't look like he believed me.

His focus snapped to my parents. "Can we move up the wedding?"

"I don't know." Mother's voice was soft, "We've already sent out invitations. Think of how it will look if we move it up?"

"But what if she runs again?"

"She won't." My father turned to me. "Will you, dear?"

I shook my head. I certainly would try to run again, but right now I needed to play the part of contrite fiancé.

"It's settled then." He crossed his arms. "And it's late. So I'll let you say goodnight and then Ashley, you'll need to be on your way."

Ashley nodded, never looking away from me as the rest of my family left the library.

"I won't run." I lied. I was already trying to think of another way to escape this house and this marriage.

He leaned in close to me. I could smell the whiskey on his breath as he declared, "I'll put people around the whole house. I'll make sure no one gets in, and no one gets out."

* * *

Ashley was true to his word. All day and all night someone was stationed outside all the doors to the house. I didn't even know he had this kind of power.

My parents didn't want to risk me running again and forbade me from leaving my room. Mary brought all my meals to me, sighing and shaking her head while she dropped off trays full of food. I barely touched it, which led to more sighing and head shaking when Mary came to retrieve the tray.

Irene came to visit when she could. She compelled me to just do what Ashley wanted to make this unavoidable marriage easier. It was her way of helping but it only made me feel worse.

When Mary came in with the dinner tray Friday night, my heart skipped a beat to see Ashley following behind her. I knew he would be coming back at some point to check on me, but it still was a shock to see him after what he did.

"Mr. Ashley, where would you like the tray?"

"In the middle of the bed is fine, Mary." She did as she was told and turned to leave.

"Mary," Ashley called her before she got to the door. She stopped and waited for what he was going to say. "Open the window please, it reeks in here."

She nodded and unlocked my window.

I had been bathing every day as a way to pass the endless minutes I was locked in my room. Perhaps the pile of laundry was giving off an odor? I didn't smell anything that warranted the reaction Ashley was having. It felt more like he was saying that to insult me.

Mary left us alone. I refused to take my eyes off Ashley, unsure what his motivations were for this visit.

He looked down and sighed, "You're scared of me now, aren't you?"

My eyes tracked him as he came to sit on the bed next to me. I scooted myself back up against the headboard, trying to put as much space between us as possible.

He leaned in close to me. "Good. I hope you're scared. I hope you remember how you feel in this moment the next time you want to defy me." He shook his head. "I don't want a bruised and battered wife but I will not spend my days worrying about you running away."

I wanted, no needed, him to leave, and the only way the would happen is if he believed I was also repentant. I knew what he wanted to hear so I started putting on my performance. "I understand."

He leaned back to study the sincerity on my face. "You do?"

"Yes," My fingers played with the hem of my nightgown. "You warned me and I didn't listen. It won't happen again." It wouldn't happen again because I had a new plan to deal with Ashley. As soon as I could, I was going to kill him. Running wasn't an option anymore. I needed to get rid of the threat. So the next time he dared to put his hands on me, I would make sure it was the last.

"Well, since you're in a more agreeable mood," He snatched my hands into his. "I have a surprise for you."

The urge to roll my eyes was strong, but I tampered it and acted eager. Ashley continued, "Would you want to join me in Washington tomorrow? We need to buy our wedding bands."

I didn't want to go with him, but I wanted a chance to get out of this house. "That, that would be lovely."

"I didn't want to buy them without you. And you'll have to be glued to me all day long. Irene and Roger will be with us as well. The more eyes I have on you, the better."

"I won't run."

He squeezed my hands. "I am going to make certain of that."

My throat worked on a dry swallow.

"I shall pick you up first thing in the morning." Ashley lifted my left hand. "And we shall pick a ring for this finger." He pressed his lips to the space that wouldn't be vacant for much longer.

"I cannot wait."

Another gentle kiss was placed on my forehead before Ashley saw himself out. The sound of the lock clicking echoed in my room.

Alone again, I started to reflect on what had happened and how I could learn from it.

Maybe I shouldn't have tried to run? I could've formulated a better plan and been able to get farther. But I only got caught and locked up like this because I ran into Ashley. If he hadn't been out, I would be far away from here now.

A loud groan poured out of me. Being locked up was driving me mad. I had reread all my favorite books and none of it seemed to help. The tray of food was still barely touched as I moved it onto the floor so I could spread myself on top of my blankets. My hand bitterly grabbed the book at the top of the stack on my nightstand. *Frankenstein* hadn't been able to take my mind off of what was happening to me, but it gave my eyes something to focus on other than the walls of my room.

Twenty Three

Matias

The buffoon was still inside her house.

From my hiding spot in the woods outside Isabelle's house, I had seen him stroll through the front door almost an hour ago and still hadn't come back out.

If he was in her house, then he was probably in her room, which meant I was forbidden to enter.

Every second I wasn't able to get into her room was adding to the fire smoldering inside me.

When I first arrived at Isabelle's house, I was so desperate to get to her that I didn't even hear the approaching carriage crunching over the gravel. A horse's neigh caught my ear and stopped me from walking out of the cover of the trees.

The carriage came to a stop, then the buffoon exited, greeting a man standing next to the large red front door, before walking into her house with all the confidence in the world. My stomach turned with jealousy. He could just walk through the front door, greet her parents, and stroll into her room because he was the fiancé.

But that was going to change tonight.

When I left Isabelle's house a week ago, I didn't go back to Richmond. Instead, I went west towards the mountains. I needed some solitude to think of where to look next for my sisters and to try to distract myself.

But it didn't work.

There wasn't a single minute that Isabelle didn't come into my mind. She was haunting me. No matter what I used to occupy my mind: drugs, blood, or bodies, she would creep into my thoughts. It drove me to turn around and start running back to Alexandria. I would get halfway back before my desire to protect her overwhelmed my desire to take her. So then I would turn around and run back to the mountains.

She would've been so much better off without me.

But I was a selfish bastard. Nothing could change that.

Turning into a monster hadn't, having my heart ruined by other women hadn't, even losing my mother hadn't changed me enough to want to be better. I was selfish, so fucking selfish.

Coming back for her was the most selfish thing I could think to do. It would ruin both of us, but it would be one hell of a wreck.

Springing up from a crouched position, I started pacing. My feet made a short circuit between two large tree trunks.

What if she wasn't happy to see me? What if she didn't want to change anymore? I wouldn't force her to do anything she didn't want to do. If she rejected my new deal, then I would respect it. And maybe a small part of me still wanted her to reject me. She should stay human so she could have a normal life.

But that small part of me arguing for her humanity was always overshadowed by the louder, darker voice telling me that she wanted to be with me. She wanted to turn. The only reason she changed her mind was because she thought she was forcing me to do it. But I was willingly coming to her now with the deal I should've originally struck.

A man's cough broke my train of thought. When I found the source of the noise, it wasn't the buffoon nor was it the man I had seen standing outside the front door. Another man was slowly walking on the outside of the house, walking towards the front door. As he came around the corner, he waved to the man guarding the door before turning on his heel and walking back the way he came. He was patrolling.

Why was he patrolling?

Had something happened to Isabelle?

My heart started thumping in my chest. The need to see her with my own eyes and make sure she was fine became more of a desperation. If the buffoon didn't vacate the house soon, I would just barge in there and kill him. She wouldn't need him anymore after tonight.

Just as I took a step to leave the shadows of the trees, the front door yawned open and basked the porch with a soft golden glow. The man moved out of the way as the buffoon came into view, twisting his body to shout something back into the house. I could see his perfectly white teeth shining from the wide grin on his face. Whatever had happened tonight, he was happy about it.

I made a promise to drain his life before leaving this town with Isabelle.

The buffoon briskly walked towards the carriage then entered with ease. A moment later, the gravel began crunching again from the horse's hooves stomping and the wooden wheels spinning.

Not a second was wasted as I sprinted towards Isabelle's side of the house. Light was still pouring out of her window.

I took a deep breath and stepped out from the woods.

My movements were slow, anticipatory. This moment was going to change so much and as much as I wanted to run head first into it, that never worked out well for me in the end. Each step brought me closer to her, ramping my heart rate back up. I took a few deep breaths to calm myself down.

"Who the fuck are you?" A stranger's voice shouted to my right.

My head flung to the side to see the patrolling man coming closer to me. The click of a revolver cocking hit my ear.

I put my hands up in the air, "I mean you no harm."

The man held the revolver up so it was leveled with my head. The Lord of Shadows loved to play a game with those guns. He would load just a single bullet into the chamber, spin it around, and then take turns shooting at me or himself. I've had bullets burning through my flesh more times than I could count. The pain that came from a gunshot burned worse than anything and the recovery took more than just a cut did. Getting shot would ruin my night and I didn't have time for that.

"Please," my voice took on the silky tone as I locked eyes with the man. "Put the gun down."

He squinted in confusion before his hand slowly dropped.

"Now," his eyes were still locked onto mine. "You're going to turn around, walk the other way, and forget all about this moment."

The man nodded before turning on his heel and walked out of my sight.

I breathed a sigh of relief, and with a quick shake of my head, I started climbing up the wall that led to Isabelle's window. The light was still on, leading me like a beacon back to shore.

As I crested over the ledge of the window, her brilliant blue eyes flicked up to me.

Twenty Four

Isabelle

Matias launched himself into my room.

His boots and pants were crusted in dirt up to just below his knees. The white shirt he wore was spotless, but wrinkled like he had been wearing it for days. Over that, was his black jacket. His brown curls were swept back away from his face and flying off in different directions.

Slowly, I put my book down and rose from the bed.

His chest rose and fell while he waited. Was he waiting for me to react?

I took a cautious step towards him, "What are you doing here?"

"Being selfish."

Within a breath, his body was flush against mine. Matias kissed me like my lips were going to give him life. I leaned into the hard planes of his form as his arms wrapped me in a tight embrace. Eagerly, I opened my mouth for him to slip his tongue inside. This kiss was hard and desperate.

Matias was here. He was back in my room, kissing me, holding me. He had come back for me.

Tears snuck out of my closed eyes but I didn't stop kissing him.

His hands slipped down my back, then my ass, before settling on my thighs so he could lift me. A soft gasp forced me to pull my lips away. I had never been picked up like this. I wrapped my legs around his waist as Matias used his teeth to nip at my bottom lip. With a supernatural ease, he walked us back towards the bed.

Matias carefully laid me down back in the same spot I had been occupying all day. A thumb brushed away a straggling tear. "Why are you crying?" His whiskey colored eyes scanned my body. "Did I hurt you?"

"No," I gripped his shirt. "I'm just so happy you're back." Another tear slipped out.

"No more tears, *mi pajarita*." He kissed the tear stained line on my cheek.

Mi pajarita.

Not *pajarita* but *mi pajarita*. I didn't understand Spanish, but I knew enough French and Latin to know that Matias had just claimed I was his. And in that moment I knew I was.

Maybe it was the sweetness of his nickname for me or maybe it was the relief that he had come back but a new wave of tears flowed out of me.

"Isabelle," Matias leaned back and I started to curl in on myself while I cried. "Isabelle, *mi pajarita*, look at me."

I forced my eyes open to see a blurry version of him. "I'm sorry, I'm-"

"No, no, you're not the one that should be sorry. I'm sorry I left you. I should've never done that but I'm here now."

If he hadn't left, I wouldn't have had to run. I wouldn't have gotten caught. I wouldn't be trapped in my room. More tears streamed down as my body started to shrink again.

Matias's strong arms wrapped around me. He laid my face against his chest. I could feel the chill of his skin through his shirt.

He kissed the top of my head. "No more tears."

"No more." I sniffled before a giggle bubbled out of me.

Matias pulled away just enough so he could look me over. "Have you been eating? You've lost weight."

I shrugged, "My stomach has been hurting."

He tsked then looked around before spying the tray on the floor. "Thought I smelled food." He left the bed just long enough to pick up the tray and bring it over to me. "At least eat the bread. The stew looks like it went cold."

I took the half eaten slice of bread and tore off a corner before popping it in my mouth.

"*Bueno, mi pajarita.*"

After I choked down the bread, I dared to ask, "Where have you been?"

Matias froze for a moment but then smiled at me, "I was trying to forget about you."

"Oh," I shoved another bite into my mouth.

"Clearly, it worked." Both his dimples were out now. "I drove myself crazy trying to keep you out of my mind. Nothing worked. I ran to the mountains and almost came back for you so many times, but each time I stopped myself saying that you were better off without me."

Swallowing my bread, I cut in, "Everything just got worse when you left. I tried to run and Ashley caught me. He hit me."

His jaw ticked, "I am going to kill him."

"I want to be there when that happens."

"You will be."

My empty hand reached out and grabbed his. "I truly didn't think you were coming back."

"I had every intention not to." He squeezed my hand as I finished the first slice of bread. When I went to grab his other hand, Matias offered me the other slice. "Eat more, *por favor.*"

Nodding, I took it, but before I started eating again, I asked, "So what made you return?"

"I dreamt of you. I haven't dreamt since I turned but I dreamt of you, waking up in my arms, and I knew I had to come back."

My eyes went wide but I took a bite to keep my mouth occupied.

"I have never felt like this with any woman before, Isabelle." Matias's grip on my hand tightened. "Even when I thought I was in love before, nothing felt like this. I had only been away from you for a week and it drove me insane. I must've run up and down those mountains in the West more times than I could count. I just kept thinking that if I left you alone, you'd be able to marry, have children, and grow old. You would get to be with your sister. You wouldn't have to leave your home. And you wouldn't have to turn yourself into a monster. When you sent me away, I didn't want to go, but I didn't know how else to help you."

The bread was gone and I drank the glass of water while Matias finished talking. I placed my hand on his before stating, "I shouldn't have sent you away."

"I'll never leave you again."

I took the tray and moved it to the floor again. Mary would come in the morning to get this tray when she dropped off the breakfast tray. It was always the long stretch of uninterrupted night that really drove the dread down deep into my bones.

But Matias was here now. I wasn't alone anymore.

Slowly, I turned to face him sitting on the edge of the bed. "I propose we make a new deal."

The right side of his mouth curved, "And what are your terms?"

"You turn me and we run away together," I paused before adding, "But we stay together. No splitting up and going our separate ways. No stashing me in a safe house. You and I can run around the world together."

A smile erupted over his face, "Have you grown fond of me, Isabelle?"

"I think we're beyond just being fond of each other."

"You're right," Matias stood up from the bed. "Infatuated is the better word for how I feel about you." He closed the distance between us. "I have had part of you already, but I want all of you." His hand went up to cup my face. "I want your body," His hand slid down to my neck.

"I want your blood," His fingertips brushed my breasts, curved down my waist, before he grabbed my ass. "I want everything."

"So take it. Take it all."

Twenty Five

Isabelle

Matias shuddered before kissing me. This one was different from the one when he first arrived. That was a wave crashing onto the shore, but this one was a calm, tender flow. The gentleness of the kiss warmed me all over.

My hands slid up his chest and pushed the lapels of his jacket up and away from his body. Matias adjusted himself so the jacket slid off his form and onto the floor without breaking the kiss.

He didn't pull away as he maneuvered his feet out of his boots, or when he picked me up and brought me back to the bed the same way he did before.

"I had every intention of doing this the moment I arrived." He whispered in my ear as he lowered me down. "I thought of all the ways to ravage your body as I made my way here tonight and had a plan to fulfill each one of my desires." He nuzzled my neck with his nose. "But I needed to make sure you were well before I ruin you."

"Ruin me?" My voice sounded heady.

"*Si, mi amor.*" His teeth scraped along my neck. "Ruin you in the best way possible."

I sucked in a breath, "What are you waiting for?"

A dark chuckle filled my ear, "We have to get you ready." I felt his hand slide down the curve of my waist and push up the end of my nightgown. "May I?" I nodded and adjusted myself so I was sitting up. At an agonizingly slow pace, he used both hands to push the fabric up past my waist, then over my breasts, and finally he pulled the nightgown over my head and off my completely. He threw the white silk bundle onto the floor with his clothes.

His hands went back to my exposed body so he could pull down my undergarments. His fingers hooked into the soft fabric then pulled them down my quivering legs. The slightest brush of his fingertips was sending pulses of desire where I was desperate for him to touch. Once my undergarments were added to the discarded clothes, I was completely bared to him.

"*Por fin.*" Leaning back, his dark eyes were shining with lust. He took his time looking over my naked body, like he was memorizing every inch of me. Matias's gaze was making me feel so desired that I relaxed against the pillows. "*Espléndida.*" He breathed out the compliment as his fingers traced the path his eyes had made.

In one swift movement, Matias pulled his shirt off, exposing his naturally tan chest. My hands reached out to trace the lines of his muscles, ghosting over his abs that hardened despite my light touch.

When my fingertips touched the hem of Matias's pants, I stalled and looked back up at him. A dark smirk curled his lip as he nodded. Slowly, I undid the buttons on his pants. My eager hands started pushing the fabric down until it bunched up around his knees. Matias maneuvered himself so he could finish undressing without leaving the bed.

On his knees in front of me, he looked like a painting from a museum. His tan skin glowed in the dim lamp light. The dark brown curls framed his angular face as he looked down at me with dark eyes. Every muscle in his hard body was tense, like he was ready to pounce on me as soon as I gave him the word.

Instead of words, I spread my legs out wide to make room for him. With a smirk tilted his full lips, he closed the bit of room between our bodies. He stretched his upper body over me until his lips hovered just above mine. I expected his kiss but it didn't come yet. The anticipation sent a wave of want down my body and to my core.

His nose skimmed my cheek, "You smell so alive."

"Is that good?"

"It's intoxicating." The words slid into my ears. "I can't get enough."

I felt a gentle kiss against my neck, just above my racing pulse.

"Do you..." My hands went to his shoulders. "Do you want to drink from me?"

"I do."

I anticipated a shiver of dread, but instead, all I felt was more heat spreading from my core.

"But," His lips started a trail across my jaw. "Not tonight. I'll taste you that way after I claim you."

I managed a nod before his lips captured mine.

My fingers tangled into his soft curls as I kissed him back just as hard as he kissed me. He pulled my lip between his teeth and tugged, dragging a moan out of me. The kisses moved down my neck, down my chest, and then his lips closed around my nipple.

I gasped at the sensation as he gently bit down. His fingertips lightly brushed down the curve of my waist before gripping my hip. He let my one nipple go, kissing his way across the small gap between my breasts, before taking the other nipple between his teeth and tugging. My hips bucked and the hand that held my hip tightened its grip.

"Matias...please." My voice was a breathy whisper now.

His brown eyes flicked up to look at me as he slowly lifted my mouth away from the peak of my breast. "So eager." I felt his hand let go of my hip, but the rest of his body was still.

My hands left his hair and gripped the sheets instead. He started to move his hand again.

Goosebumps erupted under his light touch as he slowly made his way to my core. Gently, carefully, he easily slipped a finger inside me.

My eyes closed as my head rolled back.

"You're close to being ready." Matias moved then, adjusting his body so he could curl his finger inside me. I could feel how my body responded, pooling desire between my thighs.

His lips brushed against my ear as he commanded, "Move your hips."

I lifted my hips to match the curling motion that I felt inside of me. Matias adjusted his hand so his thumb could play with the bundle of nerves, making my hips buck even more. The more friction, the better it felt.

"More." The word sounded like a moan.

Matias slid another finger inside me.

The fullness of just his fingers was starting to make the pleasure at the base of my spine coil. He started drawing tight circles with his thumb. I felt the same overwhelming pressure that came before I felt the waves of pleasure last time he touched me like this.

"Matias, it's, I'm-"

"*Si, mi amor.*" His curls tickled my chest as he lowered his mouth back to my nipple. The coil was tightening, I was so, so close to the crash that was evading me.

When he bit down, I finally felt that wave of pleasure flowing through me. Softly, I moaned out his name as I pulsed around his fingers.

"*Perfecto.*" Matias whispered as he gently pecked my lips.

My hips stilled. I realized I had been panting. I took a few deep breaths while those brown eyes darted around my face. He seemed to hesitate as he hovered above me. "What is it?"

"I think you're ready." His throat bobbed on a swallow. "Last chance to change your mind."

"You know I won't." My hands that had been gripping the blankets, went into his hair and pulled his face towards mine. "I just want you, only you."

"Only me? Forever?"

"That's the idea." I breathed out a laugh before kissing him.

"Forever." He whispered against my lips before he leaned back from me. It was the most serious I had ever seen him, as he looked at where my arousal was still dripping out of me. His eyes went back to mine. "This is going to hurt. If you can't, if it becomes too much, just tell me to stop."

"I can handle it."

"I know you can." The dimples were back as he smiled down at me. A strong, sure hand was placed on each thigh, before he spread them a little further apart.

The tip of him began pressing into me. Matias carefully moved his hips forward, pushing more of himself inside. The pressure was starting to turn painful, so I spread my legs wider to make more room for him.

Matias moved one hand back to that wonderfully sensitive spot. His thumb went around in slow, sensual circles, teasing my bundles of nerves, easing up the pleasure to overshadow the pain. "*Mierda.*" The word slowly rolled out of his mouth. "*Eres tan apretada.*"

When all of him was buried in me, he froze. The brown of his eyes was gone, all I could see was the pitch black of his exploded pupils. His head cocked to the side as a way to ask if I was okay.

The fullness of him inside me hurt and part of me was scared of more pain. I knew it was going to get worse before it became better and then pleasurable. I trusted that he would go as gently as I needed him to until I was ready for more.

I bucked my hips to signal I was ready for him to keep moving.

He chuckled, "You never react the way I expect you to." Matias pulled himself back before thrusting back into me. The sharp sting of pain forced me to suck in a breath.

He stilled then pulled back and pushed in harder this time. The pain was still there, but this thrust hit a certain spot inside me that made a ripple of pleasure spread through my core.

"Yes," I hissed out the end of the word as the movement of his hips picked up so he could keep hitting that spot.

"You feel," His hands gripped my hips and lifted them further off the bed. "You feel so fucking good. *Te sientes asombrosa.*" His body folded over mine. I thought he was going to stop but he thrusted harder, going even deeper. "I get to feel you forever."

I breathed out, "Forever."

He kissed my lips hard, before kissing down my cheeks, my jaw, and my neck.

Fangs, not teeth, scraped my throat.

"Matias," My voice wavered.

"Not tonight." He nipped the soft skin where my jaw and neck met, but not hard enough to break the skin. "But soon." The thrusting of his hips punctuated his words. "I'll taste all of you soon."

I hummed in agreement. The thought of Matias drinking my blood was enticing to me. It meant he desired my body in a different way than how he was enjoying me now.

Matias kept working himself in and out of me. I tried to keep up with the rhythm, but his hips were moving at such a frantic pace that it was easier to just lie there and let him use me.

With each thrust, the pain lessened until it disappeared completely. Our soft moans mingled together in the space between our bodies. I could feel myself quickly getting back to that point Matias had gotten me to with just his fingers.

Just a few more pumps of his hips brought another wave of pleasure. I could feel myself pulse around his cock.

"*Mierda*, Isabelle." He growled before I felt his release pumping inside me. A shudder went through his body when he finished.

As he leaned back, I sat up as much as I could, but his body was still bent over mine.

"Oh, no..." I looked down and saw the mess that was staining the blanket.

"I don't think this is salvageable." His eyes were still black as he looked at me.

"I'll throw it out."

He nodded. "Are you okay?"

It was my turn to nod. "Are you?"

He leaned back further from me then flashed a smile that showed how sharp his fangs were. "*Si, mi amor.*"

"Your eyes, and your teeth, they're different."

"Your blood." Those black eyes glanced down at the stain on the blanket. "It brought this out of me, but I won't, you're safe, I'll just," Matias stood up. "Just wait here." He moved supernaturally fast to the washroom before returning with a cloth and the bowl of water I use to clean my face. There was a tiny ring of brown around his pupils now. "Lie back."

"What're you doing?"

"Taking care of you." He dipped the whole cloth into the water. "Now, lie back, Isabelle."

My eyes tracked his path to me as I laid back against the pillows, careful to avoid the stained area of the blanket.

The cloth was cool against my skin as Matias cleaned away the evidence of what we'd done. Then he took everything back to the washroom.

He stood on the edge of the bed, "Do you want to dress?"

"Not yet." My arms opened in an invitation for him to join me. He crawled back to the bed, adjusting the blankets so the ruined one was rolled up at our feet. Together we tangled ourselves under another blanket and sheet. Matias was lying on his back with my head on his chest.

His fingers were tracing lines up and down my spine. A soft hum of contentment buzzed out of me.

"*Cuidado, mi pajarita.*" He stopped drawing the lines. "Unless you're ready to go again."

"Already? I always heard that it takes some time before a man can do that."

Matias shrugged, "Vampires recover faster."

As he said the words, I could feel the proof of his statement against my leg.

"Oh..."

His dark chuckle filled my ear as his hand slid down to grab my ass. "Have you had your fill of me yet?" As I thought about my answer, his hand slid between my thighs and a finger slipped inside me. The sensation made me gasp and arch into him.

"Well," His finger curled inside me. "Have you had enough?"

Words were too hard to manage so I shook my head.

Matias's lips captured mine. It was a harder kiss, more needy than the ones before. My mouth opened to let his tongue in as I moaned into his mouth.

His free hand gripped my thigh, found the crook of my knee, and pulled me on top of him.

"Matias!" His name bubbled out of me as I lifted my hips and adjusted myself. Then he moved his body so he could sit up underneath me. I could feel him pressed up against my ass with the intention of being back inside me as soon as I gave him permission.

He looked up at me, his full lips curled into a smirk that showed both of his dimples. "Ready when you are."

My hands moved up his cool chest then tangled into the soft curls at the nape of his neck. I rose off him, and Matias lined himself up with my entrance.

Slowly, I dropped down onto him, my muscles clenching as I took all of him in me. There was a soreness starting that I planned to chase away with another pleasurable orgasm.

A deep, low groan rumbled out of his chest. When he was all the way inside me, he cursed.

I shot my hips back off him. "Did I-"

"No!" Matias's hands softly grabbed my hips. "No, you feel too good, *mi amor*. I want to take care of your pleasure first, but," He bit his lip, and I saw the edge of his fangs. "You feel so good."

"Oh," My body relaxed and I lowered myself back onto him. He filled me up so perfectly, like I was meant to take him. But I wasn't sure what to do once I settled myself on top.

"Move your hips." He choked out the command. "Just like before."

I curled my hips in a wave, feeling him inside me while that sensitive spot at the apex of my thighs pressed against the hard planes of his lower stomach.

"*Mierda.*" Matias ground out. "You're a quick learner."

My laugh sounded different, headier, as I moved my hips harder against his body. This combination of sensations felt even better than how Matias had been pumping himself into me.

One of his hands traced up my hips, waist, then grabbed my breast. He brought my nipple to his mouth and gently bit down. I couldn't stop the moans that flooded out of me as I closed my eyes.

Matias lavished my one breast, licking and sucking, before moving to the other one. He hummed against the tender flesh as his tongue flicked the hardened peak back and forth.

The build up of pleasure was so much quicker this time. The tingling coil at the base of my spine kept tightening. I could feel myself right on the edge.

Then Matias bit the tender bud of my nipple.

I crumbled around him, moaning his name into his ear before burying my head in the crook of his neck. Wave after wave of pleasure tore through me. I tried to keep riding it but after a few thrusts I just let myself relax into his strong frame.

Then Matias gripped my hips and rocked himself into me. My body was spent. I wanted to move my hips again, but I couldn't keep up. So I just let him pound into me, grunting as he chased his own climax.

The rhythm of his thrusts was becoming erratic. The grip of my hips tightened even more as he threw his head back. "*Ay Dios.*" Again, I felt the warmth of his release pump into me.

When he let go of my hips, I started to rise off him, "I'll go get the cloth."

"Just grab the already ruined blanket."

I grabbed it from the foot of the bed and handed it to him. Matias used it to clean himself off while I went to the washroom and did the same. When I came back out, Matias was lying down, his head against the pillows, and a clean blanket pulled up to his waist. He had left one side of the bed open for me to climb in.

Without a word, we adjusted ourselves so we were lying on our sides, facing each other. When I looked into his eyes, all I saw was bliss. Pure, unfiltered, bliss.

His whispers tickled against my ear. "*Mi pajarita, mi vida, mi corazón, mi todo.*"

"I need to learn Spanish," I giggled, "I have no idea what you just said."

"I will teach you," He kissed the top of my head. "You'll be fluent in weeks."

"I'd quite enjoy that." I wiggled my hips into him.

He kissed the top of my head again. "We'll have nothing but time now."

Twenty Six

Isabelle

There was the faintest glow of sunlight spilling in from the window when I opened my eyes. I lifted my face off of Matias's bare chest. Even with the dim light, I could see his whole face was relaxed with sleep, making him look much younger than the twenty-five years he was frozen as. His dark brown curls were all twisted in different directions from the way we enjoyed each other the night before. This was a sight I could easily get used to.

Suddenly, his eyes shot open. "Someone is coming."

I grabbed the blanket to cover my chest when a knock sounded at the door.

"Miss Isabelle," Mary's voice filtered through the door. "Are you decent?"

"Not anymore." Matias chuckled in my ear.

"Matias!" I hissed at him then turned to call out. "Just a moment!"

The grin on his face was playful but this was not the moment for that. He cocked an eyebrow at me as I shooed him out of the bed and towards the bathroom.

Dropping the blanket, I quickly threw on my discarded nightgown before opening the door.

"Apologies, Mary. I was in the middle of deciding what to wear today."

"Not to worry." She moved past me, dropping the breakfast tray onto the unmade bed. Would she notice that it was more rumpled than usual? Could she tell that another had shared the bed with me?

If she did, Mary didn't show it. She looked at me and grimaced. "You'll need to wash before you meet Mr. Ashley today."

"I will."

She started walking towards the washroom.

"No!" I covered my mouth after the panicked shout went through me.

With a jump, she turned. Her sharp eyes studied me. "What's wrong with you?"

"Nothing," I moved to put myself between her and the door. "Nothing, I just want to get ready to meet Ashley alone. I have plenty of water to bathe with. I'll be fine."

Mary looked me up and down. "Are you sure you are well? I know it's been hard for you this week, being locked up here alone."

"I am, I just want to get ready myself. I won't have you at my new house so I need to start doing things on my own." The lies rolled out so smoothly, I hoped she was believing them all.

"Not if I can help it, but I understand if you want your space." She gave me a smile before patting my shoulder. "I'll let you know when Mr. Ashley is here."

"Thank you."

Before Mary got to the door I stopped her. "Could you make sure Irene doesn't come in here either?"

"I'll do my best to occupy her. She's currently saying none of the dresses she has will work for today."

"She can't borrow any of mine."

"Understood." Mary smiled and then let herself out.

I rushed to lock the door behind her.

A deep relieved breath puffed out of me as I leaned against the door. When I looked up, Matias was standing naked in the doorway of the washroom. He was scowling at me.

"You've been *locked* in your room all week?"

I shrugged before plopping down on the bed. "I tried to run away by myself and then I ran right into Ashley." My arms wrapped around me as I moved towards the bed. "And he had many ideas about how to keep me secure until the wedding."

Matias smiled at the ground, "I will enjoy killing him."

"Make sure you do it while I am there to watch."

He sat down on the bed. "That explains the men posted outside. I wasn't sure what that was about and was a bit too distracted last night to ask."

My teeth caught my lip as my eyes scanned his still naked body. "Those men didn't seem to do much good if a monster could come into my room and defile me."

The smile on his face popped both dimples out. "Should this monster take you in the light of day as well?" He leaned into me. His full lips started a trail of kisses down my neck while his cool hands started to push up the hem of my nightgown.

"I'm not sure if we have enough time." A sigh started in my throat but left my mouth as a moan. Matias had kissed a path down to my covered but hardened nipple then returned back where he started.

"I don't need much time."

"You don't?"

"No," He whispered the word against my lips before pressing a sweet kiss there. His hand had pushed my nightgown up just enough to bare myself to him. As he leaned forward, I leaned back until I was lying down under him. "If I'm going to be missing you all day," Those strong, tan hands spread my legs wider. "I want you to feel me while you're gone."

With precision, Matias thrust himself into me. It was hard to keep myself quiet as he slowly pulled out and then moved back in. "Hurry." I breathed out, worried Mary would be back any moment.

Matias instantly picked up his pace. With each turn, he went faster and faster. One hand went to draw those circles around my apex while the other was holding up one of my legs by the thigh.

I tried to keep my eyes open. I wanted to memorize the way his face looked in the daylight as he took me: the way just the left side of his mouth curled and how his hooded eyes seemed to light up as he focused on my body. But he was doing what I asked and quickly making sure I found my pleasure.

Just as I closed my eyes, I felt myself crumble around him. And a few moments later, Matias did the same.

Our ragged breaths were the only sounds as we cleaned each other up. After we were done I gave him just a quick peck. Anything more and I would never get myself ready.

As I turned to the wardrobe, he asked, "And what are you meant to do with the buffoon today?"

"Ring shopping." I rolled my eyes. Tucking my body behind the door of the wardrobe, I stripped out of the nightgown I had hastily thrown on. Matias groaned when the fabric hit the floor. I couldn't stifle the giggle. "But I'm just going to make him buy me the most expensive ring there and then we can sell the set once we're on the road." My legs slipped into a new set of undergarments.

"You continue to surprise me."

I chose my favorite navy blue day dress to wear for this forced outing. The skirt billowed out slightly and gave me plenty of room for walking around. The top of the dress was short sleeved but it had a jacket that went over it so I could cover myself if today ended up being one of the cooler October days.

Once all the buttons were done up, I stepped back into Matias's gaze.

He sat up straighter in the bed and shot one of his dimpled simples at me. "*Que linda.*"

"I'm assuming that's a compliment." I moved until I was standing between his legs. He was fully naked and I was clothed, but I still felt like the vulnerable one. There were no regrets about how much of myself I had given him. I chose who got to see and experience the most intimate parts of me. My whole life I expected these moments to happen with Ashley, but I took back the control last night. I would never regret it.

The vulnerability came from knowing I had to leave him now. What if he changed his mind? What if I wasn't what he wanted anymore?

"It is a compliment." Matias's fingers went into my unruly hair to pull me down for a kiss. He kissed me like he knew I needed reassurance that he still wanted me. I could feel myself start to lean into him when a knock sounded.

"Miss Isabelle!" Mary's voice called out. "Mister Ashley is here."

"Just my hair left to do!"

Despite the pounding of my heart filling my ears, I heard Mary turn and walk down the hall.

I looked back down at a smiling Matias, but my bottom lip popped out in a pout. "I'm worried about what you'll do while I'm gone."

"Don't worry about me." He released my hair and pushed me towards the vanity. While I sat down, he pulled his pants back on before leaning against the edge so he could look at me brushing my hair. "I'll stay here if that makes you feel better."

"But Mary will come back later to clean."

"Then I'll hide in the cemetery."

"But the sun and the guards-"

Matias chuckled as I started to twist my curls back into a low bun. "I don't see how this is amusing."

"Because I am a vampire that can erase people's memories. I will be fine. You have more important things to worry about, like scamming the buffoon."

Sighing, I secured my hair with a few strategically placed pins. "Alright, but you'll be here tonight?"

"*Claro, mi amor.*" Matias leaned down for another kiss, smiling against my lips.

Twenty Seven

Matias

With one more kiss, Isabelle finally left the room. She came back not even a second later, wide eyed and frantically looking around. "Almost forgot!" Her pale hand grabbed the ring that was sitting on the nightstand. She gave a half-hearted laugh, "He would've killed me if I wasn't wearing this."

I couldn't stop my growl.

"Not yet." She smiled. "But soon. You can kill him before we leave." With one last hurried kiss, she was out the door. I hadn't wanted to let her go, but her plan to get an expensive ring that we could then sell was genius. We would need all the money we could get now.

When my father cut me off, I was informed that he also wrote me out of the will. Any money or claim to the Ciervo fortune would've been forfeited when I didn't show up to his funeral. I'm not even sure when that was. It happened at some point while I was imprisoned.

My best shot at any real answer lied with my sisters, but their whereabouts were still unknown. Despite searching for them the last few weeks, I hadn't found a solid lead to where any of my six sisters were now living.

Part of me wondered if the Lord of Shadows had gotten to them. But the one clue I had gotten was from a neighbor who told me they were quickly married off and moved away when our father died.

Now Isabelle would be joining me on the search for them. It would be an adventure. That sounded much better than living on the run. We wouldn't be able to come back to Virginia while anyone who knew her was still alive. She knew this was part of turning, but I wanted to make sure she was still set in her decision. We didn't have to rush this. She could take her time enjoying her last few moments with family.

We also needed to discuss the specifics of our plan when she returned. I just needed to keep myself occupied until she did.

Throwing all of my clothes except my jacket, I made my way over to the window. There was a new man stationed at the ground underneath. I was certain there was another guard stationed at the front door and probably more scattered around the property after I sent the guard away last night.

Sneaking out was possible. The sky was cloudy enough that I could avoid direct sun until I made it into the woods. The guards wouldn't be a problem, as long as I could compel them before they alerted the whole house to my presence.

It didn't feel worth it to leave, just to come right back here as soon as Isabelle returned. And I didn't want to leave. I wanted to stay in this room surrounded by her.

Idly, I made my way towards her impressive book collection. We would have to leave it behind, but perhaps I could buy her replacements if we ever managed to settle down in one spot? If her family kept it safe, we could send for it later. Silently, I swore to myself that I would figure out how to keep her surrounded by books.

Footsteps hurried towards the door.

In an instant, I ran into the washroom and shut the door. My fingers went to move the lock in the crushed door knob, but my ears picked up the door to Isabelle's room swinging open then a deep sigh filling the space. It was the same woman I heard when I had to hide under the bed before.

"At least she ate some bread this time." I heard the clanking of dishes as a tray was picked up. Her footsteps came closer and I felt the wave of panic. I would have to erase her memory when she caught me in here. If she screamed when she saw me, I would have to figure out how to handle that.

The doorknob twisted. I angled my body so it would be hidden by the door as it was opened. As the door creaked open, I tucked myself behind it, willing my body to fit in the tight spot.

"And she'll need to bathe tonight because she didn't this morning. I swear, this girl." The woman sighed. In the mirror I saw her cross her arms, but she couldn't see me. My reflection no longer showed in mirrors. I just needed to wait for her to leave.

Calmly, she stated. "You can come out now. I know you're there."

I froze.

Her commanding voice continued, "Stop hiding behind the door."

As if she was compelling me, I stepped out from my hiding spot.

The older woman turned to face me. "So you're the reason Miss Isabelle has been acting so odd lately?"

I hoped my smile came off as disarming and not alarming. "I suppose I am." The temptation to just compel her was there, but I felt that would be the wrong move. She had the chance to alert the whole house that I was here, but instead she was talking to me.

Her brown eyes scanned me up and down, judging every inch of me. "What's your name, boy?"

"Matias Ciervo." She still didn't scream or try to alert anyone to my presence. I considered it a victory, for now.

The scowl snapped up to meet my gaze. "Where are you from?"

"Florida."

"They sound funny like this in Florida?"

"The ones who speak Spanish do."

She was almost two feet shorter than me, but I felt her eyes staring me down. "How did you even get in here?"

"The window." Short, honest answers were my best weapons now.

Her eyebrows crinkled in confusion, "You didn't sneak in the kitchen?"

Shaking my head, I smiled at the memory of sneaking out that way with Isabelle.

"You are aware that she is on her way to Washington to buy rings with Mister Ashley?"

"I am."

"She is already promised to him. He is going to be her husband, take care of her, and keep her safe."

"Oh, I have seen how *safe* she is in his hands."

Her eyes narrowed. "Where did she even find you? Mister Ashley never lets anyone get near her."

"Well, seeing as I'm not from around here, I wasn't aware of that rule."

"If he ever finds out about this, he will kill you and then he'll kill her." This explained the hostility. Mary cared deeply for Isabelle and any threat to her safety would bring out her protective side. I admired it. She was doing what she could despite how much control that buffoon had over everyone.

I shrugged, "He can certainly try. But he will not lay another hand on her while I'm alive."

Her lips pursed and I could see the thoughts scrolling through her eyes. She definitely didn't trust me, but I didn't need her trust. I need her silence and her compliance. The urge to compel her was still there, but my gut was telling me not to. If I forced myself on her mind and Isabelle found out, I would lose her trust.

The longer this silence stretched between us, the harder it was to resist the urge to compel. It would just be so easy.

"She expects you to be here when she returns?"

"Yes ma'am."

"I'll make sure no one comes in here today."

A long breath of relief flowed out of me. "Thank you."

The woman stepped closer and pointed a finger at my chest. "This is for her, you understand?"

"Completely. Everything is for her."

"If you hurt her, I'll kill you myself."

I smirked, "Now that I am afraid of."

Her lip quirked but that was all she would show before she turned and left me alone. When I heard the faint click of the door locking, I let out a shaky breath.

Twenty Eight

Isabelle

"Here we are!" Ashley squeezed my hand a little harder than necessary as we stopped in front of the jeweler.

Irene finally stopped the constant stream of words that she started when we all piled into the carriage together. When she wasn't talking, Roger was, and Ashley would chime in with the occasional inane joke. The pattern held as we walked around the streets, popping in and out of shops as we made our way to the jeweler. I did my best to smile, laugh, and nod when prompted to, but my mind was replaying last night.

Over and over, I kept feeling Matias over and under me.

I just needed to get through this day then I could make new memories to keep me company whenever we were apart.

Pretending it was Matias, I shot a beaming smile up at Ashley.

He smiled back before opening the door for me and I stepped inside the jeweler.

The shop was the cleanest place we had been in all day. Different cuts, colors, and sizes of diamonds were displayed under glass cases with lantern lights strategically placed to enhance the sparkle of it all. Earrings, bracelets, necklaces, and watches were sectioned together, but Ashley immediately pulled me to the case with rings.

As I stared down at seemingly dozens of ring options, Ashley turned to the middle-aged man standing behind the case of rings, "Could we see your most expensive wedding band?"

"Certainly." The man's steady hands reached into the center of the case and pulled out a pure gold ring encrusted in diamonds. "This would be it."

Ashley slid it onto my fourth finger, and the sparkle of it overtook the shine of the diamond that was already there.

From the side of me, I could hear Irene's jealous sigh. "Such a beautiful piece."

"It is." Adjusting my hand, I acted like I was checking the ring out in the light. "It doesn't quite match the ring, does it?"

"That's my grandmother's ring." Ashley leaned in closer so only I could hear him. "It's been passed down to the oldest son for the last few generations. We won't be able to find a band that matches it."

"Ashley!" His eyes went wide at my sudden shock. "You can't give me your family heirloom!"

"Obviously I can, as it is currently on your finger."

Now that I knew where the ring had come from, I couldn't pawn his grandmother's ring. That would just be too wicked of a thing to do, even if I hated Ashley. His family heirloom needed to stay in his family. Matias and I would need money to travel, but not at the expense of him losing something so important.

"No," I slid the diamond engagement ring off my finger. "No, I would rather have my own set. Something that matches and feels more like me."

"Fine," Through gritted teeth he whispered to me. "If that will make you happy." He plucked the ring from my palm before stashing it away in his pocket. I watched as his face twisted into something resembling a smile as he turned back towards the jeweler. "What matches with the band she picked out?"

As the old man behind the counter pulled out another ring, I spotted the one I wanted. A blood red ruby cushioned by two smaller diamonds on a simple silver band. "That one, please." The jeweler followed where my finger was pointing and brought the ring out.

"That one?" Ashley questioned.

"Yes," I slipped the ring on. "This is the one."

"Here is the band to match it." The jeweler produced a silver band with a pattern of diamonds and rubies. "What do you think?"

Taking the set from the old man's extended hand, I slipped the rings on. It still felt wrong because these were a symbol of my commitment to Ashley, but at least it felt more like me. "I love it."

The jeweler brought out a thicker silver ring with a ruby in it that Ashley would wear. He examined the ring that was meant for his finger. "This is really what you want?" I nodded, smiling up at him. "We'll take the set."

"Perfect." As I was taking the rings off, the old man smiled, "She can wear that one out if you like."

I slipped the diamond ring back on. "I would like that very much."

The jeweler got to work packaging everything up and discussing prices with Ashley.

"Go ahead and package this one up too." Roger motioned to where Irene was begrudgingly putting the ring back on top of the glass. "I'll need it soon."

And while the men handled the money, Irene and I wandered to the other areas of the store. "Let's see what else we can get them to buy!" She giggled moving towards a display case full of earring and necklaces that were meant to be worn together.

But while Irene gushed over the gorgeous pieces in front of us, I just stared down at the ring on my finger.

My ring.

From Ashley.

Because I had always been his, but now I was marked.

It wouldn't be forever. Soon enough I would have this ring off and I would be far, far away from where Ashley was trying to keep me locked up. I kept telling myself that everything was going to work out, but it suddenly felt like the ring carried the weight of a shackle.

"I need some air." I managed to choke out before rushing out of the shop. The bell on top of the door rang out as I exited. I heard Ashley calling out to me then yelling at Irene.

The crisp fall air was filling my lungs with a sharp sting. No matter how deep I breathed, it didn't feel like enough. My fingers started to grip the ring and pull it off when I felt the hairs on the nape of my neck stand up.

Carefully, I looked around but nothing stood out to me. There were countless people milling about on the street walking in different directions as they went through their tasks. Murmurs of conversation swirled around me but I couldn't make out what anyone was saying.

That feeling in the back of my neck was spreading to my stomach.

Someone was watching me.

Frantically, I searched for this source of my unease. My eyes were darting around at the dozens of people walking through the crowded street. That's when I locked eyes with the darkest gaze I had ever seen.

Even from across the street, I could tell that he was tall. His eyes towered above the heads and hats of those walking around him. He stood in the opening of an alleyway, like the shadows were about to absorb him if he moved just a step backwards. The all black outfit he wore just made the paleness of his face more striking. He looked like he hadn't seen the sun in centuries. Dark hair fell in waves framing the sharp features of his face. Everything about him was harsh, including the hard line his pale lips were set in.

He was terrifying, entrancing but terrifying.

Everything about him was perfectly still except his nostrils that kept flaring like an animal scenting its prey. And that prey was me.

Cocking his head, he took a step closer to me. There was a faint fuzziness on the edges of my mind, but I shook it away.

"Izzy?" Ashley's concerned voice called behind me.

I kept my eyes locked on the stranger, remembering it wasn't safe to look away from something that could kill you.

Ashley grabbed my chin and turned my face towards him, forcing me to break eye contact. "What's wrong? You look like you've seen a ghost."

"Not a ghost." Even though I couldn't move my head, I tried to move my gaze to see where the stranger had gone. I couldn't see past Ashley's shoulders as he put his whole body in front of me.

He shook me, hard. "Izzy?"

"I'm sorry," I finally looked up at him. "Did you bring men along to watch us as we shopped?"

"Of course." He scoffed. "I had a feeling you would pull a stunt like this."

"It's not a stunt. I wasn't trying to run."

His brow scrunched like he didn't believe me.

"I think," I took a small step towards him so our bodies were flushed against each other. "I think I've spent too long couped up in my room and now being outside is too much for me."

"Yes, I think so." His arms wrapped around me in an almost suffocating embrace. "Let's get you home."

"But the dinner plans!" Irene called out from behind me. I hadn't heard Roger or her come outside.

Ashley stated, "We can have dinner at your parents' house." No one challenged him.

* * *

Knowing Matias was in the same house as me but I couldn't go be with him was torture. I had tried to sneak away to my room when we arrived back at my house, but Ashley whisked me into the library for drinks before dinner with my father while my mother arranged for the sudden intrusion on their quiet dinner.

It seemed that everyone in my family was just doing whatever Ashley wanted.

Throughout dinner, Irene recounted all our exploits of the day, but left out how I ran out of the jewelry shop. No one brought that up again and I was thankful for it.

The stranger I saw must've been one of the men Ashley brought with him. He did an excellent job finding the scariest man possible for the job. His intense stare had kept me from running any further away from the jewelry shop so it was a job well done. I hadn't needed to run while in Washington. With Matias back, the plan to turn me and fake my death was back on.

When Irene wasn't talking, my father was questioning Ashley and Roger about their business deals. It all became background noise as my mind wandered to what Matias was doing while I was being forced to sit here and eat.

Was he hiding? Had he been found today? What had he done to occupy himself today? How much longer would I be obligated to sit here before I could go to him?

"Isabelle," My mother looked at me over the rim of her wine glass. "You look pained, are you well?"

"Just tired. Today was a lot for me."

"I'm sure it was." Her eyes flicked down to my engagement ring. "Do you have a safe space to keep that gorgeous ring?"

"I do. In fact," I pushed my chair back and stood. "I think I'll retire and safely tuck this ring away."

"Retire?" Irene scoffed. "But it's only-" She fished the watch out of Roger's jacket pocket. "Oh my, it's already after ten!"

Roger sighed, "I'm afraid I need to be up early tomorrow."

Ashley nodded at Roger before looking at me. "Let me walk you to your room."

"Really you don't have to. I'm just going right to bed." My smile was weak but I hoped my excuse of being tired would explain that.

"I insist."

There was no point in trying to stop him.

Roger started, "Irene, could I-"

"Of course!" Irene pulled him up from his chair and they started walking back towards the bedrooms.

"Goodnight!" I called out to my parents, and then to Roger and Irene as we passed them in the hall.

Ashley kept a hand on the small of my back as we walked towards my door. When we reached my room, I turned to face him. "Goodnight."

"That's all I get after I bought you a brand new ring?"

"Well," I backed up until I hit the door. "It was your duty to provide me with a ring."

He reached around me and turned the doorknob. "Then let's discuss your duties."

Twenty Nine

Isabelle

With a gentle shove, Ashley pushed me into my room. My heart felt like it would burst out of my chest. My eyes frantically searched for Matias, but he must've already hidden himself in the washroom.

While I scanned the room, Ashley locked the door.

"Now," He quickly closed the space between us. His hands grabbed my arms and pulled me until our bodies met. "With that new ring on your finger we're one step closer to marriage."

I tried to play my shaky breaths off as arousal. "And I can't wait until we can be together as husband and wife."

"We practically are."

"We are not."

His grip tightened, "Izzy, it's only a difference of a few days."

"Then it should be no trouble to wait just a few days. After all, you've waited your whole life for me, right?"

His eyes flashed with anger but instead of striking out, he whispered, "What I have or have not done is none of your concern. You aren't my wife *yet*." The grip on my arms became increasingly painful. "And you better not bring this attitude into our marital home, or you will find that adjusting to being a wife is more painful than expected." I worried my bone would snap from how tight he was holding me.

All I had to do was call out to Matias and he would come out from his hiding spot and kill Ashley for me.

But that would be a complicated mess to sort out right now. So I nodded while doing my best to look contrite. "Forgive me, please."

"You are reaching the end of my forgiveness."

"I won't push you further." I stared at the patch of his shirt that peaked out from between the lapels of his jacket. The seconds stretched between us and I worried he was going to escalate.

Then his grip relaxed on my arms and he sighed, "A lesser man would have just taken what he wanted from you by now. I have to say, I admire your dedication to your purity."

I nodded, letting my head fall against his chest.

"I won't be able to visit for a few days. I need to take care of some business. In the time apart, you can work on adjusting your attitude."

"I will. Can I..." I breathed to help control my frustration, "am I allowed to leave my room?"

"Not without me." He kissed the top of my head and then let himself out of my room. I heard the click of the lock as he used a key, I didn't know he had, to confine me to my room.

I sprinted to the door and placed the chair from my vanity in front of it. Slipping the engagement ring off my finger, I put it on my nightstand.

There was a mix of eagerness and caution as I made my way towards the washroom door. My heart started to pound so loud I could hear it in my ears. Anticipation was making my hands shake as I reached out for the doorknob.

Slowly, I swung the door open.

Matias was grinning up at me from the tub. "I was just moments away from coming out there but I heard you handling the buffoon."

My jaw dropped, "What is this?"

"A bath?" His tone was playful as he motioned me forward with his finger. "You need to wash the day off of you."

"How did you manage to do this?"

"I had some help."

"Help?"

"I'll answer all your questions once you are in the water."

"But I-"

"Strip." His voice lowered as he added, "Now."

I swallowed my next question and began to undo the buttons on my jacket. Matias's eyes widened as I slid the jacket down then let it fall onto the floor. "*Rapido, mi amor.* I have waited all day for you."

"Is the water warm?" My fingers unhooked the button on my skirt. When it was loose enough, the skirt joined the jacket on the floor.

"*Si,* I heated the stones myself."

"You are amazing." I took off my top and was left in just my undergarments.

"And you have until the count of five before I drag you in here with me."

I mimicked the tsk noise he so often used on me. "Patience is a virtue."

"Not feeling very virtuous at the moment." He moved his arms to the edge of the tub to start pushing himself up. Before he could fully stand, I quickly stripped everything else off until I was naked. "*Bueno.*" Matias lowered himself back down. "Now, get in."

With a newfound confidence, I sauntered over to the tub but instead of getting in, I bent over to dip the tips of my fingers in the water. "I usually like it so hot, it's almost painful."

"I can warm you up." Matias reached over the edge of the tub. His strong arms wrapped his arms around my legs. Effortlessly, he pulled me down and settled me onto his lap.

My hands shot up to grab his shoulder for balance. His skin was cold compared to the water around us, but I didn't mind. The mixing sensations of the warm water offset the chilling effect his skin was having on mine. There wasn't any space between our bodies once I laid my head in the crook by his neck. Matias's fingers were rubbing small circles into my hips.

Being in his arms again felt like a homecoming. I wanted to sob in relief, but I didn't want to ruin this moment.

Matias whispered into my ear, "I missed you so much today."

"I missed you more."

"I doubt that." His low laugh tickled my ear. "You got to go out while I was stuck here all day, getting bothered by Mary."

"Mary?" I finally picked my head up to look at him. "She caught you?"

"Instantly." He smiled to ease my now racing heart. "She was...well not pleased with my presence, but she did agree to help me hide and surprise you with this bath."

"Did you erase her memory?"

"Didn't need to. She let me know I could trust her. I didn't know if you would be upset about that."

"I-" I paused and thought for a moment. "I probably would have been a little upset."

"Understandably so." He squeezed my hips and made me jump. "Now, turn around. Let's wash the day off of you."

Matias moved my shoulders until I was facing away from him. I heard a cap twist off a bottle before the feeling of his fingers in my hair made my whole body radiate warmth. A moan escaped me as my eyes closed.

"Does this feel good?" His words were a dark whisper in my ear as the scent of lavender hit my nose.

"It feels amazing."

After a beat, he confessed, "I have never done this before."

I lightly giggled, "So I am your first?"

"And only. I have never bathed with a woman at all."

"Never?"

"No, I never bothered to stay with them long enough."

His fingers rubbed softly into my scalp. Another moan bubbled out as I leaned back into him.

"*Cuidado, mi pajarita.* If you keep making those noises, you'll never get clean."

"But it feels so good." I twisted my body so I could dunk my head underwater and rinse the soap out, then popped back up facing Matias. "I'm clean now."

"No," He tsked. "I would argue you are the opposite of clean."

"Oh?" I straddled him, and even though I could feel how excited he was, I kept myself from taking him. "Why do you say that?"

"Because you're still very, very dirty." His hands grabbed my face and pulled me into a hard kiss. Immediately my mouth opened for him so he pushed his tongue in, exploring and tasting. He pulled my bottom lip between his teeth and tugged until it popped free. "*Mierda,*" He groaned. "I missed these lips."

Matias's hands went up my slippery body and landed on my breasts. "And these." He squeezed. "I missed these more."

I was panting as he kissed my nipples. Then he moved one hand under the water and lightly touched my most sensitive spot. "But I missed this most of all."

"Matias..." His name came out of my lips in a long moan as his finger started working me in slow circles.

His lips were peppering kisses along my neck. "When you say my name like that..." His voice drifted off and he moved his fingers away from me. I softly whimpered in protest. He softly chuckled, "And you chided me for being impatient."

"Because you-oh!"

My words were cut off by Matias grabbing my hips, lifting me until he was lined up with my core, and then slamming me down onto him. He instantly filled me, my body barely adjusting to the sudden intrusion.

"Apologies," He growled. "I couldn't wait any longer to be inside you."

I wiggled my legs and hips to accommodate him. Once I found a spot that felt good, I started to rock my hips.

"Just like that, Isabelle." He started thrusting up into me, matching the pace I set. My whole body was overwhelmed at the sensation of him inside, his hands roaming my body, and his lips kissing mine.

I felt the pleasure start to coil at the base of my spine. "Yes, yes," My words were coming out in moans. Water was sloshing over the edges of the tub. Instead of worrying about the mess we were making, I focused on how good it felt to be on top of Matias. How he felt inside me. How the water helped his hands glide all over my naked body.

Matias grabbed my hips, moving me even faster. The pleasure was twisting tighter and tighter. All day I had been thinking about how many times he made me feel this way the night before. Then I would wonder what we would do when we could be alone together again. I hadn't imagined we would bathe together or that it would end with me crumbling on his cock as water splashed around us.

Matias brought my nipple back to his lips and tugged. It was so simple but it was the final push I needed to experience a sudden rush of pleasure. I couldn't stop the random combination of moans intermixed with his name as I pulsed around him.

Then a few thrust later Matias's eyes closed as he too finished. We were both panting when he kissed me softly. Cleaning up while in the water was much easier. Matias helped me off his lap, gently moving water to erase any sign of what we just did. "*Lista?*" He shook his head, "Ready?"

I nodded then began to stand to get out of the tub.

With a supernatural quickness, Matias was out of the tub before me, extending a hand to help me out. Water dripped down his tan body, clinging to the lines of muscles all over his perfect form.

"Towels?"

His voice brought me out of my trance. "The cabinet." I pointed behind him.

Faster than my eyes could keep up with, Matias grabbed two soft, white towels. He wrapped one around my whole body while his own went just around his waist. The way it hung was more scandalous than if he had just stood there naked.

He chuckled, then gently lifted my chin to close my mouth. I hadn't even realized I was gawking at him, but he was such an exceptional example of the male form. Immorality had enhanced the tone of his muscles and brought out the tan in his flawless skin. He would stay this perfect forever.

And soon I would be frozen in time like him too.

Matias tucked a wet strand of hair behind my ear. "We need to figure some things out before we go another round."

"Yes," I cleared my throat. "Of course."

He held out his arm to motion for me to exit the washroom.

We shared eager smiles as I went all the way to my vanity to start brushing my hair. Matias stopped in front of me, holding out a hand for the brush. Quickly, I finished my task and then handed the brush to him before changing into a nightgown. I settled into bed as Matias grabbed a pair of clean pants from the edge of the bed.

"Where did you get those?"

"Mary brought them in for me to wear while she washed and dried mine."

My eyebrows rose, "You must have made some impression on her."

He settled into the bed next to me. "I think she just liked that you are fond of me."

"Probably." I adjusted myself so I was facing him. The sooner we had our discussion, the sooner we could return to more enjoyable activities. So I simply stated, "I think you should turn me tonight."

"Not tonight." His voice was hard.

"But Ashley is escalating and-"

"You need to say goodbye to your family and get yourself packed for traveling. Tomorrow night I will turn you."

Tomorrow night.

Tomorrow.

It would be a lie to say I wasn't a little scared at the prospect of dying and deceiving my whole family. But that tiny bit of fear was dwarfed by the intense excitement that I was going to be immortal and spend forever with Matias.

"Perfect." I couldn't help but smile and he returned it with one of his own that showed both his dimples.

"*Perfecto.*" He looked down at my hands and then back into my eyes. "Now, I don't know how to ask this delicately, but where is the ring?"

"Oh!" I turned to my nightstand to see it was right where I had left it. I snatched it up, the jewels bit into the skin of my palm as I closed my hand into a fist. I turned back to face him before opening my hand to show him.

"*A la mierda, mi pajarita,* this is stunning." He took the ring and started to examine it in the lamp light. "The buffoon bought you a new engagement ring?"

"I didn't want the other one. I came to learn it was a family heirloom."

His brown eyes scrunched as he looked closer at the ring. "Did you pick this out?"

"I did."

"Because you like the style?"

"I do but," I placed my hand on his cheek so I could turn his gaze to look at me. "I don't care about the ring. Honestly, I could go forever without a ring. I think turning is going to bind me to you better than a marriage could."

"But I will still get you a ring."

It was the ease at which he said the words that made my heart skip.

"If I ever find out what happened to my mother's ring, I'll put that one on your finger." He carefully took my hand in his. "If not, I'll buy you the perfect ring."

"I, I don't know what to say."

"Nothing yet." He placed the ring on my nightstand. "We need to turn you first, and then get out of here and to the mountains to hide out, then go searching for answers about my family, and by then you should have thought of something to say." Matias lifted my hand to gently kiss my naked ring finger.

"Yes, by then I will definitely have an answer."

"*Bueno.*"

He laid back against the pillows and motioned for me to ensconce myself in the nook under his arm. I settled in, looking up at his face. Matias looked down at me with genuine adoration, something I had never seen in anyone's face before. It was the same way Irene looked at Roger. Ashley had never looked at me this softly before. No, Matias was the only person I had ever felt passion like this from.

But then he winced, grabbing his stomach.

Immediately, I shot up. "What's wrong?"

"Just haven't fed in a few days." He shook his head. "I'll be fine, I just need to go hunting." His arm lifted over me as he moved to get up from the bed. He swayed slightly then clumsily sat back down.

"Matias!" I softly cried out, coming around to his side and helping him lay back against the pillows.

"*Tranquila, mi amor.* I'll be fine once I get some blood in me." He tried to rise again but I gently pushed him back down.

"Drink from me." His whole body froze. My hands grabbed onto his shoulders. "Please, drink from me. You can't go hunt like this."

The whiskey brown of his eyes was gone as his pupils expanded. "You don't understand what you're asking for."

"Yes, I do. You need human blood and I happen to be full of it." I motioned to my body and his eyes tracked the movement before snapping but to meet my gaze.

"Isabelle-"

"Matias."

His face hardened. I caught his eyes slipping down to examine my throat.

"Please." I grabbed my damp hair and moved it behind my shoulder. "Drink from me."

His whole throat worked on a swallow. "If I hurt you–"

"You're not going to."

He chuckled, "You have such confidence in me, but you have no idea how much I have been controlling myself around you already."

"Exactly," I closed the space between our bodies. The nightgown provided a pathetic bit of separation between us. My neck was just inches away from his mouth. "You can control yourself."

I could feel his breath on my skin. The tips of his fingers ghosted over my hips. His brows curved in, like he was in pain from either needing to drink or the conflict of not wanting to hurt me while needing to quench his thirst. But I didn't think about how this could hurt. All I thought about was how he needed something that I could give in this moment. After everything Matias had offered me, it was an easy decision to offer up my blood.

"Please, drink from me, Matias."

His blackened eyes studied my face for a heartbeat. He kept his gaze locked on mine as one hand pressed against my back and the other wound into the hairs at the nape of my neck. He sucked in a deep breath. I saw the tips of his canine teeth extend to resemble fangs. "This is going to hurt."

"I imagined it would."

A dark chuckle hit my ear, "Did you imagine this moment?"

"I did." As I took in a deep breath, my chest collided with his. He momentarily looked down at the lack of space between our bodies before looking back up at me.

"And in your imagination, did you enjoy it?"

"Yes, but not as much as you did."

He shuddered, "You have no idea. Drinking blood, it's better than the best wine, better than an orgasm. It is literally drinking life."

My hands went to grab his arms. "Can't wait until I know for myself."

"Maybe I turn you tonight?" His nose stroked my neck. "Forget your family, we can just run away now and I'll turn you once we're safe in the mountains."

I wanted to say yes. My heart was screaming for me to say yes, but I knew that Matias was right about waiting. It pained me to admit but we needed to be smart about this. "That could work. But Ashley will come looking for me."

He hummed against my pulse. "Then we stick to our plan."

I nodded as best as I could, "Then you need to drink."

"If you insist." All of my muscles tightened up as the sharp points of his fangs scraped the soft skin above my vein. "*Tranquila*, it feels better when you are relaxed."

I took in a deep breath before slowly letting it out. My hands around Matias's arm tightened but I willed every other muscle in my body to relax.

His lips gently kissed the spot he had just scraped. Then I felt the sharp sting of his fangs piercing my skin. When my mind registered what had just happened, I let out a soft cry, but it soon became a moan. The pain of the bite quickly turned into pleasure.

When Matias started to pull my blood into his mouth, my core throbbed. His name left me in a breath. The hand holding my hair tightened its grip as he sucked harder. I could feel my blood seeping out of the small cuts in my neck. It was warm against the cool feeling of his lips.

My eyelids started to feel heavy. I closed my eyes and leaned my head back further so Matias could bite deeper. A slight fuzzy feeling was starting in my toes but that was warring with the growing heat in my core.

The hand Matias had on my back slid down to cup my backside. His lips peeled back from my neck and his tongue licked at the wound. Instantly, I felt the skin tighten and close. When I lifted my hand to where his mouth had just been, the skin was perfectly smooth again. There wasn't even any blood.

Matias was panting as he stared at me.

"That felt..." I smiled at him.

His grip on my backside tightened. "I know."

"Do you feel better now?"

He nodded. My eyes went to his lips where a single drop of blood was dangling at the corner of his mouth. I used my thumb to wipe it away before Matias's tongue shot out to clean it.

"Can't waste any." He smirked.

"No, we can't." And then his lips were colliding with mine.

I could taste my blood still on his tongue. Whenever I got a cut on my finger or bit my nails too low, I could accidentally taste my own blood but that was nothing compared to this tangy, metallic assault to my taste buds. It didn't turn my stomach like I expected it to. Instead, it emboldened me to chase the taste as I moved my tongue in his mouth.

Matias effortlessly maneuvered me onto my back. He pushed up my nightgown and freed himself from his pants. With a groan, he thrusted inside me in one smooth movement. I cried out as he stoked the heat that had been building while he drank my blood. As he started thrusting, our hips came together over and over. No words were said, just our heavy breathing and soft moans filled the room.

Matias hitched my leg up and rested my ankle on his shoulder. With my hips lifted up like this, he could hit the spot that made stars swirl behind my closed eyes. After only a few thrusts, I crumbled around him and he found his release a few moments later.

"Your blood," He panted, laying down next to me and pulling me onto his chest. "Your blood is the most exquisite thing I have ever tasted. And I'm going to taste it forever."

Thirty

Isabelle

My hand flexed against something cold. Wrenching my eyes open, I realized that it was Matias's chest underneath my palm. After he drank my blood, we recovered, cleaned up, and then settled in to sleep. Perhaps it was the blood loss or the times our bodies came together, but I fell asleep almost immediately after he pulled me onto his chest.

Matias was still peacefully sleeping as I carefully untangled myself from him and made my way to the window. The sky was cloudy and overcast, threatening to rain. The weather reflected the gloomy feelings I was struggling with.

I would have to say goodbye to my family today.

Turning away from the window, I looked at Matias.

Losing my family would hurt, but I was gaining so much more.

And I could try to come back and see them later. Perhaps I could pretend to haunt Irene? She would love that I gave up eternal peace to come harass her in the afterlife.

I would have to be subtle today. Carefully letting everyone know I loved them so I could leave with Matias feeling like this chapter of my life was closed. In between saying my goodbyes, I would have to pack and get my hands on as much money as I could.

A deep breath filled my lungs before I let it out.

I could manage it all. I had to manage it all.

One more stress filled day and then I would be free with Matias.

A content smile curled my lips.

Matias shot up from the bed. "Someone is coming."

My eyes shot to the door, and a second later the sound of a key sliding into the lock filled the room.

"Sister!" Irene's voice called out.

I looked at Matias who was already out of bed and running to the washroom.

"Yes, Irene!" I met her just as the door was swinging open.

"Sister!" She was beaming, twirling into the room. Her nightgown and robe flowed as she plopped herself on my bed. "Guess who shared my bed last night?!"

My mouth dropped, "No!"

My sister's face glowed, "Yes!"

"How?"

"Roger and I made arrangements for him to sneak back in here during the night."

"And did you?" My eyebrows shot up.

She bit her lip and looked down.

"Irene!" I squealed.

"I know, I know, but I'm in love! We've all but made the engagement official. What's a few months, a few weeks even, in the eyes of God? I've given my heart to him already. My body was part of that deal."

I plopped down on the bed next to her. "I understand."

"I knew you would."

"But you are certain you made the right choice?"

"In partner? Absolutely." The smile on her face just grew wider. "No one understands me like Roger does."

"So it's love then? Even though it's so soon?"

"Love doesn't obey the laws of time."

"No," My gaze wandered to the washroom before I reeled it back to my sister. "I suppose it doesn't."

"What are your plans for the day?"

"The same as they have been for the last week."

She stood and went over to my wardrobe. "Perhaps I could get you out of the house today? Ashley said I could chaperone you."

"Oh,"I rolled my eyes. "If Ashley has given you permission then by all means-"

"Isabelle!" Irene shrieked as she bent over. When she popped back up, she was holding Matias's shirt. "Whose is this?"

"Ashley's, of course." It was a weak lie, but I hoped she would think it was the truth.

"No, it isn't. Ashley has let Roger know exactly how far you've allowed things between you to go. Especially since the engagement, you haven't let him do anything further than kiss. So," Irene squared her shoulders at me. "Whose shirt is this?"

Frantically, I tried to think of a lie that she would believe. "Perhaps Mary accidentally mixed it in with my wash-"

"And it was on the floor, by your bed?" Irene took a step closer. "If you have been unfaithful to Ashley, he will kill you."

"Sister, we've spoken-"

The washroom door opened. I watched Irene's head twist to see Matias, half-naked, standing there. With an easy smile, he announced, "That would be mine."

Irene's mouth and eyes went wide with a mix of shock and awe. "And who would you be?" She still didn't remember Matias. Even seeing him now, she had no memory of the night of the Autumnal Ball, or how upset she was that he hadn't danced with her. Whatever compulsion Matias did on her was still working.

He looked at me then back to my sister, "The man finally treating your sister the way she deserves to be treated."

Her eyes darted between Matias and me. "So you are why she has been acting strange lately?"

"Guilty." He leaned against the doorframe.

My sister took an emboldened step towards him. "What's your name?"

"Matias Ciervo."

She purred, "Exotic."

I chided her, "Irene!"

Matias held up a hand, "I supposed for you Virginians, my name isn't common." He extended that same hand, "It is a pleasure to meet you."

When Irene placed her hand in his, Matias pulled her closer. He locked onto her eyes and started speaking slowly. "You told your sister about your wonderful night and then you left. You never saw me, never caught your sister and I, and you will not remember me. Understood?"

Irene nodded mindlessly.

He continued, "You will leave this room and return to yours. In about an hour, you will come to retrieve your sister for a lovely day spent walking around your childhood home, reminiscing about all the wonderful times you have had. You will have dinner with your parents and you will leave your sister alone until tomorrow morning."

Another mindless nod from Irene.

Matias released his hold on her. "Now go."

My sister stared blankly ahead as she made her way out of my room.

I ran to lock the door behind her.

When I looked back, Matias was tugging the shirt over his head. He let out a breath, "That was close."

"Did you," I looked at the door then to him. "You erased her memory, yes?"

"*Si, mi amor*, with a bit of compulsion in there too."

"You didn't have to. I had it under control."

"You did, but she said the buffoon would kill you and I couldn't risk that. I couldn't have her leave this room and tell her beloved Roger what she knew."

"I suppose that was necessary."

"It was." Matias sat on the bed and started pulling on his boots. "*Eschu*-Listen to me, you spend the day getting yourself ready. I'm going to go back to the mountains and get everything set up for us. I will return as soon as I can. If the sun stays hidden, I should be back before midnight."

"You have to go now?"

"The sooner I leave, the sooner I can come back." He finished putting in his boots and stood up.

"I don't want you to leave me."

"I don't want to leave," He wrapped me in an embrace. "But it'll be easier for you to do what you need to do without me here."

I nodded as my arms squeezed his stocky frame.

"I'll be back. Just stay here and stay safe and I'll be right back."

"I'll be ready when you return." I looked up into his whiskey colored eyes as he tucked a loose curl behind my ear.

He tsked, "You'll need to let go of me."

"You first."

"It's, I don't, *mierda*." Matias lowered his head until our lips met. He kissed me hard, like he would never be able to kiss me again. I held him tighter as his fingers went into my hair. He pulled my head back so the kiss deepened. I took his bottom lip between my teeth and pulled. Then when he returned the favor, he bit down enough to draw blood.

"Matias!"

"*Perdóname, mi amor*." He smiled as our foreheads touched. "I just wanted a taste for the road."

"I lo-"

He put a finger to my swollen lips. "You save that for when I return."

With one more peck, he grabbed his jacket, and leapt out the window.

* * *

Irene returned exactly an hour after Matias had sent her away. "I think we should take a walk!" She announced as she barged through my door.

"A splendid idea!" I was already in a simple green dress and comfortable shoes. We linked arms then made our way outside.

Walking around the property brought back the two decades of memories that I had from living here. We stopped in front of my favorite tree, the one where Ashley originally proposed. I would miss this tree and all the memories I had here, both good and bad.

Then we walked to the tree that Irene had fallen out of and broken her leg when she was ten. She had cried every day that summer while my cousins and I ran circles around her. We walked past the horse stables, giving our favorite ones apples as a treat.

We stopped in the garden and sat down to face each other. "Sister," I squeezed her hand. "I love you so much."

"Not as much as I love you."

I shook my head as I laughed, "I will miss you so much."

"Stop being so dramatic." Irene took her hand back. "You'll be a carriage ride away."

"It'll seem so much further than that."

"That's because you haven't been getting along with Ashley." She looked down at the engagement ring that I had returned to my finger. "Once you two are happy and engaging in the fun parts of marriage, you won't miss me at all."

"No, I'll always miss you. I need you always."

"And I'll always need you."

Thirty One

Isabelle

As I was getting ready for dinner, Mary let herself into my room. She carefully opened and quickly closed the door behind her.

"It's alright, Mary, he isn't here right now."

Her brow crinkled into a frown, "Where did he go?"

"He went to get things ready for us. He'll be back tonight."

She sucked in a breath, "So I was right to assume he was stealing you away?"

"It's not stealing if I'm giving myself to him."

"Miss Isabelle," Mary shook her head. "You are certain this is what you want?"

"More than anything."

"I can understand why. That man you chose is quite handsome."

I laughed, "Is that why you let him stay yesterday?"

"No," She smiled. "I let him stay because I could tell how much he cared for you, and it was obvious how happy he was making you."

"How was it obvious?"

"You ate."

"Pardon?"

"You had eaten food from the tray I left you. I knew something was terribly wrong when you weren't eating, but he got you to eat again."

"He did."

"Because him being back made you feel whole again? Like you *could* eat? Like you could *breathe*?"

I bit my still slightly swollen lip. "That's exactly what it was like."

"I remember this feeling, and I remember not being allowed to chase it. So," Mary grabbed my shoulders and looked up at me. "Chase after it, and don't let it go."

"I won't."

* * *

Dinner with everyone was a somber experience, at least it was for me. My parents had no idea why I kept looking at them and smiling. In fact, my mother asked, "What has put you in this odd humor?"

"I know that I'm going to be leaving you all soon, and it just, it makes my heart heavy."

"Oh, my dear!" She reached across the table to take my hand. "I know it's hard, but you are going to spend the rest of your life with the perfect provider. It'll be an adjustment, but you'll make an amazing wife and mother."

I smiled at her words, which were right but for the wrong reason. I would be spending my life with someone who would provide me with everything I wanted and needed. Not material possessions, the way Ashley would, but in love and support.

As dinner was winding down, I gave each of my parents a hug. My father squeezed me hard, despite not quite understanding why I was so emotional. Mother held me a little longer and whispered to me that she understood.

Irene walked me to my door. "You seem happier now."

"I am."

"And good thing too, with only a week until the wedding, you've finally decided to be happy about it."

"We'll see how you feel when it is your turn."

"I am sure I will feel elated, ecstatic, over the moon-"

"Alright," I giggled. "But I will remember this for your wedding week."

"And I will remind you of how sour you were in the weeks leading up to your own marriage when you and Ashley are happily married."

My eyebrows shot up. "I am actually looking forward to you rubbing this in my face."

"Well then that takes the fun out of it."

We shared a laugh and I took one last look at my sister. It was hard to tell we were related unless we were standing side by side. All of our features were the same shape, but different colorings. My eyes were blue like our mother's and hers were light brown like our father's. Her hair was so much lighter than mine, more blonde-brown to my auburn. She was a few inches taller than me, and much thinner. I hadn't been able to borrow her dresses since I turned twelve, but that didn't stop us from trying to coordinate every chance we could. I had more freckles than her now, but I wondered if avoiding the sun for the foreseeable future would change that.

Taking her hands in mine, I declared, "I need you always, sister."

"And I will always need you." She squeezed my hands.

"Goodnight, Irene."

"Goodnight, Isabelle." We hugged each other before retreating to our rooms.

Once I was safely behind my locked door, I pulled my suitcase out. This same suitcase had been packed and unpacked twice now, but this would be the final time. That I knew for certain. I packed the same clothes, but managed to fit my copy of *Frankestien* along with some pictures that I had kept tucked in my nightstand. I filled a small velvet bag with all the jewelry I could, including the engagement ring from Ashley. If I tried to take anymore of my things, my sister would notice.

Matias was going to make my death look like a suicide, and people usually didn't pack their lives away if they were just going to end it.

My family would think I was dead, quickly send me to be buried, and then Matias would come and release me from wherever I was.

The finer details would get worked out when Matias returned tonight, but I trusted him and this plan.

I didn't want my family to grieve me like this, but I needed them to think I was dead. Ashley wouldn't come looking for me if I was dead.

As I closed the latches on the suitcase, I heard a rustling coming from outside the window.

My heart skipped a beat as I ran over to the window to see Matias climbing up to me.

But I saw no one there.

Disappointed, I hummed to myself as I scanned the growing darkness in my room. There was nothing in it. Shadows started to creep out of the corners of the house.

Suddenly, there was a ripple of sensation up my back.

When I turned around, there was nothing there.

As I started to spin, trying to locate whatever was causing this, the feeling of fingers grabbing my hips stopped me.

"Hello there," A deep, barely audible voice slid into my ear. "You are even more beautiful up close."

"Who?" My body kept trying to twist around, but phantom hands were holding it in place. "Who the hell are you?"

The dark voice laughed, "You shall find out soon." A tingle started to travel up my arm. "I cannot wait to officially meet you." I could feel a hand faintly gripping my neck, but I saw nothing but darkness.

"Why not now?"

"Unfortunately, I have been called away." The soft press of lips hit my raw skin in the same spot Matias had drank from. "But as soon as I can, I will come get you."

My voice shook, "Get me?"

"Don't fret," I could feel breath against my ear. "I don't wish to harm you, or you'd be hurt already."

"That's not..." I swallowed, "That's not as comforting as you might think."

Another deep laugh, and I swear I could feel lips curling into a smile against my neck. "See you soon, Isabelle."

"Wait!" I cried out before managing to spin my body around. There was nothing there. The gas lamp seemed to burn brighter now. I searched my whole room for whoever or whatever just spoke to me and couldn't find anything.

"Matias, where are you?" I asked out loud, hoping that would magically manifest him climbing over the window into my room.

The night was eerily silent now, like all the creatures who usually made themselves known at night had suddenly disappeared. Frantically, I paced around the room. My gaze went from the clock that was slowly ticking seconds away then to the still empty window. I repeated this torturous cycle over and over but nothing changed.

Then I heard the crashing of glass coming from down the hall.

Thirty Two

Isabelle

A shout rang out. I cracked the door open but couldn't see anything happening in the dim candlelight.

Cautiously, I took a step out into the hallway.

More shouts were coming from the front entryway.

"Isabelle?" Irene stood in her doorway, the door just open enough for me to see how wide her eyes were. "What's going on?"

"I'm not-I don't know."

"Get back in your rooms, girls!" My father's voice boomed as his silhouette filled the hall. He had his shotgun in his hands. "Now!"

Irene slammed her door as I turned on my heel to run back to mine.

Locking the door behind me, I proceeded to push my vanity table in front of it. Then I went to the window and checked the woods outside.

There were dozens of men coming in all directions towards the house.

"What the hell?"

This had to be the work of the Lord of Shadows. I couldn't think of anyone else who would want to hurt my family like this. My father had made enemies through his business dealings and debts, but none of them would date to seek revenge like this. If they wanted revenge against my father, they would be burning his tobacco crops, not attacking our house.

No, this was because of me and my entanglement with Matias. He had warned me the Lord of Shadows might be looking for him, but he made it seem like it wasn't something to worry about. As I watched my home be invaded by random men, I knew that Matias had underestimated just how dangerous the vampire he was running from was. And now the only one that could save me from this nightmare, was the monster who had put me in it.

The sound of a shotgun blast came from deep in the house.

I ran to hide in my wardrobe, moving my dresses to cover my body as I tucked myself tightly into the corner. This was the best hiding spot I could come up with. I hoped Irene had also found a way to conceal herself in her room.

Several gunshots rang out in a row.

Perhaps my father and the other men who could shoot would kill all these intruders? But I had seen so many of them swarming the house like flies. As more shots rang out, it seemed impossible there would be enough bullets to kill them all.

Breathing became harder. My hand grabbed the lace of my nightgown as I tried to grab my chest. I was going to die here. Matias wasn't going to get here in time. He was going to find my dead body.

Unless by some miracle he arrived soon, these men would manage to break through the barricade I put up, then I would be tortured, and killed by the Lord of Shadows. Matias had warned me that this was a dangerous possibility. I just didn't think my family would also become victims to the Lord of Shadows.

That must've been whose voice I was hearing before the attack started.

My throat was dry, so dry, and barely any air was moving down into my lungs. A fogginess started to invade my vision, so I slammed my eyes shut.

I heard Irene scream out through the wall that separated our rooms.

Hot tears pooled in my eyes and I couldn't stop them from falling as more of Irene's piercing screams came through.

A loud banging hit my ears next and it sounded close, too close.

I moved my hand over my mouth to stifle the whimpers that were involuntarily coming out of me.

"Fuck, the door is blocked!" A gritty male's voice called out.

"Move!" A different, higher voice shouted. I heard another loud bang and then a groan.

"You idiot, you can't just ram your way in-" Wood was cracking and breaking. "Oh, guess you can."

"Told ya."

Clunky footsteps were getting closer.

"She's gotta be in here," The voice that belonged to the one who rammed their way in said. "None of the others matched the description."

"You sure it wasn't the girl in the other room?"

"No, he said she had blue eyes. That one had brown."

"Come out, come out, wherever you are..." The deeper voice taunted.

All of my muscles locked so I wouldn't shake and give myself away. I hoped they wouldn't be able to find me. I wished that they would miraculously leave the house, that my family would be alright, and this would just be some terrible nightmare.

"She's not under the bed." The higher voice grunted.

"She's not in the washroom."

"Where the hell could she be?"

"You think he already got to her?"

"Impossible, the boss said she was alone."

"Then she's in here somewhere. We checked all the other rooms already."

My panicking thoughts were thinking of all the worst possible endings to this predicament. If they found me, they would certainly kill me, and probably do worse before that. I regretted hiding in the wardrobe now. I was trapped in this tiny space with no way out. If I had gone to the washroom, I could've tried to get out the window. But it was too late now. I just had to hope they wouldn't open the wardrobe and spot me.

I heard what sounded like my desk or vanity being knocked over. Then the sound of more wood breaking.

"She isn't going to be under the desk, idiot. We would've seen her."

"You never know. They said she was short, curvy and short."

"Not short enough to fit herself under there. Check the wardrobe."

I stopped breathing, but I could hear my heart pounding in my ears.

The doors of the wardrobe flung open, the light from the gas lamps pooling above me.

"Lots of nice dresses." The one with the high voice whispered, moving some of the dresses that hung further down the rack from where I hid. "But no girl."

The doors slammed shut.

My whole body relaxed for just a second, but I could sense the men still just outside.

"Do you think she ran?"

"Where could she have gone? We had the whole house surrounded."

The wardrobe doors were ripped open. I almost cried out in shock, but I was so frozen with fear that nothing but my eyes moved. They were tracking the dresses moving down the rail at the top of the wardrobe. The hanger scraped along the wooden pole as the dresses were each pushed out of the way.

Finally, the dress that was hiding me was moved.

A man, plump but tall, stood looking down at me. His lips were curled into a mix of satisfaction and rage. His brow shot up to his bald head. "Look at that, blue eyes."

The other man hovered over the plump one. He was much taller, and thinner, with sunken cheeks and wide eyes. "Didn't think she would be hiding behind the dresses like that."

"She seems clever." The plump one chuckled. "He'll love that."

"I thought we were meant to kill her."

"No," He turned to face the thin one. "The boss wants her alive."

"But right before we attacked the house, we were told to just kill her."

With them both distracted, I bolted out of my hiding spot. My feet felt like weights as I started awkwardly running towards the window.

"Oh, no you don't!" The thin man reached out a gangly arm and wrenched me back to him by my hair. Tiny explosions of pain started to spread over my scalp. I kept scrambling against the ground, kicking out at him, but nothing made him loosen the grip on me. Finally, the plump one came over, grabbed my arms, and pulled them behind my back. Then the pain on my scalp was replaced by the ache of my arms being over extended.

"Stop fighting us, girl." The plump man shouted in my ear. But I ignored him, continuing to kick out at the thin one.

I managed to hit his knee, making him groan. "Maybe we *should* just kill her."

"No!" I screamed.

"So she does speak!" The plump one laughed and tightened my arms. "You don't want to die, huh?"

"No, no, no..." I started to shake with a sob.

"God, now she's crying." The thin one grabbed my face. "She's ugly when she cries."

His insult made me cry harder.

"So," He let go of my face. "Do we kill her or take her in?"

Through the racing thoughts, I realized I could try to bargain with these men. "I'll give you money! My father has-"

"Your father? I think that he isn't in the position to make any deals right now." The plump one laughed so hard he started wheezing. His grip on my arms eased, and I managed to slip out of his hold. I started running towards the washroom door.

"Bitch!" The thin one reached out again and grabbed my hair, but this time, he pulled me down then slammed me into the ground. "Fuck it, let's just kill her."

"No!" I started to wildly lash out at him, but my arms weren't long enough to hit him. My legs were useless once he sat down on top of them. But I kept trying, kept moving all my limbs. Nothing made a difference.

Then the plump one grabbed my arms and pinned them down.

"If we get fucked for this, I'm telling the boss it was your idea."

"That's fine." The thin one pulled a knife out from his back pocket. "I'll tell him exactly who told me to kill her." The silver of the blade was right above my eyes. "Now, where to start?" He moved the tip of the knife to my cheek and continued down my neck. It threatened to cut open my skin, but he didn't push down hard enough.

"You can't take your time with this one. We need to be in and out."

"In and out," The thin one grinned, showing his crooked teeth. "We can do that." With one swift movement, he shoved the knife into the soft flesh of my waist. At first I didn't feel the pain, but when he pulled the knife out, I felt a burning sensation start to radiate out from the spot he had struck.

"In," The knife stuck the other side of my waist. "And out." He ripped the knife out, tearing my flesh as he went.

Pain was making my vision go white. My toes and fingers were numb. I could feel warm blood seeping out of my sides.

I didn't feel the third or fourth stabs; it all just blended into the overwhelming pain that was commanding my senses. But I knew he was stabbing me again and again because he was keeping count.

He reached seven and then I felt his weight tear away from my body.

Thirty Three

Matias

I was too late.

That's all I thought as I ripped the man who had been stabbing Isabelle off of her body. In the same movement, I tore his thin body in half, discarding the pieces to the side.

I was too late.

When I had arrived at Isabelle's house, I had seen the men coming out of the doors. There were about a dozen and they were all holding different stolen riches from the house. I waited a moment, just a moment to see if he was there.

The Lord of Shadows had to be behind this. If he was here then he would be watching all the chaos with a smile on his face.

But I didn't see him or his carriage.

Once I was sure he wasn't there, I ran as fast as I could to Isabelle's side of the house, leapt up the wall, and into the window.

Rage filled my veins when I saw what was happening in her room.

One fat piece of meat had her arms pinned down, while a man who looked like he hadn't eaten in weeks was grinning wide as he stabbed her.

I watched her body convulse with pain as he slid the knife in before jerking it out of her.

Without a sound, I went behind the fat one and twisted his head until I heard his neck snap.

Then I grabbed the thin one and ripped him in half at the waist. His blood splashed up onto my face. I licked away what I could but let the rest drip down as I tossed his body parts onto the floor.

"Isabelle," My body crumbled until I was on my knees. I cradled her limp body in my arms. "*Mi pajarita*, say something?"

"Matias..." Her voice was shallow and barely audible.

I swallowed back tears, "I'm here. I'm so sorry I didn't get here sooner, but I'm here now, *mi amor*."

"I-" Her blue eyes winced as she tried to speak. "I-"

"No, no, save your strength." I sucked up in a deep breath. "This isn't how I thought this would happen, but it must be done now."

She nodded as her eyes closed.

I brushed the hair that was matted with blood away from her neck. Was it just yesterday that I had tasted her blood under much different circumstances? That felt like another lifetime ago now.

My thumb was on her fluttering pulse. She was so weak, so close to death, and biting her now would put her over the edge. But it would also save her.

Lips against her forehead, I whispered, "*Te amo. Estaré aquí cuando despiertes.*"

The scent of her blood was heavy in the air. It was pooling under her body. My fangs were already out and my tongue was anticipating tasting her again. When I put my lips on her neck, my fangs sank into her delicate skin, and I felt the warm rush of her blood into my mouth. It only took a few drags before she was completely drained.

Her whole body was now dead weight in my arms. Using my fangs, I bit down and tore a chunk out of my own wrist before holding it up to her lips. My blood soaked them, dripping down the sides, to the point I wasn't sure any of it was getting in her mouth.

"Drink, Isabelle, *por favor.*"

I expected her to move in some way to indicate it was working. I closely watched her throat to see if she was drinking. I waited for her chest to start to suck in breaths.

Nothing happened.

She wasn't moving.

She wasn't breathing.

She was dead.

I couldn't remember how long it took to turn into a vampire. I could barely remember anything about my own transformation other than the overwhelming pain I was in.

I would wait for her to wake. I would wait as long as it took for her to wake. And if she never did...I stopped my mind from following that train of thought. She would wake.

I kept my wrist against her lips until the skin had healed itself completely. Enough of my blood had to be in her system now. Even if she hadn't swallowed, enough would have slipped down her throat. I hadn't swallowed much blood myself and was still able to turn after I had been drained of blood. This had to work. It had to.

I took in a deep breath, then lifted Isabelle off the ground, and brought her to the bed. I laid her down in the same spot she had lain when we were sleeping together.

I was afraid to leave her for even a second in case she awoke. So I curled up in the bed with her, and just held on tight.

* * *

I didn't sleep.

At the slightest noise or movement, my whole body would tense. My eyes would instantly focus on Isabelle. I kept thinking she would wake and I needed to be the first thing she saw. Then we could go to the cabin in the woods that I rented for us. Dreaming of the life the two of us would have kept me awake.

The sun had risen but the sky was so cloudy that I could barely tell it was daytime now.

Still Isabelle didn't rise.

I had tried to rouse her throughout the night, but nothing worked. I was so careful as I held her not to hurt any part of her.

I had just adjusted my hold on her so she was laying on my arm when I heard voices, and they were getting closer.

"What the hell happened here?"

I recognized that voice. It was the buffoon.

"*Mierda.*" I quietly cursed before slowly moving Isabelle off of me. I could hear other voices I didn't recognize guessing at who caused the violence in the house as they made their way closer to this bedroom. The buffoon would come to check on Isabelle. As much as I wanted him dead, now wasn't the time to confront him.

Reluctantly, I pulled myself away from her before locking myself in the washroom.

A moment later, I heard the buffoon cry out, "Isabelle!" His hurried footsteps moved, then stopped, and I heard the bed creak.

"Oh my Lord!" Another voice called out. It sounded familiar. "They're all dead then." It belonged to Mr. Middleton, from the party.

"It would appear so." Mr. Smith was also here.

"How the hell did this happen?" The buffoon's rage was evident in his voice. "I had men posted up outside! I had taken every precaution!"

Mr. Middleton responded, "Whoever wanted them dead clearly came prepared to deal with those obstacles."

"Someone will need to go tell Roger." The buffoon's voice was heavy with grief now. "He wasn't able to leave the office, and he'll, he'll-" There was a pause.

"That's alright." Mr. Smith spoke. "We'll send word to him so he can come say his goodbyes tonight or tomorrow. We won't be able to do anything about burying the bodies until the rain clears. You said you knew where Haller kept his important papers?"

"Yes, he showed me the other night when I was here. Said now that I was going to be his son, I needed to know where all that was kept."

"Almost like the man knew his days were numbered."

"Yes," Mr. Middleton added. "I wonder if this had something to do with those odd deals he was making."

"Tobacco was hit the hardest after the war." Mr. Smith replied. "He made it seem like things were going well, but we all knew the truth."

The buffoon scoffed, "I was fixing all that."

"Clearly it wasn't enough." Someone cleared his throat, and then Mr. Middleton continued, "Not that I think this is your fault. None of this is your fault."

"Why don't we give you some space to grieve." Mr. Smith sighed. "Haller's brother needs to be sent for, but we'll handle that. We can all reconvene at your family's home to make a plan moving forward."

"Thank you, gentlemen."

I heard hard pats against backs and then footsteps retreating.

Carefully, I cracked the door just enough to confirm that the buffoon was indeed alone in the room now. He took a long look around at the two men who had killed Isabelle, shaking his head before going over and kicking the fat one. Then his gaze settled back on Isabelle.

"Izzy," Her name was a whisper out of his mouth. Slowly, he approached the bed. "I shouldn't have left you alone. If only I had been here." His hand reached out to stroke her hair. "If only-"

Without thinking, I shoved the door open. "Don't you fucking touch her." I growled standing on the opposite side of the bed from him.

The buffoon paled as his eyes went wide. "Who the hell are you?"

My chest was heaving with anxious breaths. I wanted to just rip him apart, but I held myself back. Isabelle had wanted to watch him die, so I wanted to respect that wish. Perhaps I could hold him hostage until she woke up.

"No," The buffoon's eyes settled with a knowing look. "No, no, she didn't. Good Lord, it would explain..." He looked down at her then back at me. "You and her?"

I nodded.

"So did you do all this?" The buffoon motioned with this head to the rest of the house.

"No, I would never hurt her."

The buffoon laughed, "It all makes so much sense now." He eased closer to her body. "Izzy, I underestimated you."

"Get away from her!"

The buffoon cocked the pistol in his hand and pointed it at me. "I don't take orders from some disgusting foreigner who seduced and defiled my fiancé."

"That's not-" But that is exactly what happened. I couldn't deny it just because I didn't like how he had worded what had transpired between Isabelle and I.

"Now, be a gentleman and take this shot as punishment for what you've done here."

I couldn't help but smirk at him as I spread my arms wide. "Go ahead."

The blast of the gun hit my ears before the bullet lodged into my chest. It was so close to my heart, which would have made recovery so much more painful, but thankfully this would be an easy fix. As my fresh blood mixed with the dried stains that Isabelle's blood had left on my shirt, I could already feel the bullet being pushed out and rejected by my body. Within a few seconds, the bullet was all the way out and fell to the floor with a clink.

Now the buffoon's countenance paled. "What the hell are you?"

"Not human."

As he cocked the gun again, I pounced, leaping over the bed with ease. He crumbled underneath my strength and even though he started flailing his arms, it was useless against me. I pinned his arms at his sides and then leaned down to taunt him. "She hated you." He writhed under me, but I kept going. "She hated how you were going to use her, how you saw her as nothing more than property, something to covet. And she knew, like everyone else knew, that you were bedding other women. You were never worthy of her."

"You piece of shit!" He spat back, fight lighting his eyes up. "You'll rot in hell!"

My laugh was vicious. "And I'm sure I'll see you there."

He started to scream something else but I tore the words away as I bit into his throat. With a hard yank, I ripped out a chunk of his neck, letting blood spray all over our faces. In the few seconds he was still conscious, I licked my lips. His blood tasted like stale cigars and cheap whiskey. But the fear that flashed in his eyes right before he died was worth the foul taste in my mouth.

The buffoon's body went limp under me.

So much for honoring Isabelle's wishes.

As I stood back up, I went over to Isabelle. "*Perdoname,*" I sighed and grabbed her hand. "But he needed to die now."

I could almost hear her voice telling me that I did the right thing.

"Isabelle, *mi amor, por favor* I need you to wake up." My grip on her hand tightened. "Just give me a sign that you're alive. I'll let you rest, but you need to let me know you're going to wake up."

Nothing happened.

I was still struggling to remember anything about my own turning. "Perhaps some human blood would help?" Quickly, I went back to the buffoon and put my mouth to his open wound. I sucked in a mouthful of blood. Instead of swallowing, I held it in my mouth. Gently, I used my thumb to open Isabelle's mouth before pressing my lips to the opening. The buffoon's blood dripped out of my mouth and into hers.

"*Necesito que esto funcione.*" I could feel the remnants of the buffoon's blood dribbling down my chin. Not a drop was spilling out of Isabelle's mouth, but her throat didn't move. Nothing indicated that she was going to wake at all.

I am not ashamed to admit that I have cried quite often in my life, but I hadn't cried since I was turned. Until I sobbed over Isabelle's body. My heart, whatever was left of it, was cracking with each second that she didn't wake. It had been over twelve hours since I had tried to turn her.

She wasn't going to become a vampire.

Isabelle was dead.

The realization was the final crack that shattered everything in me. I cycled through wailing, shouting, and holding her close to me. I cried out to a god that I knew had abandoned me long ago, begging him with whatever religious loyalty I had carried in my human life to trade her life for mine.

But that went unanswered.

When I recovered, I noticed the sun was going to set.

The buffoon never went to his family home. His family would come looking for him soon. Which meant that unless I wanted to kill more people today, I needed to leave.

I looked down at the mess all over my clothes. There was so much blood that my blue pants were now black and there were barely any white spots left on the shirt. If I left the house like this then I would draw too much unwanted attention.

But maybe unwanted attention is what I needed now. If I was caught by the Lord of Shadows, then all of this could be ended.

With one final kiss on Isabelle's forehead, I leapt out her window for the last time and headed North.

Thirty Four

Isabelle

Vivid dreams swirled through my head. I heard Matias's voice calling out for me. I tasted metallic blood, and even though I couldn't swallow, I could feel it sliding down through my throat and spreading out through my body. Then I felt warmth, uninterrupted warmth.

That warmth cradled me for hours, like the sun while I laid out in my yard. It was a shock when the warmth was suddenly replaced by a chill that rattled pine trees in my dreams.

I heard Ashley's voice, and two others that were familiar but too far away for me to hear well. But Ashley's voice rang out, mixing with the cool wind that was blowing. Even though I couldn't hear what he was saying, I knew he was sad and then angry, so angry I could taste it. The pine tree in the center of my dream cracked and fell over into freshly fallen snow. The other trees around shuddered.

Then the warmth was back. The trees faded into a bright sun, so bright it hurt.

I wanted to run away from the heat, it was too much, too quick. I wasn't ready for it.

There was nothing else to run towards, so instead I stayed put. The bright sun hovered above me. I could feel sweat dripping down my cold body. The mix of temperatures made my heart race.

Matias's voice was in my dream but I couldn't understand him now. He was being blocked by the sun. Somehow I knew he was on the other side and if I could just get to him, everything would be right again.

I couldn't get around it, no matter how far I ran.

Stepping up to it, I had the idea to go through the sun. It would hurt and burn, but if I was reunited with Matias, the pain would be worth it.

My hand reached out to test touching the sun. As soon as my fingertips grazed the surface, pain exploded up my fingers, into my arm, and hit my whole body. Wincing, I recoiled, holding my burnt hand against my chest.

When I opened my eyes, I realized that I was no longer in the dream. I was alone in my bed.

Where was Matias?

Pain hit my senses. I felt it coming from my fingers, like in the dream. When I lifted my hand, it shot towards me. I barely stopped it before I hit myself in the face. With a close up view, I watched the burn marks on the tips of my fingers heal until my skin was smooth again.

I laid my hand back down so hard that the bed groaned. Within a few seconds, I saw a tendril of smoke start to rise and the pain start to ebb into the same spot it had started before. Taking extra care to move slowly, I pulled up my hand to watch the burns heal themselves again.

"I turned." The hoarse words were barely louder than a breath but they sounded like a shout to my new ears. My fingers moved to my neck but I felt nothing there but dried blood. Matias must have healed the wound.

Carefully, I sat up and saw that I was surrounded by the carnage I barely remembered. The memories hit me at once. My family home was attacked. Men had come into the house to do terrible things. Two of them had attacked me.

Blood on the floor caught the rays of sun that were illuminating the dead bodies on the floor of my room. I remembered the two men, but didn't remember them dying.

When I looked down to check the clock on the nightstand, I saw Ashley's body crumpled on the ground. Ashley hadn't been there that night, had he?

How long had it been since the attack?

The sun continued to creep into the room, hitting more of my body. Small burns started to pop up everywhere my skin was exposed to the light. I cried out, quickly hopping out of bed. Without thinking, I rushed to the washroom. I almost broke the door as I opened it, so I carefully closed it behind me.

The small window in the washroom wasn't allowing as much sun in. It was easy to avoid the small stream of sunlight while I figured out what to do next.

"Where the hell are you, Matias?"

I started to pace, keeping careful track of where my feet were landing to avoid the sun. If I was turned, but I was alone, something had gone terribly wrong. Otherwise, Matias would be here.

The tears started before I could stop them.

He must be dead.

That's the only thing that could have kept him from being here when I woke.

I tried to put all the pieces of what I remembered back together. The memories of what happened rolled around and jumbled in my mind, like a language I could read but couldn't understand.

"Perhaps he's somewhere else in the house?" There was the faintest glimmer of hope as I opened the door. Careful to avoid the sun's rays, I made my way out of my room, into the hallway, and stopped in front of Irene's broken door.

"Oh!" I cried out at what I saw. I didn't need to go inside. I could see my sister's broken body lying on her bed. Her eyes were closed, and if her limbs weren't bent in unnatural directions, it would look like she was just sleeping.

"I'm so sorry, my dear sister."

Irene was so close to getting her happily ever after. Now, she was dead. She'd never get to be a bride, never get to be a mother. I took her future away.

Because this was ultimately my fault. Those men came here because of me.

I hesitated at her door. I wanted to go inside her dark room, but I knew if I went any closer to her, I would break. I couldn't see what I had caused up close.

A fresh wave of tears blurred my vision as I made my way towards the center of the house. Different servers and workers who had been caught by bullets were lying in the foyer. There were only a few bodies, and I hoped that meant everyone else managed to get out.

My father was lying on his stomach, his arm stretched out towards his shotgun lying a few feet away. A dark puddle of dried blood spread out from his body. He died trying to protect my sister and I. Even though my father and I hadn't seen eye to eye on things lately, it still deeply hurt my heart to see him lying there. My father, the man who raised me, who worked hard to give my sister and I everything we wanted in life, was dead.

I didn't want to keep going, but this whole event was my fault so seeing all the death my selfish actions caused was almost like a penance. I was on the other side of death, living a cursed life. Something none of the others were offered.

I owed it to them to have their deaths haunt me.

So I took a hesitant step towards the other wing of the house. There were a few more bodies of staff that I didn't recognize. My mother had hired more help as the party and wedding approached so I hadn't had a chance to meet them all.

Mary wasn't among the dead that I saw. I silently prayed that she had made it out alive.

The doors to my parents room were ripped open. I took a deep breath to try to steady myself but I instantly regretted it. The smell of stale blood overwhelmed my senses. I bent over as my body threatened to vomit. I managed to keep whatever was in my stomach down and straighten myself. I needed to see what happened to my mother.

When I went in the room, I saw her in bed. Blood was covering the sheets and floor. Her blue eyes, the same color as mine, stared lifelessly at me. "Mother," I cried out, sobbing harder as I went to her. The first thing I did was shut her eyes. I couldn't take them looking at me. "I'm sorry. That isn't even enough to cover how I feel, how I ruined everything. You and father and Irene and everyone, I never meant, this wasn't, and now..." I couldn't finish speaking as I cried.

And all I wanted at that moment was for my mother to wrap me in her arms and tell me she understood. I wanted to smell the wine on her, see her rosy cheeks, and feel her hold me close to her.

But I would never feel that again.

It was all my fault.

I curled onto the floor of my parents room, letting my sobs shake my whole body and my wails fill the empty space. I cried and cried until I ran out of tears. Then I laid there staring at the ceiling thinking about what to do next.

I couldn't just stay here in this house, surrounded by death. I needed to get out of here once the sun was gone. I would head West, towards the mountains, to find Matias. He had to be alive.

I would find him.

* * *

I washed myself the best I could with the water that was left in my washroom bowl. When I looked at myself in the mirror, there was no reflection. I had forgotten that would be a problem once I turned. Even if I couldn't use mirrors now, there had to be some reflective surface I could see myself in. I fumbled around my room until I came upon the gaslamp. There was just enough sunlight in the room to let me see a very faint reflection in the glass. It wasn't enough to see the finer details of how I looked.

With a sigh I gave up. I could feel there were still patches of dried blood in my hair, but I had cleaned everything away from my face and hands. When I was able to, I planned to take a proper bath.

I changed into the simple black travel dress that I had planned to wear when I left with Matias. My suitcase was still packed and in the bottom of my wardrobe. The men hadn't touched it in their search for me.

As I adjusted my grip on the handle, the weight felt daunting. This wasn't how I pictured any of this happening. I wasn't supposed to be alone. My family was supposed to be alive. Everything had gone so very wrong.

I couldn't fix what happened. I'd give anything now to have my family back. I would give up this immortal life to see them all alive again. There wasn't any way for me to do that. But if I could find Matias, then a part of me would be fixed. He was the only thing propelling me out of the house and into the growing night.

My eyes avoided looking at any of the dead as I went. Their faces were already seared into my memory. I stepped through the threshold of the torn open doors and onto the front steps.

I heard gravel crunching but didn't see anything.

My feet faltered just as I got to the bottom of the steps.

The crunching sound was getting closer.

A carriage I didn't recognize was coming up the lane.

I wanted to run but there wasn't enough time. The driver of the carriage locked eyes with me. He encouraged the horses to speed up.

My shaky legs retreated back up the steps, ready to run back into the house and hide from whoever this was.

The carriage came to a stop several feet from the first step. The driver sat there, staring ahead, motionless. Suddenly, the door swung open.

Dark, black hair emerged from the carriage first. Then the head it belonged to swung up to reveal eyes with blown out pupils. I recognized this face. It was the stranger I had seen in Washington.

His lips curled in a smile that revealed fangs, "Found you."

Acknowledgement

This book is decades in the making so thank you for taking the time to read it! I always dreamed of writing a vampire romance novel that combined my love of all these different vampire stories into one. This wouldn't have been possible without:

Danny for the love, support, and input.

Mitchell for always being the first person I ask to read anything and knowing just what I need to hear and fix to make this story make sense.

Sarah for making sure it felt like a period piece and getting the jokes.

Amy for hyping me up and giving me feedback when I needed another opinion.

And finally, Josh for always making amazing cover art.

A Dance and a Deal With a Vampire

www.ingramcontent.com/pod-product-compliance
Lightning Source LLC
Chambersburg PA
CBHW032019310726
48972CB00002B/464